Proph..
of the Past

Mario Paluan

To my wife Dafne

To my son Edoardo Simone

TABLE OF CONTENTS

ACT I

How three anchovies and butter spark hell, and how a coffin strolls down the road

My left eye differs from my right. What a shame. I am certainly not making this up. One of them is sharp, like that of a hawk, the other is spent. One perceives the tedious unfolding of unmemorable events characterising my days, whilst the other admires everything else. Others would stash these views in their safe of recent memories and allow time to inexorably erode their certitude. However, when I try to do so, things go so terribly wrong, and the day's symphony progresses in a crescendo of confused staccatos. I would like to see you in my stead; avoiding curious cousins, dilapidated condominiums and cellars where the tree of folly finds root. I tell my reflection: "I must have used my wrong eye; things cannot be like this." Never was I so mistaken.

Cascades of galloping light pierced through the mansards, and the purple reflection of the setting sun soon followed like thunder follows lightning. The bedroom doors were permanently locked on this floor, they were one with the walls. Windows faced an array of uninterrupted roofs, where through them one could behold islands of mysterious hills far beyond the vast aerial sea. In that ocean of light, the wind heralded Spring, joined in its tune by the lifting of dandelion seeds, vagabonding up the dwelling's rooftops. They waltzed on the wind's fingertips, with petals of mysterious flowers as companions, disregarding gigantic cockchafers which clumsily bulleted into the glass. The heat would have been unbearable in those mansards, just like every other Spring.

In one of those many burrows, there lived a mother and her son. She was over inflated, as though too much stuff had been jammed in that purse of human skin, with a badly defined pernicious smile, pale and a widow since before anyone could recall. The son was a tram driver, snaking the number sixteen to the foot of the hill. He confided in no-one and felt no need to. To malign spectators, the two were suspiciously intimate. Never a fight, never anything really. The son was indispensable to the mother, the mountain of pale blubber. Mother and son had each other and that was enough for them. *"After all, with such a mother, the tram driver could have never stood a chance with other women."* Or so my mother said. The son sits in the kitchen with the parent, shielded by a cone of shadow projected by the shutters. They linger, like walruses in the sun, lying next to the icebox, a monument to shabbiness in that torrid summer. The nylon tablecloth is bodily warm, as is the marble basin, the ceiling is a mirage as the air pirouettes like dancers on ardent coals. The tram driver extends his legs and dozes away. That very afternoon, the mother comes and goes and falls asleep, enveloped in her nylon under-gown, with socks rolled down to her shin, she mumbles something inaudible without moving her mouth. Everything is still, in anticipation of the event. A ceremony takes place every time the pair allow *"Chicco"*, the two-year-old, to come and play with them for a while, giving the toddler's mother some breathing space next to the mansard. The day lingers on, half asleep, waiting for the event. Even the mother's belly starts laughing when that small sprout of blonde hair protrudes through the door.

"Some more food would not hurt the baby. Please madam, do not give him anything to eat otherwise he won't have his dinner." Says the mother.

Chicco diffuses his way to the coldness of the attic; already an explorer, already getting to his destination. He is as beautiful as a heart, as a delicate heart, even his tummy is delicate. *"Zizzi"* and *"zizu"* and *"piri"* and *"piru piru"* is the background noise to the mother's anxious recommendations. Such anxiety would be out of place if its sole foundation lay in the eventuality of an infant missing its dinner. No, one should look with more malign eyes, void of restraint, in a bid to understand where this prejudice originates from. Mother and son together, always alone, cutting the bed sheets in two, what is there not to think? Fantasies. All fantasies, or gross embellished accounts concocted by my mother, the official house spy. My other eye starts recording now, in a time before the horrible revelations lurking in the cellar and before Dino Serra demanded the neighbour for an explanation as to why bras and panties were dripping onto his mother's laundry.

* * *

Chaos ensues : prologue, entr'acte and epilogue

The child sat on the marble of the kitchen table surrounded by the dim light of the attic. He looked more like a sausage waiting to be chopped into little pieces and thrown in the stew. The child's mother, having learned it had eaten forbidden food, gripped by a nervous fury, threw herself at the door shielding the tram driver, punching it as though her hands were battering rams.

3

"If I lay my hands on you, I'll ruin you," she exclaims, *"you and that son you have. Witch! You know nothing about me and my husband, you have not endured us ever since we got here!"*

"Let her be, she is old," the neighbours tell her. *"What do I care if she is old? She gave my baby anchovies, butter and even the wine. Witch!"*

"Ovies, ovies" the child utters, like a drunk gargling from one end of a bottle, *"Utter ovies ine."*

The mother collapses to the ground, a fitting stage exit to her nervous breakdown, with bloodless lips, every sign of life in them vanished. *"Do not let me find you on the stairs, I'll ruin you, you witch!"* The last bloodless warning. A spit void of any saliva hits the disdainfully closed attic door, and there, the mother finally falls onto Rita Rambaudo's sofa, in a crash as epic as that of the Colossus of Rhodes. I was temporarily entrusted to Rita after the incident. Fine, I should not have eaten butter and anchovies in the tram driver's attic.

But what fault did I have? I had only just discovered how to convey feelings of pleasure and disgust from my taste buds to my plump toddler face. The burst of electrical hatred my mother left on the stairway quickly died down, but it lasted for eons in the condominium's collective memory. The following day's main event was hosted by Madama Serra, as she bawdily wondered what had happened the previous day. Not a week goes by without a misfortune plaguing a family, dismaying, or entertaining, the whole building.

Engineer Silvano was married and with a child. He is the one who worked for an American patent company, he is also the one who was unceremoniously cleaved in two by the wheels of the *23.13* fast train, just outside Central Station. They said it was exhaustion, they say it was a suicide. The newspaper mentioned the incident as well. His wife Ada told everyone how he was always so tired. Ever since his migration, he had become myopic and his waxed floor, to which a mirror would have paled in comparison, would no longer be usurped. The macabre honour of identifying the engineer's mutilated corpse fell to Basovici. He explained to the policeman how his friend had had a nervous breakdown, and how they no longer played cards on a Sunday. Then he began to think about it.

4

Day and night trying to understand what denied him sleep... the reason why that body was now cleaved in two. In a past life, Basovici had stood in front of the Kremlin and shouted his enthusiasm as a communist from Turin to the Soviets, but now, after seeing that corpse so... absent he shouted his desperation. He touched it with his probing hand on the sliding bed of the morgue; the last necessary proof required to reassure him of his friend's absent presence. All the while, a powerful rage mounted inside him. *"But good God why are you in this place of death? And how did you do it? And why you did not tell me anything? We could have at least departed for Moscow to have some fun!"* Basovici ruminated all this while fixating the recomposed manikin. At two o'clock his wife asked him if he wanted a chamomile.

Of course, he had other things in mind, more important than a chamomile. He had never been on a trip with his friend, what better opportunity than now? He thought about how he could do it all night. Giovanna heard him come and go in the kitchenette. He took the wine bottle out and attached himself to it like a patient on insulin. He ignited the disgusting filter-less cigarette butt; it felt worse than sucking on rusted iron. Nothing else would calm him down. An eclectic desire to act grew within him. Basovici was not violent, but when in the mood, he could lift a table or make you hover twenty centimetres off the ground solely aided by two fingers. He would pinch your ass too but would then go and cry in the restroom because he could not find a way to apologies.

That big nervous giant; he was as good as butter, but electric and with yellow eyes that could strip your flesh off. Basovici gazed into the night, thinking it was a trap. The condominium, the courtyard and the balcony were asphyxiating. *"You are not coming to bed, Nanni?"* Giovanna said. He stared at the dim lights flickering behind the house, where my cousin Lory and her sinister groom were fornicating. *"In bed doing what? Good God, things just don't go as planned and when they start to digress too much from their original path, they break you in two ... just like..."*

The third gargle of wine suggested to Basovici how he could stay a little longer with his dead friend. There was no evil moon to guard Basovici's sky and soul, only a heart-breaking melancholy which whispered unspeakable things, otherwise he would have despaired, forever, alone. He looked over the rooftops, towards the hill that stood out like a jungle burning with heat; he wiped away the tears, multiplying the city's dim lights a thousand-fold in the process.

No one will ever know how Basovici managed to make everything work so smoothly all by himself. The morgue guardian mentioned how the whole affair had seemed a bit odd, mostly because of the time; *"Usually the dead are not taken out past five o'clock in the evening, however, as there were no funeral workers I could not deny the dead man's release."* After all, the police had already done what they had to do.

The funeral was to take place the day after, at the deceased's birthplace. *"Corridor A, room six. I will open the gate. You may enter with the van from behind,"* said the guardian. Basovici had loaded the box, alone, lifting it with two strands of tape. Chronicles do not speak of the journey. *"I hope he does not slam his head inside the box, it is already quite worn,"* thought Giovanni Basovici, as he ignited the engine and started talking to the dead man. The engine's loud stuttering disturbed the night. The same priest who had married Basovici and Giovanna would soon forgive him for that night's folly, after all, Basovici was not allowed to transport corpses, even if it was just for old times' sake.

* * *

How Fiorillo's only son loses his mind over the beautiful Figheira, and how he ends up in the barracks as a result

A motorbike was added to the boy's arsenal of toys with which to impress women with. One such victim was the gypsy who lived in the farthest attic.

A third-hand flame red Aermacchi was parked near the door. It irritated Iotti, the doorkeeper, because she did not want it there, or anywhere for that matter. She ritually blemished the fender by splashing murky water every time she was face-to-chassis with it, she looked bemused at her opponent's incapacity to react. It was an old motor bike, you could not ask it to confront a woman few dared to confront. She must have felt the same way, incapacitated, when she lost her daughter to a throat infection.

The Fiorillos lived on the lower floors and the beautiful Figheira was a recluse in her den, how could the boy ever reconcile seeing her with his shop's impossible work schedule? Giuseppe had reduced himself to embers because of the witch's gait. An abyss divided her from the others. According to legend, that outgoing woman of the world did not eat and did not sleep. Nobody wanted to give her importance but they all glued their eyes on her figure and let their imagination take a ticket to ride. The beautiful Figheira had a slight limp to her, but this did not jeopardise her arcane beauty. Thus, the fame of the one who had nothing to share with anyone grew.

"Shall I stop her on the stairs?" Thought the only son of the Fiorillo tribe. Who visited her? Shadows in the darkness ascended five floors to mount the lame spider, attracted by the open book she carried on her lap. More than one found itself entangled in the shiny lace of the bras and underpants spread out to dry in the yard. A liquid stare and reddened ears, those were the indications to be sought in rare customers. However, it was not easy, the lady only welcomed shadows to her hatchery of desires, and Giuseppe was no shadow.

He had changed his schedule, bartering his weekly rest with more flexible hours which would allow him to see her; what else could he do? Nothing. Giuseppe had crawled as far as the great patch of damp that bloomed on the wall, adjacent to Pezzuto's toilet. *"Was anyone inside? Was she in bed, naked?"* He had once managed to steal a memory of her deep neckline in the dim light of the entrance. These details gave him the thrills. Did she smile at the man who, furtively, already headed downstairs? Could this door of opportunity open for him too? Now that he was so close he could clearly hear them.

Pezzuto's turtledoves moaned inside their cage. *"Giuseppe are you looking for something?"* He jerked into the air, they had seen him snoop all the way to the top. *"Me? Nothing... the turtledoves..."*

"They are hungry," intervened Madama Pezzuto; *"I give them food and they stop their cooing,"* she said while closing the window giving onto the main staircase.

Giuseppe had no longer any pretext to be buzzing near beautiful Figheira's den, however, she who had ruined his opportunity had inadvertently procured him with a better one.

As he rushed down, the witch of desires ascended. They had never been so close, almost touching. She slowed down, lingering her blue eyes on him. To then storm off. Giuseppe carried the witch's gait within him for evermore. It was the only thing she had deemed fit to give him. He had returned several times to the obstacle which separated them, he had returned to the door.

The house doors opened easily, even when trying to unlock them with different keys. He thought of slipping into the dimly-lit apartment, into the woman's bedroom, perhaps, stealthily, like a lover, like a thief.

"What time was it? First you said five o'clock, oh!... you were confused. And who did you think you were going to find there? First you said she was at home, why didn't you ring the doorbell? You could have knocked. Did you think she was home? You wanted to invite her, where to? If you say she was not there, and if, as you still say, you did not force the door because you simply walked in... Listen, I would not come to your house if I knew you were not at home. Did they find you inside or did they not? Well, do you know what we are going to do now? Here is the official complaint. Now, let us start again: so, you say that the doorbell was malfunctioning... continued the policeman.

Giuseppe left the barracks at dusk of the following day. Nobody saw him again for a good three months. He fled back to his home in the south. On his return he answered with lowered eyes to those who greeted him.

They had seen him force the beautiful Figheira's door and enter the empty attic, enough to last a life sentence in the eyes of the condominium's jury.

* * *

Condominium and whereabouts

In the epoch which saw the refrigerator replace iceboxes in multiple homes, I was just a stripling. Official documents portray me in a number of different poses: with a camera case and curled hair, astride a rock in an unconvincing pose; with a telephone receiver and a dubious expression after having vainly chased Basovici's cat; with a scoop and bucket, adorned by a toothless smile, near my father's bronze, athletic body.

Other photos portray subjects whose stories weave into my own. Carlo, the cobbler who had baptised me, Aunt Antonia, my father's sister, who along with her second sister had formed a coalition against my mother, the unwanted and unforgivable sister-in-law. Mother was well aware of the misdeeds that occurred behind her back.

My aunt appears embarrassed in the baptism picture as she holds my head, embarrassment probably originating from my mother's absence. She had fallen prey to her usual spasms of dizziness. I was a newborn with ideas which destiny thought fit to confuse, right from the onset.

Back in those days there occurred a series of thunderstorms that are still remembered by those unfortunate enough to have been flailed under them. Streams of electrical discharges split the heavens. Strands of violet and white light broke the horizon in perpetual flickers. A ruckus of water followed as though summoned to drown the combined tortures of the Pezzuto's, the Black Children and the entire condominium; sadly, to no avail, history and memory would not be cheated.

The mysterious hill promontory stood like an abandoned fort, besieged by waves of air and water. Premonitory oracles for Fiorillo, Pezzuto, the Black Children, Gilberta and Dino Serra, spoke. Seven years ago, the post-war period had started to blossom in all its slowness, fatigue and hope studded the future which was struggling to sprout from its past.

The carpentry shop spat splinters while making tables and sideboards, one of which had struck me at the height of my neck, according to Iotti, it should have permanently disfigured me. Around the corner of the street there is a minute dairy connected with a damp cave illuminated by flashing neon tubes.

There, radishes exploded in their aromatic smells and bunches of hot pepper sprouted between casseroles of escarole and rocket. But it was not there that Gilberta, a friend of my mother and her family, was hanging out.

* * *

9

How Gilberta gives in to anger, while trying to avoid being smashed on the head with a bottle

Gilberta lived with her tribe several blocks away, near her mother Eugenia and her father Carlo, who was both a blasphemer and my honourable godfather. Gilberta was generous yet abrupt, with skin pulled tight like a drum, she was as fat as a stretched goatskin, and routinely cursed her mother, Eugenia, in the name of the jealousy she proved towards her sister.

A highly ranked doorkeeper, loquacious as one needs to be, she was a servant to the mother, the sister, the husband and the children who kept being churned out, and this all added to her official summary: a concierge in a beautiful building, as dark as Cagliostro's cave, overlooking a garden in which clematis plants languished.

The terrace, set among the courtyards of dilapidated houses, still dominates the surroundings as though enchanted. It became the glorious destination of all those exhausting journeys I went on with my mother. Now somewhere, now nowhere, just to let time pass by, she visited friends and relatives and friends of relatives, immigrants from the country.

She had no business to attend to which was not confined to the house. According to an unspoken and poorly shared thesis, this was due to her invasive nervous breakdowns, so we were free to do whatever we wished. At that time, I was still a stripling, and could be placed here or there, like a parcel, delivered to whatever address these unstable maternal wanderings required.

One of these wanderings included a pilgrimage to one of the thirty-four houses managed by Gilberta who used to acknowledge my presence by sniffing me with a rough dog-like greeting. I looked and nodded, entirely lost, on that damp terrace populated by spiders and worms shivering in the cold. The new houses were on the other side of the river, shimmering in the water's reflection. The city was still struggling to recover, more than seven years after the end of the war.

I was bored and wanted to quickly see what there was to see to then move on to something else. To the elegant paths, sprinkled with rotten petals of magnolia, I preferred contriving stratagems to get caterpillars out of the vases. A light mist stagnated on the floor and laundry line, onto which some soft cloth of water always hung.

Gilberta's beauty resided in her soul: generous, excessive, overjoyed. That body could not contain the energy within it, it overflowed, as did her desire not be alone, to revel and indulge in an attitude of excesses. Sometimes bouts of anger would land like thunder on her husband, who was curved and thin like a willow branch. I was on the terrace visiting Gilberta and her third child, who was trapped in a cradle of chairs and broken stools stacked on top one another. I hear her hiss: *"And instead where is that drunken stink of my husband? If only I could, I would strangle him..."*

I was picking up a ball of celluloid as I heard this, and other charming comments aimed towards that star of a new dad. Gilberta's storm intensified. *"... See if the key is on the lower floor, ... If it is not in the box, he will have forgotten it. What the hell do I know? Lower floor? Yes? Third floor, the doctor is not at home. Look at this stuff ... adultery? You know how they inflate words,"* she tells my mother. *"Adultery! ..."* making her jump, *"there's no good, they must go with the van, no, there is no one on Thursday. Hello? Ah, he is on the phone: all day every day you know?"* she tells my mother. *"But please stay, that I may let off some steam for a while."* She continues. *"Adultery! The first time? Tse! You tell me I have to make a complaint. And what will they do to my husband? A reproof, that is all. A reproof to that stink, oh, his mother had warned me: do not mingle with someone like that. Now he is cheerful! As though nothing has happened, he... No, it is not good over there, they have to open the door, they have to get out, put it there! How many bags are there? The administrator does not even tell me, he does not care. But if there is no order the cement will not be discharged. Stay here, I'll tell you more..."* she tells my mother.

"It is always that harpy, she makes everyone spin in a confused state. The commissioner talked to me, what is he ever on about? Abandonment of the conjugal roof! He comes to sleep here! After that he goes to his jezebel; and I still have to wash the laundry and keep that stink away." The first of Gilberta's tears drops as she caresses the newly hatched baby, asleep in the basket.

"He searches for me in bed you know? You can see he is not exhausted enough even after his pimp's trick. Once I found her slut right here in front of me. Just think about it, that dirty face. He was waiting for her around the corner. I ran after her and in doing so lost a shoe which I never found again. What in devil's name do you want from my husband you dirty stinking witch?! He comes at me

waving his fists; come if you have the courage! Aren't you ashamed?! Come, I will ruin you, come on! Your own mother told me you were worth less than a cigarette butt. Try to lay a hand on me and I will ruin you, you and that family-ruining gypsy... What did I have to do with the cement bags?" She said, towering out of the porter's lodge to the little man who insisted on unloading the sacks. *"If the administrator did not issue an order, there is nothing I can do,"* she responds. *"For Heaven's sake!"* She slams the door in the bricklayer's face. *"For Heaven's sake! All the while he did not know whether to run after his witch or smash the bottle on my head. I go to the judge and this time they lock him up for good. It is not enough for him to make me have children, no, now I must take care of them by myself as well. Slanderous knave! But please stay here, you have only just arrived!"* Said Gilberta.

Gilberta's last tear begs us to stay a little longer and she has not yet offered us biscuits. I admire her beautiful gold framed oil painting, the figure possesses a slightly cross-eyed look, worthy of a fat Venus.

We have tea in the atrium; I am not a fan of the sugar-coated biscuits, so I vie for a wet plum cake; outside the sun must be shining and spiders are tentatively peeping out.

"Who am I? I am nobody and they have always treated me like a sock, starting from my mother. Do you treat me like this because I married a fool?"

By this time the bulging caterpillars must have holed up. I take a second plum cake, a little less moist than the first. The cup is filled with a liquid whose color resembles that of lubricating oil, perhaps the taste will confirm its nature. Gilberta shrieks at me; *"You do not like it? Drink! It is good for you. It makes you go to the toilet ... No, I will not sign anything...I let you unload the cement sacks in the yard without permission, and I must sign too? It is not even my bloody concrete!"*

I could smell it, all the while we were at Gilberta's, a familiar odor reminiscent of broth and celery, a smell that makes you utter 'I'm home', as it emanates from the damp wall. A smell like that of rotten magnolias, or dog pee, raging, stale moods, which hypnotised you while evoking your past.

A long time has come to pass here, stables and horses still live in Via Mazzini 61, the hooves beat on the pavement, the carriage wheels screech when a pebble gets caught between iron and stone; it must have been some three, four hundred years ago. I still smell that peculiar scent which evokes lost worlds. I dream of dreaming, I go in an ecstasy; it has happened before. Is there horse drawn carriages or is it this great torpor which plays tricks with my eyes? I discern a swarm of lackeys, bums, usurers, tavern-masters, prostitutes, and fancy gentlemen, or is it all a dream? Everlasting friend of striplings who fall asleep after drinking hibiscus tea? Is it Gilberta who shrieks? Or is it the jangling barkers in tailcoats? People with top hats, wastrels who go to the market rummaging through vegetable baskets, to jostle, to bet and squander their money.

There must have been a market in place of the porter's lodge. I'm talking about the same odor that put me on their trail, on odor of a few centuries ago, still present in the lodge. Distilled through the door's wooden molecules, through the pavement, through the grass among the stones, and through the water and lye, sinisterly murky. I inhale and discover that the hibiscus tea has ceased its effect. The smell has vanished, so too has the market.

***

First strikes and dismissal letters

Basovici said that if it was up to him he would have put the owners to eternal rest, because he had learned stuff when in Russia, and you could not expect the average worker to act subtly, with ever inflating prices and owners who took advantage of you, while leaving you in your knickers. There was no other talk on the stairs save for that regarding the dismissal letter, which went something like this: *"Well, we do not need you anymore, many greetings and thank you for the past collaboration."*

Workers had had their heads smashed in three different squares, and the police didn't seem to mind joining the fray. It was like this everywhere in the city. Houses grew like mushrooms to the point where you did not know where the suburbs were.

People who still did not have a home television made routine trips to the bar, they marched to see these new boring tv shows: *The Musichiere* and *Lascia o Raddoppia*. The first seaside vacations were already threatened by the economic doldrums.

Muller the widow did not care about letters of dismissal, death had fired her husband for some time now and her eyes still had a tint of red at the thought of it. After the broken heads came the processions and the newspapers filled with boisterous headings and photos, however, they downplayed the foment, presenting it as: *"Social tension gradually slowing down"*.

It did not slow down one bit, as the new houses remained void of inhabitants and the shopkeepers complained, including Ginetta's mother, who had a prodigious yet minute drug store just around the corner. The letter of dismissal sent to my father's colleagues never landed at our house; triggering my mother's comment: *"If they did not send it to you, it means that you are worth more than the others, it is time to ask for a raise."*

As my father was a constantly embarrassed man, in perpetual awe with the world and with himself, he unwillingly resigned, pushed by my mother, to chase after a few extra coins, and became a worker in a motor-pump company, which he despised. It was around that time that from my family's native country came a host of letters which were as confusing to read as they were tiring. Sisters writing to sisters. Mothers writing to daughters, sister-in-laws who turned to their sister-in-law complaining about their mother-in-law.

"Your brother told her, but she does not listen. Tell her something, maybe she will listen to you," or: *"Send some money, his uncle cannot sell that piece of countryside near the ditches; and he never asks anything of anyone."* Ancestors were about to kick the bucket and their imminent passing was to be announced.

The dying man had sold a house in his youth. He deemed it right to deprive it, and therefore the acquirer, of its windows, which he stealthily removed during the night. He claimed that *"bare ownership"* meant having walls and nothing else. The buyers could turn to the lawyers, but he had the law on his fingertips and it was in that way that the dying great-grandfather had managed to sell blinds and windows separately, removing them from the already sold building. Malice inspired missives, it was a well-known fact that the fray of letters brought with them animus, which hovered above the table like virtual food so indigestible to make the real one tasteless.

* * *

How a heredity fades into nothingness because of a dripping tank top, lying on the washing line

One of these letters read: *"Dearest... I hope you are all in good health as we are. I am writing about our brother Sostene, who, after the death of Yole, has not come to visit ever since our mother came to live with us; he went to sleep in another room because he regrets marrying his second wife."*

Sostene, my mother's brother, lived in Mantova in a bright two-story building which gave onto a garden where hens, expertly trained by one of my cousins, managed to stand on his bicycle's handlebars.

A row of trees acted as a watershed between the garden, where capricious carrots were struggling to find their space in the world, and the grass from the ditch. There was water a plenty in the great channel, slowly flowing, of a cloudy green.
However, this oasis was an ordeal to him, everything there reminded him of his first wife. My mother's brother was as small and fat as he was not quiet and peaceful, he was diseased with a pernicious apathy. The memory of his first wife was the acid that eroded his life away through bouts of torment.

His first bride's qualities inflated his heart with widespread affection, poisoning any relation he might have with his second wife, sons and brothers. He conserved the dress Yole had worn when she first came to him, a rag hanging in the closet, faint remnant of a bygone age which had faded away along with his happiness. There were also the wedding shoes, shirts and socks, he kept all these memories in his mind's wardrobe. After his second son's birth my uncle had holed himself up in the upper floor's closet. The bride's new house had come to him as a dowry. He grinned as he recollected the mischief perpetrated by his relative: the sale of the windowless house. He grinned the same way at his sister Luigina, who resembled an Evergreen monkey with an ever-red neck. His new wife served him with rude benevolence. The mutual care between the two, which should have represented the marriage seal, was nowhere to be found. Perhaps it had been passed onto the stepdaughter, perhaps. My uncle remained segregated in the closet with the creaking wooden parquet signalling his movements, now on one foot now on the other, as he put on his vest and shirt.

The new servant bride initially felt motions of affection for that sullen and melancholy man, but those soon withered and died.

My uncle was to be found less and less amidst the blue and cream-coloured wooden furniture. *"Sometimes I do not even know if he's at home, I do not hear him during the day,"* his second wife told my mother. *"He is not evil, but your brother is just like that."* In that place, scents were the real masters. Hourglass scents, indelible markings of dissolving epochs. Scents of the soul, scents of uncle's fresh, white laundry, acknowledging the day of his son's first communion. *"Why isn't dad coming?... Why does he not come to church too?"*
Scent - the taste of my cousin's tears on the day of his first communion, a day where he would have never imagined presenting himself in front of God without his father. Scents of my uncle's freshly ironed shirt, stretched in the drawer where it will be stored, never to be worn. And then there was the odor of incurable pain.

Focusing back to the indigestible missive, thus concluded my mother's second brother: *"... I know why our brother Sostene is mad at us, it is because of the signature on the will. However, my wife treats our mother well, ... and I did not ask anything of you, where will our mother live? I can still provide for a roof over her head. Our brother believes I forced my mother to leave me my heredity for crackers. But I leave holding my head up high, as it is clear to everyone that I did not do things in secrecy. With this I salute you. Your brother."* End of the indigestible reading, end of this table's appetite.

My mother had read the letter, which she held with her left hand, fluttering it like a flag of surrender, as she was stirring the rice. Her comment was: *"He keeps my mother in his house for his own selfish interest. I saw her, she was crying because my sister-in-law let the tank top and petticoat drip over her head, out of spite, on the washing line over the bed..."*

* * *

How I discover Muller's son's revolting secret

Five floors and no lift. The wet stain on the wall was expanding beyond the pencil lines the tenants had traced in a bid to analyse its growth rate.

The house had been built immediately after the war by a certain Professor Savasto, who died of a heart attack because he had difficulty climbing his house's stairs. The top floors were built with cheapness in mind, attics gave directly onto the tiles tangled together with bamboo and lime reeds. *"You see?"* Pezzuto had once said, *"One only needs a finger to pierce through the wall."* Quite right.

The mother of one of the Black Children had nodded and Miss Pezzuto, closing the door, cursed the heavens for the smell of fry coming from their quarters. Michele, Silvio and Pino and, more rarely, Muller's son, used to touch their nipples or chain themselves to the gas pipe which exuded a sinister odor.

They sharpened arrowheads on the rough concrete handrail and seldom resorted to using the sophisticated aluminum blowpipes that were starting to creep into the homes. Charcoal and wood were still used to imbue the condominium with warmth. Fuel sacks were carried up the stairs by primitive people with tong-like hands.

The boys immediately explored that cornucopia of half baked-wood, looking for the most interesting pieces: those which possessed long liquorice-coloured fibres. Globes of coke and anthracite were not handled because they dirtied you as soon as you set eyes upon them. You had to rummage hard to find their traces, but in the dormer's sterile forest you could occasionally find dry larvae bathed in the smell emanating from dead wood.

It was a sorry sight to see it devoured by the kitchen stove. Then one evening another kind of heat was trialed, that from the gas stove living with widow Muller, who had invited us to watch her black and white television.

There was nothing else to do apart from spying Muller's son, a stripling who was two months my junior. You had to be quiet and still, sitting on hard chairs, one in front of the other.

Only the grandmother, the silent, lady-like skivvy with a wild desire for strawberries, had the right to sit on the sofa as the TV slop streamed by. We place ourselves under the dim light of the dining room.

I begin to spy. His hands. He raises one, then another, then both at the same time. What is he playing at? He moves his fingers, first slowly, then abandons all caution. He is quite into it. He does not know I am spying him.

I look around and notice how his face, like that of the other bystanders, is absorbed by the flickers of changing light on the screen.

I do not like the TV show. My head collapses and after some ten minutes I awake. I see myself observing Mario Riva's face, along with everyone else's, including the Marshal's pea-coloured one, Rita Rambaudo's and that of Muller's son, who fixates one hand now, then the other, observing their contents. The condominium's elite have come to see the *Musichiere*, presented by the giant of all presenters: Mario Riva.

"And what do you think of this situation?" The austere Muller begins, addressing Madama Serra's son. He stutters, already fiery red in the face, wondering what he had done wrong to become the target of such an embarrassing question. He mumbles something about a situation he has no idea about. *"Which situation?"* What must Dino Serra answer? He is clueless about what situation he should talk about, and the situation dies in his mouth... did the situation refer to his dog or his mother? *"Everything increases; ah it is not a nice situation, what with the price of fruit and vegetable skyrocketing, and the strikes. Ask Basovici what the situation is like in Russia."* This was said.

The advertisements ended, ending the situation. Muller shakes her head towards the video. I take a furtive look at her son again. I can imagine what happened in the dark when I was asleep. What the child encloses within his claws are small, compact, well-made balls of treasure, the result of one skilled enough to make such masterpieces. More than a vice it is a skilful craft, using techniques and diverse materials.

He carefully placed them on a piece of cardboard, ripped off a match-stick box. He admires as many as four small balls, made of compressed phlegm coming from each nostril, amalgamated with chomped chewing gum, ruminated in great secret. The horror knows no bounds. I do not know if I should tell someone.

* * *

18

Behold the aquarium's mermaid

I usually get sick during the month of March, as I endure its bristling and glittering days. No medicine can cancel my appointment with the March sickness. Few know that November is not the month of the dead. March fully deserves that accolade.

During this period, shining coffins sink hurriedly into the ground, I have seen so many, some escorted by nightmares. It is indeed a deceitful month, sitting on the fence separating shaggy Winter and Spring's loving womb. I try to keep it at bay, but it always finds a way, with its cold bursts of air.

March makes me inconsolable and I cover my sickness under a veil of sadness. Neither the caramelised sugar, nor the honey, nor the promises could soothe my cough and melancholy.

The cold and sadness did not seem to find a dead end. *"Your son is not ill at all."* The doctor said. *"But doctor, when he starts crying, he doesn't stop."*

"He's got nothing," said the doctor, *"please do not be alarmed."* He turned his head and stared at me. I looked at him and he warned me: *"Is it not true? You will not cry anymore young man?"* He was giving me a ton of responsibility, I felt crushed by the weight of that guarantee. I was able to stop, not because the doctor had shamed me, no, it was because March was over. Tomorrow is the first day of April, and tomorrow I am cured.

No one understands this phenomenon. Wishing to avoid any relapse, my parents thought of giving me a present; an aquarium. An aquarium as big as a room! It was not something to be taken lightly. An aquarium! My parents really wanted me to heal and stay that way. Its layout was surprising, the fish turned out to belong to an alien species. Every time my mother's cousins came to visit, the opportunity to introduce new fish into this extraordinary world presented itself.

The fish came from that side of the family and a legend was required to make sense of anything in that fumble of fins. I never understood why their house was always bathed in sunlight.

Underneath it there was a shop selling bottles, adjacent to it; a bowling alley, shaded by a row of lime trees as big as a ship's masts. The whole area was reclaimed by a monstrous building, erupting from the bowels of the earth to satisfy the needs of the wealthy. Whenever Vera, Fidelio's daughter passed by the bottle shop, she was followed by whistles coming from therein. Anselma, Vera's mother was a woman who would curl up close against you every time she wanted to greet you. She declared it was not her daughter's fault if they whistled. *"Have they never seen a beautiful girl's backside before?"*

Fidelio disapproved of such frankness. Before the visit, we voided the corner shop of its pastries. We plundered trays once full of biscuits, resulting in the plunder of our parents' wallets. *"Well we will not get any richer or poorer,"* uttered my parents, a tame justification for such a theft. The afternoon unfolded following a script.

Greetings, confirmations, prayers, igniting in denials, a great bedlam, all prelude to Sunday's apocalyptic meeting. Erri, who was my mother's second cousin, had a wife, and she adored her mother-in-law.

Passers-by mistook her for Milva, the famous singer from Goro, she had a beautiful mouth and every time she uttered a compliment our way, it felt like she had not seen us for years. I thought she was a truly great human being.

That family hoard was like a musical box, optimistic and revelling. It produced an articulate melody, with sometimes dissonant nuances, but it had a background tune to it embellished by harmonious chords. Its continuous chirping heralded good omens, understanding and harmony. That very same afternoon, like many before it, the cheerful music box began playing.

Milena, one of Erri's sisters apologised because her baby had a cough. My archival memory pictures her framed by a collar made of the finest Persian lamb fur sewn on her suit. After the whistling, Erri's saxophone began to sing, I was certain he would have invited us all to admire the big night-blue tinted letter H he had drawn himself on the living room wall, a testimony to his originality as an industrial designer. *"I don't think it is that big of a deal,"* my mother whispered, *'What is that thing? Did he dirty the wall? I really don't know."* She said ever so quietly, but not enough, for Erri exploded in uproarious laughter. The sun leapt into that festive theatre: a heavy multicoloured Murano glass ashtray, a wooden and ivory box filled with honey candies, the table of cut crystal, with sanded patterns, all was covered in gleaming gold.

One had to wander from one room to another of the great lodging to not die of a heatstroke. Streaks of light assaulted the entrance, protected by a heavy green velvet curtain, held by an even darker twisted cord; a curtain as functional as a wall, aiding our friend Nicola, the Neapolitan guitar player in his search for freshness. Nicola knew how to move the *"oldies"*, women like my mother, to tears, with melodies from Naples.

Vera stood spying from the corners of the rooms, her back dusting the wall, while she sucked half her thumbnail, to then throw herself in the arms of guests and relatives with no restraint. She was a great condor, attacking its prey with calculated furtiveness. Fidelio showed us one of his latest inventions. He was a precursor to the great inventors of the time, messing with wires, valves and magnetic fields. Fidelio spoke in a faint voice, aware that his creations were far too ahead of their time.

He had a crazy idea, set aside due to a lack of customers; to turn on the lights with the touch of a button. He went as far as proposing to connect the metal pipes that chimed in the living room, with the entrance's doorbell. Such genial uselessness accompanied him till the end of his days, it consoled him, as it provided a distraction to his daughter's dubious interests.

Vera's mind seemed to be saturated with romantic photo-novels. *"Not much will ever come from that one, but don't tell her mother,"* whispered Fidelio to his first cousin, my mother. That day Vera locked herself up in her room and read about her half-naked heroine, pursued by a thousand scoundrels, Erri's wife showed my mother her new blender, which was posing on the kitchen's marble table and the mother-in-law boasted how the Prosecco had to be opened, otherwise the whole event could not be called a feast. *"Wait a moment mother,"* said Erri, *"tell Roberta to go and get the bottle opener."*

"Roberta! Roberta! Where is she?"

"I am here grandmother."

"Go and get the bottle opener, no go and open the door."

"I will go."

*"Vera haven't you had enough of those filthy magazines?
They make you stupid!"*

The doorbell rang again.

"May I have the honour of introducing you all to my dear friend?" Said Nicola after presenting the little man to the confusion. Nicola's friend was immediately welcomed and enthusiasm for him grew when the contents of his shoulder bag became public knowledge.

The little man did not say much, as a matter of fact, the bare minimum to not appear rude, a thank you here and there, he sipped some Prosecco, dried his toothbrush-like moustaches and started playing his joyous melodies. His fingers ran, marvellously agile on the accordion's keys. It felt as though all the hot air had flown through the open doors and windows to surrender the stage to the dancers. The chairs and tables were moved; the carpet was rolled up. *"Go and call Ester, go, go and call her, she will be so happy."* Roberta, Erri's daughter, went to call on the neighbour.

Erri's wife was already pirouetting with my mother, holding onto her back with one arm, my father was dragging Fidelio's wife, with composed skill and the right amount of awe while Erri was can-caning with her children, making them twitch up and down.

Fidelio went to the bathroom to freshen up a little, he did not feel like participating in the *sarabande*, however he was still smiling.

Nicola's friend intoned different motifs with absolute mastery, seemingly never ending them, he was so focused on his music, jumping between songs in a strange but agreeable legato of syncopated melodies. Here is a polka, now a mazurka and a tango, dances which nobody could dance to.

Vera came out of her lair, sucked her thumbnail and performed a single dance step with her brother Erri all the while holding her magazine. *"It is so hot, too hot,"* she said, *"a shower is way better than staying here"*. The dance had taken over, the dancers were silent, enraptured by the magic keyboard and Nicola's guitar. The music invigorated everyone, promoting a burst of *"do, re, mi, fa"* and wide-open smiles.

After the low notes' embrace he plunged back into a deluge of trills, like he was a chess piece, bouncing once on the white, once on the black, here and there with hopping notes, as though they were made of rubber. Then the music stopped, the dancers, dragged by the bizarre little player's nets, took a break. *"Get me an orange drink from the fridge!"* Exclaimed Erri's wife. Nicola and his friend's performance ended in a crescendo of *"hurras!"* and *"bravos!"*

The excitement the music brought was stamped on everyone's face. The sun's fury had given way to an orange-yellow color, which changed into ocher as it creeped onto the tiles. Someone shrieked from the bar, promptly echoed by a passing swift's screech.

A few days later, accompanied by Anselma and Fidelio's blessing, Vera entered our house. *"The fifth floor without an elevator, as if!"* She glanced up and asked: *"Where can I put my stuff?"*

In a large square not too far away, there was an amusement park she intended to go to. She had only come for the fairground. *"Aren't you happy she came to see us?"* My father asked me. *"Oh, I am so terribly happy!"* I spied my distant cousin as she was combing her long silken hair, and I stuck my tongue out at the large mirror looming over the entrance.

I followed her everywhere, without asking myself why: she often came back to the mirror, as though to check that the three strides she had taken had not thwarted her meticulous appearance, I then grimaced again in her general direction. She spoke little, she did not hold me in high regard, I was of no use or interest to her.

I had given her magazines a bit of a peek, she was passionate about viscount Hembeck's adventures, and fell in love with his slave plantations in South America, then there was Jade's story, a heroine dressed in tattered blouses and thigh high boots, lusted for by infamous people. After a night of sin, she finally understands the mistakes she made and decides to become a nun. This was the garbage she fed her eyes.

"Do you want to do something?"

"No," she answered, *"maybe in the afternoon, if you guys go to the fair."* The carnival had lasted well beyond what it was meant to last. *"Why are you called Vera?"*

"What do I know? Why do they call you by your name?" Not even her eyes could betray a smile. Every now and again, in an attempt to season her monosyllables, she tensed the corners of her mouth, simulating a smile, this was more a habit than a movement inspired by the soul.

"Do you like going to the beach?"

"I've never been to the sea." I said.

"It's not bad, there are people, you take a bath and you sunbathe."

"Do you go to the sea?"

"Yes, with Erri, you know Erri, right?"

"Of course, he is your brother."

"Anyway, go there in the evening, that way you'll go to the open-air cinema."

I looked at her avoiding eye-contact, I knew she was looking at me; her legs were wide open, her skirt flapped like a sail in the wind, she did not care, she walked barefoot in the attic.

"My mother says you will catch yourself a cold."

"Your mother is not my aunt, you know?" she said, *"she is just my father's cousin."* She continued, as did her stare. Now I was feeling uncomfortable, Vera was proving to be a costly parenthesis to pass over quickly. I could do without such surprises.

"You will go to the rides, she will sleep with us, aren't you happy?"

She was fifteen, she looked so old to me, with all those magazines. A fish out of the water, in our own house, what was I ever going to do with her? It was during Vera's stay that my special eye came into action. From head to toe that electrical pulse traversed me, I had been bewitched by the vision!

Characters, interpreters and objects in order of appearance are as follow: the lock with its dusty hole, the frosted door glass, the eye of a stripling rummaging in the kitchen and a siren, who else would have been fit to embody such a being if not my distant cousin Vera? I focus on the zinc tub, the one which lay in the closet in front of the firewood, because I hear great splashes! Splashes of water which trickle down and down in the never-ending crevices of the great canyons.

A foam-covered siren swims; spreading sparks of water infused with love. Radiant.

The foam drums in my ears as it inconspicuously descends into my soul. This is how we get ill and how certain fish begin to swim inside our head. The mermaid washes her armpits, raising her arms. Pale pink rosebuds followed by the darker tinted ones of bigger roses heighten my thirst.

Roses, sponges and rubber nipples emerge. They tremble, caressed by hands and water that streams down towards dazzling forests. *Splash!* Golden apples, rubber apples, the mermaid dazzles, sinks, rises, dripping a melody of awe from the basin.

Vera is the fifteen-year-old mermaid swimming inside the zinc tub. Inside my very blood. It was the same tub in which my little repudiated cousin, Olga, got soaped by her aunt, my mother, because her own mother Prisca neither had the time or the desire to do it!

There is no time left to waste! The stripling has forgotten his eye inside the keyhole and he cannot escape. Vera, the shining mermaid, rises up from her folded stance in the tub, stretching: naked and soapy. A tuft of wet hair, to the south of the navel, releases a trickle of water. From there, my cloudy eye will never reemerge.

They put me to bed early that night. My head and everything below the hip hurts. *"It might be the season, it might be that returning cough, or the wind." My parents said.*

No, it has nothing to do with the season nor the wind, it was Vera, the siren, who reduced me in such a state, the naked one, whose landscapes I saw under her clothes, she might have suspected someone was peering through the keyhole! You cannot even begin to imagine how she is still wading under the sea and inside of me. How cheeky of her.

* * *

How war was declared on a stripling's mother

My family's history is typified by a piece of wood-hard salami and cheese wrapped in a damp napkin. Salami and cheese both oozed out their grease and their rancid smell mingled. Salami and cheese were locked away in the kitchen table's drawer. The kitchen was as wide as a parade ground, so spacious you could ride your bike around the table. It was surrounded by three large windows and their slim internal windowsills, which lacked a curtain's caress. The floor should have been sprayed upon because it released red dust, like that of an arena.

A shotgun with a shabby leather belt, in as a disgraced a state as the rifle itself, was hanging on the wall. Above the fireplace's great black mouth there ran a wooden shelf, shelving nothing.

On the blackened wall, on a piece of wood attempting to be a rack were three bunches of cobs and on the hooks protruding from the fireplace hung a cauldron soaked in soot in which beans and potatoes were cooking. Beneath one of the windows lay a trunk filled with blankets and aprons.

My father's mother was hardly ever there. She made hemp, gleaned in the fields and prepared exquisite pork pies. When it rained, the barnyard filled with stinking mud which inevitably splashed on her long black skirt. The mud's color contrasted with the brick's red hue.

Harsh, dark and taciturn; these adjectives perfectly described my grandmother, who would have soon declared war on my mother. She came home at dusk, kicking the cat away from the kitchen door. She took her apron off and wore another one to stir polenta. Her life did not have much more to it, except for the salami and cheese in the drawer and the gift of meat occurring around Christmas and Easter. Her husband was a land surveyor, but not a farmer.

He was occasionally friendly, one could describe him as an oscillating man, due to his wife's grim character. One day, they caught my grandfather poaching, what gave him away was the drip of rabbit blood from under his jacket. However, a reproach from the brigadier followed by a visit to the tavern ensured no hard feelings prevailed. There was my father, the aspiring inventor, an emigrant in the Eldorado composed of the city's factories. He bequeathed onto himself his bride's capricious burden. The house was slightly out of town, behind it was a small stream, a little further on, the minuscule latrine house, made of wooden planks, facing the river.

Processing hemp was a lot of work, hard work at that, it had to be macerated, dried and cut. There were ropes, braids, skeins and fabric, there were fields of tobacco and corn behind the house, in the miserable countryside which kept grandmother alive.

The town was a reflection of the countryside, uninspiring, dusty, with a large square; at the time of the fascists it filled and emptied with the regularity of someone gasping for breath, until they had all left to become soldiers. Many of the ones who made it back were like my father, who, after six years of war in Libya, decided to marry the metamorphic and moody creature.

He made the grave mistake of having her stay over at his place, she was as nervous as a pregnant filly. She had always been like that. She also had a tendency to speak when not requested, drawing upon her all sorts of antipathies and ridicule. The two sisters-in-law observed and stayed silent. For now.

"Why did they not come to our wedding? So, kind of them isn't it? For them to stay at the bar smoking and not come to the parade. They only came to Church and hid behind a column. Do they think I am just a nobody's daughter? Do you think it is kind of them? Hu?"

"Lower your voice, speak softly," says the groom.

"If you do not talk to your mother and sisters, I'll go back to my mother. What grudge do they have with me? What did I ever do to them?"

"No no, stay calm, they do not bear you any ill will," her father-in-law used to say.

"Really? And what about the bucket she threw at me? She says I am stealing her son. Go to hell."

"Do not make pancakes anymore. Go away from here, go with my son, he loves you" said my grandfather.

"And the pancakes I made? Not even a thank you! What have I done to your wife? I then see her in the kitchen, eating the pancakes in secret, from under her apron. Is this the way to ingratiate a daughter-in-law?"

"You saw it too, how she wanted to hit me with the rolling pin."

"There's nothing left to do here, she is not evil, she is just like that. Take the train, go with my son's last salary and do not stay under the window, if she sees you she will surely throw a bucket of water straight at you. May you and my son tread down your own path. Otherwise that one will stick the rolling pin in your belly. She's jealous," my grandfather used to say.

"She is mad at me because I threw away that piece of salami and cheese. For Heaven's sake, they stank! All of you saw how the salami had gone bad."

Sostene came one Sunday morning, saying that if things did not work out, he would have taken her sister back to his house, partly because she got along well with his first wife.

Instead, there they went, away towards the city. Grandma had lost the game.

She had lost her son and daughter in law. Meanwhile my father's sisters remained silent. That was the first and final condemnation.

They would later have had the cheek to say: *"Nobody sent her away, she did not get along well with our mother. Imagine, she wanted to tidy up our house! Someone like that!"*

My father wanted to ignore the fact that his sisters had disapproved of his marriage and had ignored the procession of pages, altar boys, Sostene and the three band players. The wedding procession composed of floppy hats, shining shoes, and fresh, starched shirts had commenced, and my father pretended nothing had happened. His family was absent.

The bride wore a dress visibly altered to suit her figure, it had already been worn by her sister Luigina-Uistiti for her marriage, but not by her other sister, Prisca, who had married in secret a guy who seemed to want to claim rights on the stepdaughter and on Prisca herself.

The bright forsythia flowers are all lined up all along the avenue and light up when the Sun kisses them. The procession treads along the avenue, under the stark blue sky. My future parents can be found in its fulcrum and will soon pack their dreams.

A procession composed of flowers, hearts and open wounds, with my father's sisters inside the smoking lounge. My magic eye pierces the fabric of time itself and replaces the hourglass.

I wanted to scrutinise my birth place's geography, but it was not an easy task. After my father's sisters declaration of hostility came the time of reckoning. My aunts preferred a fellow countrywoman who, like their mother, treated hemp and had no sudden flares of rash madness, over my mother. *"Ah! Mena, that villain with a ramshackle ass of a Mena. What a bargain!"* My mother commented years later.

* * *

Time goes by, bringing with it the unavoidable

The dying evening brought with it a familiar stranger, who knocked on doorkeeper Iotti's glass door. Brusque sovereign of the condominium as she was, distressed by her daughter's passing caused by a throat ache, Iotti looked from the courtyard where just a few moments ago she was busy throwing sardine heads and scans the intruder, before shouting: *"Who is it? What do you want? What are you looking for?"* in her usual surly way. The disdainful greeting is met with a mellow inquiry:

"Is this where Mr. Such and such live?

"Yes, he lives here, with his wife, what do you want?"

"I am his sister, and I wanted to talk to him."

"Go on then, they must be home at this time." Iotti says briskly.

"I will wait for him," the visitor says, *"I will wait for my brother."*

"But why are you waiting for him if he does not know you are here? He has just gone up!"

"So how does one warn him? Can you not go tell him I am waiting for him in the reception?"

Iotti eyes the interlocutor. She marches to the porter's lodge, an inaudible ruckus ensues, and marches back out brandishing a cardboard cone. She carefully positions herself and empties her lungs shouting my father's name in the cone. *"Now he knows someone is waiting for him. Good evening,"* and slams the door.

What happened next pertains to the genesis of a cascade of effort and hysteria. A large tree branch had snapped. My future mother was dismissed with a: *"She made our mother cry. Poor brother, who did you ever get yourself with!?"* Meanwhile, my mother peers out over the top floor's railing, looking for her husband, like a bird of prey seeking for a squirrel. He was hiding at the bottom of the stairs, talking to his sister. My aunt did not want to see her.

Chronicles narrate there was a cascade of angry sobs, recriminations and clenched fists on chests all evening and for the better part of the night. Cries and curses followed suit. From that moment onward, my father knew what destiny had reserved him and sealed all dreams of aspiration in hermetic abandonment. His wife definitely went down her own path; existence's vicissitudes were interpreted as subtle plots against her.

My aunt had come to inform my father how their father was not at all well and that a visit would have been useful ... on condition that he was the only visitor. This was also partly because the second bed, the one my mother had usurped, had been unmade and burnt to ashes, like a leper's clothes.

* * *

Basovici's fury leads to an unexpected event

June brings with it an unbearable heat. Pezzuto's turtledoves stink more than usual and continuously coo with the same plaintive cry of those who seem to fear an evil come to pass.

It is late evening, and half the condominium hears a great bang, an earthquake of broken glass and screams from the top floor. Muller looks out and shakes her head, followed by the Marshal neighbour, the Black Children resume their exploration of nasal cavities and Madama Serra's son, rushes to the balcony in his vest and shorts brandishing the iron rod used to free the clogged trash can.

The turtledoves moan flap their wings, *"flaaap frap laaa,"* against Pezzuto's laid out net. The hurricane's epicentre lies in Basovici's mansard. The scene is one of desolation; broken glass from the backyard window, broken glass from the restroom giving on the stairs, two chairs with broken backrest, glass shards from the two-litre flagon and cutlery scattered like bodies on a battlefield. The wife picks up the fragments.

Giovanni lies on the kitchen sofa, biting his hand because of the great nervousness that has just devoured him. *"Stay calm, stay calm, ok Basi? It's all quiet. It is all in the past, Basi. Do not hurt yourself. Do not bite your hand. Rest Basi, rest."* Basovici's wife is distressed by her husband's exhaustion which routinely breaks him in a hundred pieces. The same man who can lift a bull and who votes blood-red communist, from time to time falls prey to a nervous panic that traverses him like an electric shock. His face is disfigured, and the fury arises from a cooing of turtledoves, from the rain that does not fall, from the sky being too blue, from a cry in the street.

Only half an hour is needed for everything to return to normal. Basovici's face recomposes itself, life is imbued onto it, conveyed via brush strokes of color. He gazes at the ceiling, peering through the window bars giving onto the little balcony where Giovanna planted her basil. The heart palpitates, he brushes his forehead. The current has abandoned him. He is exhausted. It had to be Basovici, he was ready to fuel the working class', his class', redemption. *"I will go live in Russia if things do not happen here. I swear to God I will."*

But now he is too tired to think, too tired for anything. He is leaning on the small balcony's window sill, watching the flickering light dance a tango with the shadows. It has been two nights in a row now that beautiful Figheira's shutters let rays of light filter through.

They come from the second room. Someone who is not her, since the woman has a bedroom on the side of the road, right next to the turtle-dove's cage. *"I see it too, she will have forgotten to switch off the light,"* says the marshal to Madama Serra.

Iotti mumbles: *"It is her business, until that light starts bothering someone."*

"One moment," says the Marshal "she has to pay more in waste tax if someone lives with her."

"Who is up there? Does that slut have permanent lovers? She does her things in utter silence, all day and all night." Someone on the opposite side of the building, who lives in the barbarity of the studios deprived of a toilet, swears she saw her at the window, with a guy on-top of her.

They break that black flower into thousands of pieces, spitting fantasies against her, fantasies soaked of loose bras, garters, black petticoats, smuggled money and unmade beds in the dormer's shadow.

Mud is thrown against the building's black virgin. Only Iotti says: "Did she kill someone? Did she hurt someone? No, so?" Iotti slams the glass door again.

They want to throw her in the garbage. Does someone have the guts to ring the brothel's doorbell and inquire why the light is always on? Hurried steps, a slamming door, a dull thud and a female voice, asking "Who is it?" The silence continues. Then, again the voice. Silence. Crying. Then silence and still nothing. The door opens. "Ah! was he her father? Dead? When was this?" Asks Madama Serra. "Yesterday." a voice on the landing replies, losing its composure.

"The father, who was not very well, had come to stay here."

"To stay at hers? And who knew?"

"Nobody. And how did he die?"

"He fainted, but he was very old."

"Yes, ohh! Falling, he banged his head against the stove's pipe."

"Fallen? Mhh, tragic thing that, but she is still young."

"Still a beautiful woman."

"And the funeral?"

"Tomorrow."

"Oh, I'm not going."

"Neither am I. Are we insane?"

"Eh, she might just not be a monster. It is hard to be one when you come face to face with death."

"Ah yes, well for that matter someone will go, at least to church."

"With death... there is little to do."

"You are so right."

The turtledoves' whining recommences. Such manifest disrespect.

* * *

How an evil spirit torments uncle Bizzarrone

One cannot expect events revolving around me to have much temporal coherence. I know something was out of time and place. I admit it. I might have confused stories I heard with events I witnessed.

It matters little. Sometimes, events that occurred in the past have replaced events which occurred at a later stage, perturbing time's linearity. Stuff like this happens you know? As it just so happens, I was not there when the body was stolen. Giovanni Basovici's friend's body. Giovanni the merciful.

One might ask: *"What is your alibi?"* To which I would reply: *"Well, I was not born yet."* However, I believe I was present at little Muller's nasal explorations, actually, no, I was absent, because this episode stems from the commencement of time itself, as old as the disappearance of the *salame* and cheese from my grandmother's drawer.

Ennio, husband to the sister of my mother's mother, came to visit us, he left his bicycle in Iotti doorkeeper's lodge. My mother's lye-dripping hands open the door and her voice exclaims with a suppressed annoyance: *"Here you are Ennio! It was about time! Come in. We have not seen you for so long."*

33

Uncle Ennio regains his composure and at the second glass of Marsala commences his narration.

"This is all I know, and this is what I came to tell you. One does not joke around with these things because one can die of such things." He sombrely says. *"It has already happened."*

My mother winks and does not know how to weave this new thread of facts to the canvas of frayed news in her possession, this new version adds so many details.

"Tell me, Ennio, is it true? Did all this really happen? And my sister, how is she now?"

"Ah! The priest came as well, to put things right, the priest came to bless her home. This is what I had to say." Uncle Ennio tells my mother. *"You have to stay calm. Certain in your faith and pray… without the priest, there was no way Bizzarrone would still be alive!"*

"But Ennio did it really go like this? Is this really how it went? And how is my sister now? And who told you all of this Ennio?"

"The Gualandis, they are their neighbours and I also heard it from the butchery in the main square. They told me the very same thing, I swear it." I was already bored, Ennio's distraction prompted me to reflect again on March and April, so contiguous yet so different. Ennio needed no one to prompt him in narrating the whole story for a third time, the story of what had happened to Bizzarrone and his wife.

Bizzarrone resided in the country side, it was only slightly livelier than the paternal land which extended far into the delta's desolation. A land full of tobacco, hemp and chard, one where the earth was less disheartened, partly due to its inhabitants' strong character. The land was littered with villages that had known the syncopated rage of first the fascists and then the communists. It got increasingly flat until it finally merged with that of my father, there among the river's delta.

Grondonia road was an insidious snake meandering through the valleys. The deceptive shadows of plane trees strewn along its sides covered it and its side roads with a mantle of translucent darkness.

Side roads cut the countryside in untidy polygons of emerald hues, slithering until they plunged into the river bank. In short, it was a nice view. Deep in the countryside, where the sky, embankment and field met, lay a village whose name was a pain to remember, and in that village, one could find the home of Luigina Uistiti, Lory's mother, my mother's sister.

The house was constructed of a red brick reminiscent of that used in cellars or storage facilities. Its other inhabitants were the great Bizzarrone and his tank top. His own mother, with no acrimony, defined him as a: *"pig ready for slaughter"*. Adorning the room were two beds and a sideboard which could have been mistaken for a block of half cut wood.

The roof and walls gave an impression of precariousness, hard work and fatigue.

A badly placed armchair emerging from reed baskets, bags of corn and beans was a vain attempt at showing some notion of hospitality. It felt like a shelter, the door was always open and the curtain, which was nothing more than a potato sack, continuously waved visitors in.

Hen and duck chicks traversed this crossroads to easily reach the other side, where the earth was damper because of the stream. There they fattened, feeding on a banquet of earthworms, larvae and insects. Resting inside the storage were hoes, shovels and saws with big rusty teeth as well as two picks, a broken spade and a chipped sickle. Behind the house there lived other tools or half tools, there was a morsel of a plowshare sunk deep into the ground, a rusty iron wheel with brown circles and iron wire touching every object it could stretch to.

A creamy, grey slime, similar to pestilent batter, covered the bump separating the threshing floor and the sludge drain, losing itself in a jagged puddle behind the knotted cherry tree.

From there came sweet and sour fumes. The tree stood crookedly tall in front of all the filth, it was so disheveled in appearance that at first glance one could interpret it as being a bizarre three-branched candlestick, however, on closer inspection one would be overcome by its morbid resemblance to the hangman's gallows. That cherry tree had never been much of a worker, its productivity seemed to slump into unnoticeable mediocrity. When it finally decided to fructify it produced hard, pink wood-like spheres that abruptly rotted. To the locals, that was the hangman's tree. Tall and black, a crazy cherry tree, which could not even produce a shadow, let alone fruit.

Under the vault of salt-peter bricks was a jar of fat, demijohns and pointed ash stakes, further on there was the pigsty fence.

My aunt is weak and very thin. Her skirt no longer fits, so much so that one can tell the time of day by measuring the distance travelled by her skirt in its inexorable descent. Her characteristics included: skin, bones and a little patch of hair and the right side of her inflamed neck. She is enjoying her first days as a stay at home mother, loving her house, the pig, the hens. She also loves Bizzarrone, who has a blue tank top over his skin, which is permanently oily, throughout the Summer and the Winter. Uncle Bizzarrone looks at her with that loving cloudy pupil of his. He loves her too, in his own way.

That love for her was justified by her laughter, which was competition to the muted giggling of gunshots, by her serving him, and by her reaction to almost having a miscarriage eight months into her pregnancy as she was tending the hemp.

After she lost blood, she returned to the fields, as though nothing had happened. *"That is how I like my Luigina."* thought Bizzarrone, as he peeled the beans before carefully popping them into the basket. She was a real working mule, a certified countrywoman. Had she been left to her own devices, she would have stepped into the countryside at one o'clock in the morning to work, to look at the moon, while clutching her apron to her hips in a bid to save it from the same fate that waited her skirt. Bizzarrone thought women like his didn't exist anymore, only his Luigina knew how to tend the pigs, look after the chickens, treat hemp and glean, all this was a real pleasure to him.

That passion made her grow thin, living off of air and apple peels. Luigina was part of his stuff, much like the saw or the spade. He was fat, big and strong like a bull, his neck permanently beaded by a double line of droplets of sweat. He laughed too, but only at other people's jokes and he only had at heart his own interest, and that of his beloved.

Luigina was a great woman. She cost him nothing, kept him happy, even in bed, and worked the equivalent of ten men in the fields. But that evening neither he nor that rag of a wife would laugh.

"Stay calm Luigina," and Luigina would stay calm. But she asked why he had heard those voices again. Loosing twelve pounds worth of weight was no joke. Bizzarrone wet his pants and his food got stuck in his throat. His throat turned dry and his guts suddenly became as agitated as the tempestuous sea, he always ended up that way when that topic was brought up.

"You still hear them? Even now?"

"Well yes Luigina. They have not stopped, ever since you went to hospital you know…"

"They continued?"

"Yes."

"Even by night?"

"Yes."

"And they did not stop?"

"No.

"And what are they?"

"I do not know. Sleep now. Stay calm."

The crazy cherry tree was struck by the blowing wind, much like a hand shaking the thin strands of hair on a head. God had forsaken that countryside. Even war left it alone; the English had bombed far in the distance.

"They are jealous."

"Who?" said Bizzarrone, pacing back and forth.

Aunt Luigina picked up the bundle without looking at it. She was as lean as a shadow and quite dead-looking. Here follows the description of the newborn; the rate of daily silence was measured in minutes; any other moment was characterised by high pitched litanies of breathless wails. Bizzarrone looked at him and not too brightly thought: *"What have we done to deserve this? It is most likely the child's fault.*" He went to the cradle, overarching with a smile-less stare.

Then he raised his big carrot-like finger. "*What are you doing?*" cried Luigina, alarmed.

"*Nothing, what do you have to fear?*" Bizzarrone barely touched it, his big finger tickled the little boy's cheek. "*Is it the child's fault?*" he thought.

"*They never stopped? Not once?*"

"*No, I told you. Let's go to sleep.*"

"*There is still some light.*" Says Luigina. "*You cannot sleep when there is light.*"

"*We will, I tell you,*" insisted Bizzarrone. He took off his shoes and, still dressed, mounted his bed and as if by enchantment, started snoring. Luigina already hears the torment.

"*It never stopped.*" Bizzarrone had said. Now it is dark. "*It never stopped.*" It will come tonight as well. When asleep, she thinks about thinking, the anguish she felt before giving birth reappears in her wake.

When she thinks she is dreaming she is deceived, and when she thinks she is awake, she is sleeping. Dreaming is in every way the same as staying awake, and it is in that great chaos that Bizzarrone picks up the child and slams him on the floor.

"*Wait! Stop!*" She shouts in her muffled voice. Bizzarrone turns around, full of blood. "*Wait! Stop!*" and Bizzarrone throws himself to the ground. "*What are you doing? Good God. What are you doing? Look at all this blood!*" All the drawers are slamming, just like the first day. All the drawers empty their contents, underpants, aprons, one after the other fly away from their wooden cells. It was the invisible hands.

The wood slams against the wall.

"*Do you know or don't you?*" Gargles Bizzarrone the giant.

"*We should not have had the baby! They did not want us to.*"

"Them who?"

"The spirits did not want it!"

"Luigina, sleep!"

For twenty days Bizzarrone had to live with the incessant *thump-thump-thump* against the walls. The scythe, the sticks, the hoes, the shovels and the pick with the broken handle, all struck the ground in unison like soldiers at war. Bizzarrone wet his pants; they come from neighboring houses to hear what happens here.

"What have you done Bizzarrone?"

"Me? Nothing!"

"What if you find something hanging on the crazy cherry tree?"

"What could I ever find on its branches? The stinking dead?"

"No, the baby, hanging."

"So, they are here."

"What? Who?"

"In a procession. Listen to them."

From the cherry tree they fall, two or three at a time, they descend.

Phosphorescent discs, like fast moving fingers connected to a hand, they quickly descend the cherry's tree trunk, six, eight at a time, they head towards the newborn.

"Is it even true?"

Bizzarrone nods. Luigina says yes. Everything calms down. What the hell. Bad dreams come frequently. Calm pervades the area, it is almost peaceful.

Luigina has never hurt a fly. She looks out towards the latrine on the field, not far from the crazy cherry tree. She is as awake as an owl. She touches Bizzarrone's shoulder, *"They even spat on his face ... Who? Shadows. Even the moon does not come out tonight,"* thinks Luigina, in a pool of her own sweat, sitting on the mattress stuffed with corn leaves. Even the moon is not out, how can they be here if there is no moon?

Fingersofagitatedhandswhichseemtopointtoashapehangingtothecherrytree.

Bright, transparent fingers lined up on the window sill. Luigina cannot be sure of anything anymore, the phosphorescent spirits are back and close in on her.

"But if all is true, how do they manage to go on living like that? And does Lory know?" My mother asks, distressed.

"How else could they have gone on living like that?" Rebates Uncle Ennio, who was getting ready to depart. *"The neighbors called the priest. He came and did all the things a priest usually does."*

"And everything was fine after that?"

"Everything."

"Come back when you want, come back Ennio. What do I have to listen to! What extraordinary things! Poor Luigina!"

* * *

Afternoon at the z'dora's house

A special woman still lives in the generous motherland, she is an incarnation of ancient virtues, a compromise between earth and sky. Interpreter of tenacious feelings, overflowing with practical and moral qualities. Part caretaker, part domestic, wife and mother when required, she is a wise manager of assets, of things and animals.

She never loses sight of her qualities, qualities matured between the oven and the cutting board, or between the vegetable garden and the hen house, between controlling the bills, and carefully choosing fruit and vegetables, always aiming for the best quality to price ratio. She was the unfortunate abbess of a home convent in a still dull post-war world. Such dullness felt threatened by the TV's sporadic incursions into people's homes and by the populace's desire to emigrate. She is a *"z'dora"*. In truth, she was the *"z'dora"*.

Edvige was Salieri's wife, first and foremost however she was the incarnation of one of these virtuous creatures. Salieri was a tailor and an Emilian like us, he lodged, as did his frown, on the second floor of a beautiful apartment, sculpted of stone and marble.

The memory of Edvige is as clear as red flame, she was always smiling, open and serene through the good times and the bad, wise beyond words and always willing to partake in the troubles of others. She was a little woman, with a hair bun kept together by a burnished iron pin, her kind demeanour married her gentle looks.

Edvige and Salieri had generated a bevy of daughters whose wavelengths could be located anywhere along the marriage satisfaction spectrum. Regina was as superb as a great duchess and had married a Neapolitan who had gifted her with a daughter; a certain Aurora. I once had to swallow my pride and surrender to the little beast as she wanted me to be a page, I can still remember her fluttering around with a strip of pink lace, diamonds most likely grew up her highness' nose. The shop-house experienced a hullabaloo of shop assistants, gentlemen, pieces of cloth and luxurious clothes. Among this confusion, towered Edvige, the z'dora, there to meet and greet and to deferentially serve her husband.

Salieri's frown deceived no one.

Those eyebrows looked like greying whiskers placed on his visage to expressly frighten any who had the audacity to stand before him. The tension would dissipate as soon as Spring was heralded on his face via the grafting of a smile. The man's belly was wrapped in a grey satin waistcoat and the trousers were an effigy of perfection, with a fold as clear cut as a blade, capable of splitting a hair in four equal parts. Salieri, like the great Mogul, stood out with his yellow teeth, which were the pillars to his big smile stretching geodetically across his world of expressions.

As my mother could not possibly work because of her mephitic and irritating character, she found a habit in taking me to people's homes at any time of day, including immediately after lunch. So, she took me to Salieri. To see things that could have only happened there, for example, bringing the fabric back to life.

One could only remain gob smacked when Salieri the artist caressed his fabric. He had raised a brood of simpering daughters, all the while ironing, marking cloths with chalk and cutting them with cyclopean scissors.

He fashioned jackets and trousers to such millimetric accuracy, that buyers would feel uncomfortable wearing them, unworthy of being adorned by such works of art. One would not wear a Rafael, a Buonarroti, or for that matter, a Salieri. The secret lay in the fabric; when he treated it, he imbued life in it. He used primordial instruments for example, an iron with a cork handle. Such items were forged by their use, brought alive by their symbiotic relationship with the craftsman. The scissors' tint was of an oxidised silver, a dull blackness which tended to the anthracite on the back of the handle.

Great Guignol scissors, the nut, forced the blades into an indissoluble, but elastic grip, meant to facilitate the cutting of the fabric, the handle, monitored your every move with different eyelets, one larger than the other, aiding in the thumb's articulation. Wonderful scissors, which refused to cut any material which was not prized, and ineluctably cleaved the fabric marked by the slippery chalk. Menacing, they were the companions of another tool: the iron. Its presence was gargantuan, like that of a ship's keel, a superb find, with a handle clamped by two burnished nuts. The impregnable fortress of perfection was equipped with a treacherous weapon: steam.

Its jet was such that it caused turbulences and almost made me feel dizzy when I saw it emerge out of nowhere.

I knew it was there, latent, ready to emanate its clouds of wonder. *"Do you want to try boy?"* This is how he used to call me: *"boy"*. *"Boy,"* was how he knew me.

"No, thank you, Mr. Salieri." It certainly wasn't a normal iron, more like a clumsy prow, a steel rampart with its battlements and a three-millimetre-thick lapel that smoothed out every fold. The current passed through some kind of circuitry and the switch occasionally crackled, making you jump.

"Do you want to try boy?" The Great Salieri was one with the spent Tuscan iron, stuck to his lip. If I had not had his nephew Aurora

forcefully involve me in her women's games, I would have enjoyed the atmosphere of sartorial fervour.

Instead I had to sustain the siege of this virtual castle, dashing on steeds to defend the princess with my stupid smile. We flowed from one room to another, followed by the looks of mothers, workers and that of Edvige the z'dora, looks which derided my clumsiness. As expected, the floor began to move, and the steam iron was charging towards me. I did not notice it and continued to tumble, to lie down between bastions and cushions, to crawl under horse bellies, brandishing hypocritical banners. The second blow of nausea knocks me out, forcing me into a regurgitating retreat.

The beautiful pink grit floor centrally located past the entrance spills over me and no iron can come to my rescue. Vomit everywhere. Indigestible meat, peas, a hail of buttons and burnished hooks which were once insurmountable walls on my pants flap, got dirty with gall, all together on the magnificent floor.

It is my stomach-brain that avenges itself, my twin brother mocks Aurora and her fairy games, the fact is that I can see the maiden retreat, disgusted.

".. Do so and so .... to the boy .... Meat ... digested ... you see ... not ..."

Edvige accompanies us to the door. Understanding. There are no such z'dore around these days. I hear her say: *"It is nothing, he is only a little weak, make it a light dinner, a bit of rice."* And the floor? Have I ruined it forever?

ACT II

Elegance, tabacco and the hamlet's aroma

"Helegant Hosieur" or *"Charmant Tres Helegant Moister, Elegant Monsù, Pour les homme tres chic Hosiery elegant."* Perhaps there really was written: *"Elegant Hosieur"* on the sign of a place which was: *"tres charmant."*

Brown letters in calligraphic style on a beige background. The shop was in front of the tram stop, where a large poster loomed, outlining a brown-white striped man drinking from a large cup attempting to advertise HAG coffee. The owners behind the counter ceremoniously whispered: *"Could you please show us the size of your fist? There you go, please close your fingers, just like that. Perfect. Thank you. I would say we need a third, or a second or a half measure."* This they suggested, treating me quite respectfully indeed all the while finding unlikely relationships between the size of my fist that of my foot and the distance between the Moon and Saturn.

Husband and wife were innately elegant. He was always tanned, him, the Humphrey Bogart of the village, he awed people at every whisper: *"There you go, please close your fingers, just like that."* And my hand was clutching the ball, to show him what foot I was equipped with, for him to understand which sock best fitted me. It was the go-to shop for the son of a migrant worker coming from the southernmost parts of Reggio Emilia. He wore a damask waistcoat with trousers whose crease was an ironwork masterpiece. One of those *'Helegant Monsieurs'.*

The wife, who was even more reserved, had her hair pulled across her temples and through to the back of her head, terminating in a chignon, which looked not too different from a giant cream *cannolo*. Wide and long skirts woven with a beautiful tobacco-coloured fabric frolicked about.

Among those noble promoters of charm there loomed a relationship of tacit professional entente that seemed to marginalise the conjugal bond. A protective orange plastic filter ran high, shielding the treasury of socks and gloves from the sun. It set forth an unreal light, like that of a tropical aquarium morphing the interior into an oily atmosphere of uncertain proportions.

The mustard-stained wooden counters and the row of gloves stuck on severed hands were on display, protected by a sliding showcase with a notch, satin on the edges. Those gloves were metaphysical greetings.

The decor was completed by a heavy glass vase filled with steel clips and three iron buttons with *poussoir*, with some torn labels bearing the inscription: *"quality yarns"*, and by the pincushion, a tiny pudding with a tender heart, covered with crimson velvet, pierced by an array of sharp needles.

All these objects had voices of their own, yet they chanted in unison just like the shears and the iron of Salieri the tailor. They sung in complete juxtaposition to the utensils one could find in a very different shop, that of Mario, the great man, who was greatly two-timed.

Half a block from the infamous condominium, on the same side of *Helegant Hosieur*, was Mario's tobacco shop. He ran it with his gypsy bride. Mario is the ceremonious quarreller who spent as much time in small talk as he did being two-timed. So, they said. He would come across as a guy who knew everything about you, from what color were your underwear to what you did in the last twenty-four hours.

Were the gypsy's eyes traitorous? Maybe. A long time ago. Who will speak of it now? Whoever slept with her was quite fortunate, Mario, a little less so. She was dark and silent, with a miserly smile and wide necklines, monitored by her spying mother. Mario was the candid soul, it was rumoured that he had been double-timed so much that there was no more time available for it! Poor Mario.

Their cat was perched on various pipes. He pretended to be dozing but never lowered his guard. He was the third store manager, the real store manager. A cat who, alone, managed to run the tobacco shop. Some things are beyond belief.

Sneaky, magnetic, receptacle of his mistress' mysteries, no one had ever seen her smile except him, that black pillow with big dangerous eyes. On leaving the shop, Mario's mother-in-law looked at me, I never understood if she had greeted me. In doubt, I waved three times. The first wave was to Mario, I was certain he had heard me, then I said goodbye to his wife who had just looked down at her crossword-littered magazine, and finally to the gypsy's

46

mother, who no one could really ever spot, as she camouflaged so well among the packets of cigarettes.

I turned around to check if the cat was there, he always was, and I always felt some regret in never performing as much as a nod in its general direction. The stinker was always awake. Having closed the door without a salute, his eyes turned into incandescent slits.

He threatened me: *"Oh is it so? You leave without saying goodbye? Go ahead, villain, one day I'll make you pay for your affront."* This is why I often left the shop so dissatisfied. But that cat was not receptive to compliments, it definitely was not.

If in the *"Charmant Hosiery"* one could fall victim of the smells emanating from the old wooden floor tangled with the fragrance of dried flowers confused with a breath of bergamot, in the tobacconist there was a symphony of succulent aromas.

Toscani, cigarillos, Agio evoked a dry forest. A live forest just touched by the rain had to emanate from the soft tobacco of the Samson and the Drum, and what is there to say about the aromatic Clan which made the customer dream of liquorice bushes and ferns?

Glues and dry paper and small bags of Bofil with mouthpiece and yellowed postcards. Materials with their odours, transparent, discreet; dry glue of the stamps and soft glue of the *Coccoina*, symphonic harmony of an aroma that thrived in the memory of smell.

How could we forget the packages? Illustrated by enchanting images. In the desert one would smoke Jubek on the back of a camel, in an aromatic sandy expanse and in the company of scorpions and pyramids. Hardened smokers chose Disc bleu and Gauloises which split their lungs. Lucky Strike was for the tram-drivers and gamblers, Pall Mall Red package for the spoilt and for the murderers, Chesterfield for directors and musicians, Benson & Hedges for traitors and office workers. Gallant for hysterical ladies, Senior Service and Player's for sailors with swollen dreams. There was also Peter Stuyvesant for students.

An encyclopaedia of aroma and taste perfectly crammed into order, right up to the top shelf, where the boxes of noble tobacco pipes towered.

Tin containers of a yellow-orange hue, in elegant packages like they were meant for perfume, and then Turmac, flat Mercedes, dark and light tobaccos. Crispy chopped crumbs, some strong, some soft, blond and soporific crumbs from Goodman Steven's. Cigarettes for the soul, cigarettes for betrayal and love. Cigarettes to kill oneself, used to celebrate love or resentment.

There was also some pretty poor tobacco, like the one for Ennio, the messenger uncle, or the sour one the great Salieri was accustomed to have.

Disdainful tobacco, an insult to its very name, was the one from National Exports, the one with the filter, which my father smoked on the balcony, after dinner, not to be seen. There was also tobacco for people who did not want to be seen, people like me. It is easy to imagine that this forest of packaged aromas exerted a magnetic attraction to all in the village.

Mounting guard to this treasure-trove there were the concubine, Mario's wife, and her sphinx cat.

* * *

You could not get away from Salvatore

Talcum powder, more talcum powder and a cologne which fuelled a never-ending fire burning on the reddened neck. An appointment at the hairdressers guaranteed being pinched by that sheep shearing machine which tore hair from your neck with no regard for precision or comfort.

Salvatore was dignitary to a court of spies, the chastiser of local customs, he was mad at all who spat in front of his shop. In the end, he just got mad at everyone.

"Let the devil take them, vandals." Ceremonious, gruff and gleeful, the great village spy had a name, and that was Salvatore. He was a barber by trade and fed those unfortunate enough to find a seat on his chair of tortures clouds of talcum shot from the chrome bottle. *"And do you know of any young ladies? Uh?"* He asked me.

"Your son will go far; it is beyond any doubt." He informed my father. *"I can already see what kind of man he will be."* I definitely did not want to disappoint him.

That sturdy, old Figaro, was combed like a village-grade Rudolph Valentino, his grim look never betrayed his thoughts. His wife, who was struggling with piles of white towels, took care of her husband's and the shop's reputation. The woman's virtues resided in the exemplary dedication she had towards her husband. Their infertility had been sublimated by their involvement with customers. Thus, did the village work, seven years after the end of the war. Everyone knew everything about everyone, or so they believed.

"But do not tell him too much, he already makes up half of what he says, he is a loud mouth." I heard Madame Rambaudo say to Giovanna Basovici.

Chatter for the sake of chatter, like a toxic talcum powder raised in the air. Chatter like nervous serpents. Neither Fiorillo's falling in love with the beautiful Figheira, nor the timely death of her father, went unnoticed to Salvatore.

"Yeaah! Who knows if he truly was her father?" He said.

Sometimes I found him on-top of me, like a gargoyle protruding from an archway, looming with the sadistic eeriness of a stalker with the deadliest of scissors. They revealed their murderous secrets with every *"tick-tac-clack"* noise they ushered, blades for a killer.

"That kind of woman, maybe…they go with the first one that comes their way … they go, you know? Take Carmen for example, wuhhh, Salieri's daughter." Did I hear that right? I only knew Aurora's mother. Who was the sneaky barber talking about? Who was the unfortunate target of his perennial mutter, shooting his words of poison into the back of my neck, with a breath that also spoke of coffee and mint?

I shrivelled under the torture of those murderous scissors, oppressed by his breath. *"Keep your head up please!"*

He ushered sly insinuations as a means to stimulate people to talk, uttering their unheard confessions, and then baste his oblique stories on-top.

A skilled investigator with thundering shoes, their vanity accrued by their mighty sole and exceptional splendour. They were of a brown bird poop color, but sometimes appeared to be as black as death and shiny, in the summer, they morphed into lighter, braided hoofs.

"And how are the uncles?" Oh no! not the uncles! I exclaimed internally, in the vain attempt to protect them. What did he know about my uncles? Did he know about Aunt Luigina Uistiti and the balls of phosphorus? Or did he know about the wet laundry dripping on poor grandma's head? Or was it… … Vera?

I almost blushed in front of this fake inquirer who invoked every last one of your secrets. *"And how are the cousins?"* He even had the nerve to snoop on my cousins! My eyes closed forming a crack of angry resentment. All the while, however, I was tilting my head now to the right now to the left, obeying his intimations.

You could not escape Salvatore. *"And tell your mother to stop pouring junk over your head. Why did she ever put this petrol?"*

I knew the reason why, but I would not have told him for all the money in the world. *"And do you still see your mother's fat friend? She is a nice lady, friendly … Ah! She is the doorkeeper? Where?"* Accc!

Gilberta also knew. It was enough for him to see a person, put them next to another and he could lay out their lives, spices, beards and bits of hair. Amazing Salvatore, the insidious hound.

"And mother? How's your mother?" At that moment I did not know whether to reveal her nervous tumults, caused by the rows of skeletons which danced in her maternal nightmares. I answered: *"Good. They're all fine, thanks. Mum too, all good."* I tried to get him to drop this investigation, to little avail. *"Nerves are a bad thing ... you know? Stand up and bend your head."* I obeyed with a second to spare in a bid to make him understand my resentment.

"When you go to Salvatore, do not tell him anything." An unnecessary recommendation indeed.

What would I have ever told him? Would I have mentioned Sostene? My uncle who was about to hire a lawyer because of the inheritance his brother deprived him of, and because of the laundry which drips on my grandmother's head. Would I have made a ruckus about Olga? Olga who spent her days damning that burdening fate passed onto her by an unknowable father. All this because of Aunt Prisca's shame: to become pregnant by a stranger who was already married and with children.

You understand that I could not have him know any of that don't you? Did Salvatore already know all of it? What about Bizzarrone and the spirits, did he know about those too?

"Does your father still run experiments? His attempts at fusion occur in the kitchen, right? There is fire there, that should be where he fuses things. He is a bright one your father, Geeeshh." Who could have told him about my father's experiments? From whom did he know?

"Not like that wretch who ran away with the daughter of the doorkeeper of the red house. I refer to him because they are the same age, you know, that wretch and your father." He said. I was stunned. Not even three days had come to pass since my mother's last wandering and he already knew all about it. A friend of hers, had brought us to Carmen's mother's place on the ground floor.

"Come on, let's go pay her a visit."

"Let's go then," my mother said. She was ready, clutching her bag in anticipation, excited to meet all the future misfortunes that kept her

interest in life high. Small, with a big sad face, dignified and with her daughter's lips ... the woman welcomed us. *"My daugther did not like to live this kind of life,"* said the widow looking around distractedly.

"I have to clean both this and the other condominium staircase. Luxury. My daughter likes that. And money. But if one is born poor, like us..." She was introducing herself in her own way. She had never properly got to know us, but she was letting off steam as though we had been her confidantes for decades.

The three women sat around the kitchen table. I was dead and lying on a red sofa. Roses. Presents. Beach house. Sons, weddings and promises. They spoke of all this. And then the saddened face of the woman who said: *"Two months ago. Everyone told her. Escaped ... no. With him. I do not know."*

"Does his wife know?"

"I do not know. Two children, how can you even get married if you have children?"

Three women talking about a girl. *"It is not just a whim,"* said the widow.

"It's easy to jump to conclusions. He has even gifted her a fur coat. I would call it destiny. I do not know, I do not know."

"I'm packing mum. In his house by the sea. He is a director. He owns the factory."

"I slapped her twice." Tears sprout from the doorkeeper. *"Who is going to marry her now after all this publicity? Will he still be with her, even if she is pregnant?"*

I looked around, the open window was facing the courtyard. You could see the red house that had been investigated by Salvatore, it stood with its two large columns of chipped cement. No child was around. Neon light filtered through the lumberyard's frosted glass panes.

Grey day, grey sky, bricks and grey shingles. Grey Carmen. No, not her. Beautiful mouth. Sensual bearing. *"Not here, I will not stay here mother."*

Handbag, high heels and off she goes. *"Do not go, Carmen. You will ruin yourself."*

A fresh mouth, one to eat. I only ever saw her a couple of times at the milkman's, her veil of grumpiness covering her beauty. *"Come back soon. Be careful. At first, she went out with an engineer. I like him mum, he is to die for. She said. Then she went out with the industrialist. This time, mom, he is the right one for me. I told her she deserves better."*

"He kissed me. The groom. He will marry me. I will leave him. It was him."

"It's not true. He is the one who left you."

Another man. Yet again another man. Sea and mountain, Saturday and Sunday.

"This time yes. It's the right time."

"Carmen, you are a whore."

"I do not want him anymore."

"What don't you want?"

Carmen's face is pale, her lips are grey like the walls after she had an abortion. *"This time it's different, she says. But I do not believe her. I do not believe her anymore. My daughter…"* Tears finally come streaking down. A necklace of a thousand tears adorns her neck. There is an affinity of tears between Gilberta and the doorkeeper.

Was this the story Salvatore knowing about?

In his shop lay secret and unconditional love stories. Wads of cheerful little women with their legs high in the air, depicted in the small fragrant calendars, held together by a braid of red thread.

A barber's pin-ups, how many times had they winked in the general direction of Dino Serra, of the Renna brothers, of Pezzuto, of the old Fiorillo, of Mario the tobacconist and the carpenter who almost beheaded me with the splinter that jumped off the planer? All these characters were Salvatore's customers.

For once my different eye got along with the other one, they focused on the graceful movements of young ladies in lavender bras. Inside a glass of champagne, a cyclamen-coloured little devil with a loose corset winked my way. The delightful brunette with her red garter belt holding up white silk cobweb stockings smiles at me. Dreams of scented paper, delicious barber *cocottes*.

"You like them? Take them if you want." I winced. A gift from Salvatore!

Confused, I put back the voluptuous object, "grown-up stuff", close to the chrome sphere holding the talc. I ushered a *'goodbye'* as I closed the heavy glass door, wearing a mask of confusion.

I thought I heard the barber say: *"A good lad. Good, like his dad, if he does not wander off while growing up. Too bad, he has that shocked mother, he does not look like his mother at all …!"*

* * *

How Prisca abandons the maternal house, getting into all sorts of trouble

The fire station is located behind Via Fischietto. Around the corner, there is a market covered by lead-coloured tiles, where people trade fish, birds and small domestic live animals, including cats, dogs, chicks and chickens.

On Saturday's half the city comes to the market, condensed in an electrifying frenzy of expense. There is a perennial congestion of machines, rags, fabrics and shirts sold in the adjacent market on the same esplanade. Some southerners come from the far South, from distant Sicily, and others like us, come from the closer Po delta. Bags galore, crammed boxes of fruit and vegetables, beans, dried peas and lentils in voluminous bags of concrete, chestnuts and chickpea flour scattered here and there.

The bakery is working around the clock, but it still cannot dispose of its orders. It bakes the crispest bread in the city. On Saturdays, people descend from the mountains to sell honey, goat's cheese and sheep's ricotta. Via Fischietto prospectively connects with a city that slowly extends beyond the river. Here you behold new houses and new faces with the same look of abandonment and the same aspirations. This is a fulcrum of activity for everyone, everyone except for Prisca the red skin, my aunt. She is Luigina's and my mother's sister; dried-up like a herring, toxic like gall and like it, indigestible. She took the number thirteen tram and stopped six stops from the market, in front of the fur factory, where she worked.

She never talks and never smiles, she only quarrels with the neighbours and insults those who happened to cross her path. Such animosity was never justified, it just occurred.

Treating the countryside, getting engaged, having fun or hanging out with friends were all things which Prisca would hear nothing about. She had forged her own solitude, a self-inflicted punishment, all day, every day, including Saturdays and Sundays. She was as surly as the frogs which paid her a visit every now and again.

Could anyone understand her? What was there to understand about her? I do not know. I have to use my special eye for her but I'm not sure it will work. Everything had already happened long before she took refuge in Via Fischietto; she was a fatherless orphan, like my mother and aunt Luigina Uistiti, an orphan of everything really, she took care of her daughter Olga who was beginning to understand what kind of mother and stepfather destiny had reserved her. At the time she was still with my grandmother, whose head had been used to dry the laundry. She learnt how to sew, cut clothes and keep quiet.

She went to Norina's sewing courses willingly, and brought these acquired skills back home, where she would perch like a condor next to the window, sewing, silent. She would sow until she felt her needle more than she could see it, in a bid to save money. The war was still raging on. When Luigina Uistiti had married Bizzarrone, Prisca isolated herself in the stables the whole day, to then migrate to the barn and finally ended up at Norina's place, who inquired: *"Why don't you go to your sister?"*

"I do not have the gown." she answered. Norina scolded her: *"Liar!"*

Prisca shrugged. She was as stubborn as a ram, with red hair, she kicked the world, mocking it. Her future would have paid her back with interest.

Only brother Sostene succeeded in dragging her to church. He had married Yole, the first wife who would have left him a widower shortly thereafter. *"If you do not come to church I'll take you, as you are,"* she was barefoot. *"And I will tell everyone: who wants someone like this? I do not know what to do with a sister like you."* They did not speak for some thirty years after that. And neither of them had lost out.

To tell the truth, Prisca had half a mind of going to Luigina and Bizzarrone's wedding, she would have liked to try on the dress she was secretly sewing. The front was wonderful, the fabric fell very well, slightly pleated, but she had stuck it in a corner of the room and it would have ended up in the closet of Via Fischietto. There to forever rest in peace.

She possessed an unmentionable joy in harming herself and making others furious, which nobody could understand. Indeed, she was quite bizarre.

In an episode stemming from before the war, aunt Prisca found her sister playing in the fountain one afternoon. She ran to her and grabbed her by the hair. *"You play, I work ..."* She kicked Luigina, all the way to the house's door, where my grandmother whispered: *"Leave her alone, she will get sick like this."*

Luigina's neck has been red ever since. *"She was playing by the fountain in the square."* shrieked Prisca.

My grandmother did not speak. Luigina was crying silently, holding her head as she diminished into a heap on the ground. Prisca sobbed: *"She must work, like me, she is good for nothing."*

A man was missing from that family. My grandfather had died early, leaving no rules. Leaving nothing really. There is a confused and photo shopped picture of him, a man with a hat who does not know where to look; aged around fifty, who died the same year my mother came into the world. My grandmother had given birth to some thirteen creatures, one of which died of fright as a cat jumped on his bed. A rumor circulated; whenever my grandmother was pregnant, my grandfather would tell her: *"What are you crying for? I will rent a cow for the milk, we have the money for it. What are you crying for?"*

That family had been orphaned too soon, and there were too many women. Those who lived there, seemed to be governed by anarchy and by the forfeit of choice due to a lack of opportunities. Marriage was a road which could have acted as a loophole and was therefore taken in high regard.

Prisca had received some interest from a guy who had a workshop beyond the Po river, one whose face was unknown, since she did not let him get any closer. *"Far away."* she said. *"What interest is he to me? Let him stay at his place."* There was nothing more to discuss.

When she became pregnant she still did not live in the house in via Fischietto, which she would have polished like a clinic's waiting room until her passing. She cursed fate, time, the toilet on the balcony, the houses, because *"people passing by look at your backside,"* she cursed the missed opportunities life never brought her, relatives, sisters and brothers-in-law, but especially she cursed her daughter, the living incarnation of her guilt.

She had disowned her even before the foetus started budging. After the birth, the very knowledge of having first held her in her stomach and then ushered her into the world provoked intense bouts of nausea. Cousin Olga begged for love until the end of her days. Her mother bore the sentence to the crime of having given herself to that dark-eyed southerner. And when the incautious child breathes a complaint, Prisca discharges all hatred on her, like a storm, and this for years to come.

Is there anything else to add? Of course! But it is best narrated by Norma, Prisca's countrywoman, who came to sell flowers near the tram station in via Fischietto. Norma had hosted Prisca, immediately after the war, because of a lack of housing, courtesy of the men and their belligerent games.

"I get home late at night, it is already dark. I have time for nothing." Norma says. *"I get my flowers at the wholesale market, and there is always a lot to do… Tell your mother you got pregnant… Are you ashamed? What are you ashamed about? You're pregnant, you had to think about it first. Now you keep it, the baby. She does not say anything. She makes the bed and washes the dishes."*

"Does it hurt? She does not speak. She does not even know how long she's been pregnant for. By the way, she cannot stay here, we are already squashed between the two of us, let alone three."

"I see you hold your belly." I see her place her fists on her tummy and she pushes. What are you pushing at? Leave the child in peace! Do it again and I'll tell your mother! I will tell her! She looks at me with two frightened eyes. "You will kill the baby like this. Stop it, you mule!"

"It's what I want." She said.

And so, I gave her a slap. Can you imagine that I have to take care of someone like this? She isn't even my relative.

Keep working, you are worse than a mule." Says Norma, the florist.

She eats, vomits and works. Then I come to know that in front of the flower stall there is someone waiting for her. So, I tell her to cheer up and look good, asking her: "Are you not happy?" Had I never said that, she almost jumps at me, screaming: "Who do you think I am? A slut?"

"What are you screaming for? Shame on you!"

I heard that he is a worker and I do not know if he knows she is pregnant. I think he did, because now the bulge is clearly visible. He is not the southerner who put her in trouble. Easter came, and I gave her an egg. She looks at me and says she is getting married. She could have thanked me at the very least. She is capable of leaving without saying a word. I ask her: "Who put you in trouble?" And she does not answer, I would not be able to carve a name out of her even if I had a scalpel.

They have only recently installed a phone and I receive a call from the hospital: "Are you a relative?"

"No." I say.

"Come anyway because they gave us your number at the switchboard."

She has a bundle near the bed. She gave birth. As soon as she sees me she says, "She's not my daughter, she's not red. They made a mistake." What does the child have to do with any of it? At least say something. "Now I'm getting married, I'm leaving. I will not bother you anymore" I look at the baby sleeping next to Prisca's bed.

She gives me some money for the food and shelter I gave her for the last two months. She says she is in maternity leave. "But after that? What will you do?" She does not answer.

I still go to see her. She does not see me coming. There is an open window. She is standing in front of the windowsill with the child in her arms. "What are you doing?"

"I will throw it away. I do not want it. She always cries, she never sleeps."

"Say that one more time and I will throw you over, mule! Now I will tell your mother."

She never came back to my place. I heard she married the worker.

Word of Norma the florist.

There are five floors, accessible via grey stone steps. Patched walls and balustrades, with Turkish toilets. It is 1950 or thereabouts. Communal toilets are arranged at an angle, with wooden doors and chains, where walls and indiscreet looks die. It is the first price to pay for staying in the city. Run! Run to catch the future, it frankly does not give a damn about you. But the countryside was worse for sure. Via Fischietto. Gates, bars, railings stuck to the pearl-gray wall. Houses there were worse than the one we inhabit with the Black Children. Via Fischietto is at the periphery of everything, including hope. And then it is full of southerners, and from Emilia and Veneto.

On a large iron shield that looks like a city banner, a late eighteenth-century mask is painted, the sign is rusty, characteristic of the city. Ponytails, wigs and cocked hat, carnival masks of the famous Gianduja. The sign must still be hanging, in front of the firehouse. *"C.C.C. Cantoni Cucirini Coats "*, was engraved under the second sign.

We lived in those houses, on the fifth floor without a lift, '*it was temporary*', or so my parents said. We spent fifteen years in the attic, temporary indeed. You could not have asked for more after the war? A factory is a factory, an iron dream, so are we, Europe and its ruins.

Families who would learn the diaspora of new life. But yes, let's usher the word overflowing with flattery, that word called: PROGRESS. Little is known of the worker who had accepted Prisca the red and her illegitimate daughter. The timing of such events is unclear, corrupted by the approximation of memories.

Olga is Prisca's bad conscience, she has ten years' worth of experience more than I do, naturally I start to admire this young lady leaning against the loft of the attic where I live, to me she is: *'pear-shaped-breasts Olga. Daughter of Prisca and a man called Nobody.'* In a few years she will have to dislodge from the zinc basin to make room for Vera. Same basin, different mermaids.

Maybe we have reached our destination. Only five minutes ago Olga was a red-cheeked lady with cheerful tits, how is she now crying her heart out on her poor stepdad Mario's knees? It is really true that the past is composed of jumps and reverses. I will have to rely on the paraplegic attempt to recreate her life in the house. They revealed to the young girl that poor Mario had nothing to do with her birth, and naturally she takes it quite badly. And how else did you expect her to take it? Mario was fine with her resentment, after all, Prisca showed gratitude towards her husband and stopgap father. And that was enough for him. The resentment towards the man called Nobody rises, the man from whose loins my cousin was born.

* * *

Lamentations of Olga, called the mule

"She does not want to tell me," Olga tells my mother. *"She shouts. Does not speak. She puts on his stern look. She says it is none of my business. But how is it none of my business? And what will they write on the official documents? Nobody's daughter? Why doesn't she tell me? I am not asking for the moon. Tell me at least who my father is. She's afraid I will go find him, and that this would complicate her life. After all these years he will not even remember he has a daughter. Why is it your concern? I have never been a burden to her. I do not take anyone home. I found a job, which might not be great but at least I do not weigh on her. As we are talking about money, 'Lend me something, then I'll give it back to you,' I asked her. Had I never said it! She asks me what I would do with it. I tell her I want to get married. I need more money. I have a job, I can easily repay. A storm erupted, aunt, the end of the world."* She tells my mother.

"You should first repay me everything you have cost me. Now you also want to get married?"

"Where would I go? I have a skirt and a shirt, she never even bought me an ice cream cone, never ...my mother is good at turning the tables. She does not want to talk about that. She becomes crazy. And what fault do I have? Is it my fault she never married my real father? At least tell me where my father is. At work they ask about my family. Which family? When my mother starts crying, she shrivels into a hump. I do not pity her, with what she made me go through. Can you now tell me my father's name?

Why does she and my stepfather look at me with those pairs of big eyes which speak to me telling me I should be ashamed? What was my mother doing when you washed me in the basin, aunt?"

"Oh, you know…" my mother answers. *"You know how much she worked, she has always worked her socks off."*

"Yes, but for me, she never did anything." Word of cousin Olga, as she rose from the tub. I find some of her figure's features delicious, she has nothing to do with the little ladies housed in Salvatore's micro calendars. Take a look at her, she is leaning against the door jamb ready to complain, as she usually does. She is a star. When she talks about her problems, her cheeks go red and her lips thicken, and she is always moved a little, with her voice breaking every now and again into silent sobs. Then she releases her arms and the puff of the blouse flattens but the two joyous headlands remain on the front. Nun heels, knee-length skirt, but she emanates freshness, and I almost want to squeeze her. Unfortunate Olga, nobody's daughter, because nobody ever wanted her.

* * *

Ennio, the messenger uncle, has something to add

Why were Olga's boyfriend and her stepfather drunk together? This most embarrassing tale was revealed by Ennio, who came to our house at nine in the morning.

"They vagabonded under half of the village's windows and made a ruckus on every street they explored. They woke up people. Then they called out for Olga." My mother's answers now are exclusively monosyllabic. Doubt stimulates fantasy. Are all of Ennio's tales reliable? This revelation forces us to reconsider Mario, Olga's stepfather. So far, he has been presented as Aunt Prisca's integral saviour.

Let us recap: Mario marries Prisca, welcoming her daughter Olga, a young girl whose father is Nobody. Then he waits for her to have a boyfriend so that he may go with him, at two in the morning, to Prisca's birthplace to visit my grandmother. They enter the only open tavern in the square and fill themselves with wine and walk down the full length of the street, arm in arm, shouting: *"Olga ooohhh ooohhh,"* and laughing; someone says he has heard some dirty words. But Ennio does not remember. Someone was going to call the Carabineers. *"What are you saying Ennio? And why? The Carabineers? For such nonsense!?"* My mother asks.

Malice is not yet my forte, but I feel there is a rumor lurking around the house which mutters that Mario liked Olga, and that he waited for all those years to scream her name out loud in the street, combining unflattering epithets with the names of the stepdaughter and wife, just to confuse Olga's boyfriend. It is almost as if he meant to tell him: *"We're joking, look here, I also make fun of my wife!"* Things a drunk would do. Moreover, Prisca would not have dared ask him for an explanation, she first had to tone down all the dedication she showed him by several notches. Every time I think of Olga I imagine her stepfather and boyfriend shouting her name and that of her mother in the middle of the street. That is, if one is to believe uncle Ennio's stories.

* * *

You must tell him about that filthy woman

The intemperance of Dino Serra's mother causes him to have an ulcer. He tangles himself with his thoughts. He would like to smash her head every time her stubbornness arises like a weed. This time it is not the stink from the rubbish, nor Lea the bitch's piss trickling down the stairs, it isn't even the gate's key stuck in its lock. No, this time it is something entirely out of his control, something which, to be put right, requires balls of solid steel. Having gone shopping early in the morning was not enough, nor was exiling the brooms and hammers cluttering the house to the basement. He tried to avoid her insistence. And now the mother, hidden behind the curtain, requests him to do that thing.

"Because that filthy woman does not care and continues to turn everything grimy. Luckily there are still honest children like my Dino who do not go with

sluts, not to mention the diseases they carry." This does the parent think and say. *"The disgust I have at the mere thought of having a brothel over our heads because of that filth. Tell her, tell her, tell her!"*

When he does not know what to do, Dino Serra dangles. His ear lobes become fiery red and he starts stuttering. He spent the whole weekend looking out of the balcony, gazing at the toilet-deprived studios, a realm of first-class terrors.

"Do you understand what I want?"

Time passes.

"Tell her, tell her!"

What's the hurry? First, he must find a suitable place to rest, then he must take a breath before ringing that woman's doorbell. Dino Serra climbs the stairs and goes to the landing where the boys sharpen their arrowheads. His legs become softer, they are turning into strands of spaghetti, how will he ever bring himself to do what his mother asks of him?

"Tell her, tell her!"

"You tell her, you're so good!" Dino Serra thinks sombrely as he gives his mother one last look. There is little to think about, nowhere to escape, he has to tell her. He can hear the turtledoves cooing, he has passed the point of no return.

"Did you tell her?"

"Hey, wait a mo ... mo ... ment, no no body w w w will die." But what could I have possibly had to say to her? *"That she is making it drip?"*

"Fool. Mind your own business. Fool of an o o old wo wow mm an, I have to do everything myself."

"Scscchh!" He whispers.

Dino Serra is crouched in the corner of the landing. Nobody sees him. He pulls out one leg, then stretches the other. *"What do you care? There are others who can ring the doorbell. I have to go. What do I care if it drips? I have to look after her. And to the do... do dog. My sister comes three times a year. It is not good to come so little. I have to put up with the old woman. Even during Christmas. Then she starts to whine. But I turn smart."*

"Tell her, tell her!"

"Just imagine the scene at my marriage. Pull the curtain and mind your own business. Stay calm!"

Dino Serra checks at his nails. The turtledoves end up in a tangle in the great cage and *"fla laf flap"* with their wings against the net, just like his thoughts.

"Instead, I look into my binoculars. Who will have the audacity to strip me of my binoculars? Quite superb binoculars at that. Military marine model! Nobody can bother me."

Dino Serra rubs his nails on his shorts' stitching, thinking: *"We could stay at the village. What business do we have here? At least the village is fresh. Not like this place. The village provides you with air, changing the air is not g-g-goo-o-good. We came to stay here, one on top of the other, doing nothing. And then she says: it drips. Of co-ou-course it drips, she is right over your head. It is not her fault if it drips."*

Dino Serra was starting to feel warm. His sixty years had passed with nobody there to notice, those sixty years were a weight. The only thing that bitch ever gave him was problems. She is old too. *"Today she has not pi … pis… sss …pissed"* thinks Dino Serra.

"Like my mother and her cystitis."

Whatever is going on in his head? Hammers, screwdrivers, glasses, binocular lenses, handkerchiefs, rope slippers and short socks, sparkling water, the gas stove's knob, tank tops and soap, a curtain separates the internal toilet and the handle that does not work. Underpants, shutters, wires to hang more underpants on, bras ....

"Drrrinnn!" Dino Serra's finger crushes beautiful Figheira's doorbell. *"Driiin!"* He is going to attack!

The mother spies if the child is doing his duty. She went out onto the balcony to eavesdrop. He hopes that the beautiful Figheira is not at home, he hopes he need not reproach her of the terrible crime of having her black lace bra drip onto his mother's sheets.

The third ring already …. *"It is not for me to wait,"* he thinks, as the door slowly opens up unhinging Dino Serra's bowels. Beautiful Figheira was home! *"Curses!"* He swears inside.

The filthy woman's face appears, absent. *"Dr err rii drips, yo you your st st tt stuff dr err drips. It t t st sta stains the la laundry laundry."* He manages to utter it all in one breath, ridding himself of the weight.

"Excuse me?" Says the sorceress.

"Excuse you? I do, but for what?" He thinks. He does not remember what else he has to say.

"Excuse me?" Says the woman, slapping him with a faint voice.

Beautiful Figheira has already said too much and is about to return in her dark lair's gut.

Serra tries to repeat the sentence. She finally answers.

"I am not lying, it is not my stuff that drips." Says the hairy virgin as she closes the door which seemed to crash down upon Dino Serra like boulders falling from a mountain. He runs, runs away tormented by the snake of shame. *"The underpants belong to that filthy woman,"* barked the mother, *"you had to insist! She stained my underwear! Go tell her! She made a fool out of you! Go!"*

"She t t to told m mm me that t they a are not hers."

Dino Serra stands his ground, ready to remain silent until evening. More extraordinary events than water dripping from underpants and bras were starting to see the light. One began to see radiators, aluminum pans, refrigerators and televisions pop into every home like mushrooms. The pressing slogans of the future were crowding our lives. It all began with the surrender and subsequent appeal of Alcide, a most honest man, hat in his hand, who, in the name of an Italy in ruins, would have told the United Nations: *"We were wrong and lost, give us a hand, it is also good for you."*

It was 1946 and cousin Olga was already wallowing in the zinc basin, my future father-in-law started to roast in front of oven number five located in Europe's largest aluminum smelting factory. These might be boring details to listen to, but to listen to them now makes other vicissitudes much easier to understand. Everyone set about looking for the best, doing double shifts at the factory, rushing to raise vineyards again, fixing bolts, raising condominiums, cursing or blessing fate, depending on one's inclination. Back then everyone knew what war and defeat meant. They wanted to leave that behind, and quickly too. How can one not agree with them?

* * *

Refrigerators and subtle pitfalls

He came straight from America and his name was Karson Tecumseh. Practically perfect, his polished chrome handle greeted me at every handshake; his size seemed to dwarf everything in the attic, attic included.

Everything from the enamelled metal, steel and unbreakable plastics for fruit and vegetable drawers was engulfed by his shadow. He was diabolically efficient. You saw him triumph, pulsating with his own and mysterious life.

Karson Tecumseh, the fridge.

But his arrival was preceded by an even more unique event. The great hunt for the sneaky little animal that liked to play hide and seek in a forest.

I remember that day like it was yesterday, I was pushed back near the woodshed located in the dormer, no man's land, in a bid to not attract too much attention and to not bother the plumber at work. Even before the man said *"good morning"* all hope that there was no substance to the suspicion had collapsed.

The animal was there, all right. Three o'clock in the afternoon, light on, as is the anxiety, coupled with the doubt of not being able to drive the enemy back. The curious plumber seemed to have a rough guess in deciphering the tension in the air.

Cousin Lory, daughter of red-necked Luigina Uistiti, held her grin, because she too would take part in the hunt. I looked terrified and exhausted as I gazed towards the imponderable, towards cousin Lory and my mother, who pretended to answer to the man wearing overalls. *"To change? What? Ah the tube. Change it if it needs to be changed. Come when you can. Would you like a glass of water?"*

"What is he doing, bent with his head under the sink, if the missing piece is missing?" We wondered. My hands, knees and head tremble. The man finally goes away taking with him the pipe piece that needs to be changed.

As I close the door, the connection between the plumber's eyes and mine is severed, leaving a taste of hopelessness in my mouth.

I have to deal with two wild Erinyes. I am innocent I swear it, I oppose no resistance.

"They will scold me at the very least," I think.

* * *

I have three enemies, one worse than the other

Lory's breath is oppressive; her protruding eyes rejoice when the enemy is suppressed. Mother and nephew would like to undress me and leave me there, naked.

"Come on aunt, come on, maybe we can find it again!"

I try to protest. *"Here it is aunt, here it is,"* shouts the hyperthyroid Lory, *"another, look how many there are! Good God!"* A high-pitched scream accompanies the attack, similar to the cry of Shilluk warriors, rushing into the darkness. The two, to see better, have secluded me to the pillory with a cardboard collar running around my neck, an effective means to understand my enemies' strategy.

"Come on, let's kill them all!" cackles Lory. *"That one is so big!"* *"Tic"* Killed. *"And this one is a goner too"* *"Tic"* Another goner.

I examine my cousin's palate. Her crown of incisors and canines are grafted into my flesh, she is the murky daughter of aunt Luigina, the one with the red neck.

My eyes hurt as they rummage across Lory's neckline, I am the unlucky host of a terrifying battlefield. My mind falters, while in the dark November afternoon I am massacred, as fingertip-riding eyes scout for louse eggs.

My battlefield hosts immanent forces, ready to unleash havoc; I have them on me now. The wrath of these Gods of war has nothing do with my father's docile manifestation of force, or the blind one visible in Giovanni Basovici, all actors in a cosmology composed of invisible energy.

On this dark November afternoon, my mother is not herself anymore, cousin Lory is not Luigina's daughter. Both are incarnations of the Electric Force. New modern Erinyes.

"Where did you ever get all these lice?! Set fire to them! Only then will we be sure they will die. Have you never heard that lice die with alcohol?" Suggests Lory.

"Not with alcohol, but another oil will do the trick." The second Erinyes says. Shortly after, a handkerchief impregnated with a stinking substance slaps my head, downgrading my dignity. Who will save me?

"Stay still! How can I do this if you keep moving? They will escape. Oh my, a beast, what a big one, that one here!"

I do not know whom to turn to for help. I do not know who the greater evil is: the Erinyes or the lice. I feel like a civilian caught between the crossfire of armies I never asked to have on my turf. All this occurs as I think about the day, which slowly consumes itself, in this atrocious November afternoon.

Lory stops laughing, her gaping cave-as mouth was large enough to let a fish swim into it with ease. Her strength has vanished. She too must leave, and her aunt, still breathless, talks to her about the dinner and the new refrigerator, which, according to her, buzzes suspiciously. I will wear that oil stench for life. Salvatore, the great village Figaro, he suspects something, and will no doubt complain, according to him, petrol oil ruins your hair as much as it does your reputation.

* * *

One never forgets the first refrigerator

They pulled him up five floors without a lift. The mule men, picking up the straps say: *"Where do we put it?"*

"There…Not even a little water for your efforts? …"

"No. … Thank you and goodbye."

"Aren't we off to a good start?" I thought.

A fridge goes where it can. In doing so, he captures half the kitchen from us. The illustrations on that American magazine exalted him; they heralded him as a milestone of the future. He was struggling like a metaphysical giant, with his steel decorations. Graduated lights celebrated him while the mind recollected the pieces of rancid salami and cheese, in the paternal grandmother's drawer. One would have to be used to seeing the parallelepipeds of dripping ice slowly disappear, unloaded from black trucks along the way, every other day.

Had the lice not invaded, the fridge would have had a much different greeting. He had arrived in the turmoil of a wrong moment. Anyway, now there he was, as thick as Sostene, the sloth-swollen uncle. However, it was not good! That mass of technological prowess resulted DEFECTIVE to someone in the family. Noisy and nothing else. There was conspiring talk about bringing it back to the appliance store.

"I can do without it. It is you who wanted the fridge, not I." The maternal Erinni concludes. Yet another family diatribe coincides with the arrival of the Karson refrigerator and his chrome handle. The verdict was an unpronounceable sentence. The disputed refrigerator had a secret life. It was a totem, an Apache refrigerator, branded with the mark of the American Indian, the one with all those turkey feathers. My father proposed to replace him.

"Here it is, and here it stays, you sleep well, I'll stay awake all night, pity" It did not break. It never broke. It worked, without fail. It became noisier and noisier, with its impertinent *buzz* that admitted no responses. *"You hear it, too don't you? I am not going crazy, am I?"* The new silence became his *buzz*.

69

Only then could we rest, pretending to believe that silence was now the hiss of that electric heart. That pact fed our family's precarious peace. Kit Karson, the Frigidaire, could have also worked under water.

Turning to his electric heart, I begged him to reduce his volume for the good of the family. I begged that technological heart. I thought the fridge would have understood me, I thought he had a soul. One time the defunct spirit of the great Apache, incarnated in the Tecumseh engine, departed from the cold carcass to tell me: "I listen to you, speak." Even today, fifty years later, in the end even, "he" had to die; his remains still exist, hospitalised in the house attic. The fridge, the corpse, the tombstone, with engraved:
THE INDESTRUCTIBLE.

* * *

The emporium of desire

From the noble village crowd comprised of Salvatore, the lynx eye, Mario, the two-timed tobacconist, Salieri, the virtuoso tailor, one figure stands out, affectionate, surrogate of maternal attention, sublimated of welcome and care.

Big, tall and pale; she hung forwards a little because of the cumbersome melons that weighed her down. Ginetta's mother ran the grocery corner-shop. Rice, coffee, pasta, stock cubes, dried beans, and even chickpea flour, toothpaste and soaps of infinite scents, everything was there, in bulk. In her delightful emporium, the apparent realm of chaos, you could experience paradise through your nose.

Therefore, I captured the fragrance of jute bags, of scaled soap, which hinted at sunny morning and clean clothes. Just perceptible scents coming from the pile composed of sheets of wrapping paper, the aroma of shortbread and that of pasta poured into large exposed containers, whose cracks nestled strands of stray spaghetti and shell-shaped pasta. Sacks, barrels and boxes hid the real size of Ginetta's mother, identifying her was not an easy task. She would offer a balsamic greeting, which made you feel at home.

One had to defend oneself from the swirling preparations of cousin Lory's marriage, from the melancholy utterances of uncle Sostene and of Olga, the illegitimate cousin. I had to find a safe space, one free of problems, to which only I had access.

Ginetta mother's emporium was the appropriate hideout. That is why I pretended to leave behind this or that food, purchases which I forgot on purpose, just to be able to cross the emporium's sacred threshold again, hastily saying: *"I forgot …!"*

In the store surrounded by floral cretonne curtains, I was welcomed like a prince, as if I had been the only customer on the face of the Earth. Immediately inebriated by the smells, the food courtesans told me their stories as my eye fell over the vanilla cakes, sprinkled with multicoloured sparks like a dotted night sky. *"Are you still here, darling? Did you forget something?"*

I do not know if Ginetta's mother ever understood. *"Do you want something else?"* She asked. I did not think she imagined I had come back just for her, for her gratifying greeting which flattered me. I did not want to tell her that maternal rages were oft unleashed at my house. *"Did you want peas darling? Tell mom that the tuna brand she wanted so much has arrived. Do you want me to write the name of the tuna on a ticket?"*

Touched by Ginetta's mother, I went out, with a gleaming smile on my face. *"Dear darling"* whispered the big woman with a golden tooth protruding from her gums.

In the loving cradle, a welcoming surrogate of my family, in the organised disorder of anchovies, mackerel, cod and green olives, where the rice swelled the jute bags, which supported delicious boxes of golden tuna, I found new life, and pretended to forget about the soap and toothpaste. I was going to go back there. The need to give back what was so gracefully given to me ... but I had nothing to reciprocate with.

Today, in retrospective, I should be angry with Ginetta's mother. She made me believe I would become master of the world, that the roads I tread on would be paved with gold, smiles, crowded with loving women, cheering, simply at my own existence. Ginetta's mother had the power to make me feel like someone important, a feeling that came in bouts of confidence and dizziness. Sometimes

I was surprised that no one had come to pay me homage. Perhaps my fame was not known to most yet.

The budding Narcissus rummaged among the windows that had better reflect his figure, he wanted to appreciate himself more. *"Oh my, how well combed are you?! Was its mom? Are you going to go for a walk? Come, I'll give you a surprise."* I came out like that, brandishing a chocolate bar, the first tribute, chased by the scent of scaled soap. What a present!

* * *

Cousin Lory's muddy marriage

"Did you not see them? The light turned on, only sometimes. They are always in there."

"Can nobody see them?"

"Nobody. What are they doing?"

"You can imagine."

"Day and night?"

"Yes, she likes it. He likes it too. She was always a bit weird. Well, they happily found each other. I don't really think she is a candid Virgin. What white dress are you on about? They started doing those things when they were kids."

"As long as they don't erupt into a scandal, they are like all modern couples."

"She will get thinner if it goes on like this."

"He is in love, so much! He only sees her. I do not know what he saw in her, she's small as well!"

My mother and her friend, who accompanied us while visiting the usher of the house with columns, talked about Lory and her husband Albino Purusa. They were in one of the railing studios in front of our attic and they been holed up in there without being seen, one could only imagine what they were doing. I do not know if they were also looking at pictures of scantily clad women in magazines.

After the lice story I would only see Lory once more, and that at her wedding. She wanted to get married in her parents' house, the one next to the hangman's tree, where the spirits had appeared. However, let's go by order, memory sometimes deceives.

"I'll see you aunt, I'll wait for you." She shouted at our attic's entrance, slamming the door. Balancing the little bag of wedding favours, my mother said: *"At least my niece is not bad, look how many confetti she has given us!"* Almost double the usual amount.

A cousin had emerged seemingly out of nowhere. He was calmer than Lory, he would permanently borrow money from his mother, making her die of a broken heart in the process. So, the stories say.

In my eyes, everything was new. The place where the incursion of the phosphorus balls had occurred was a large, poorly placed house, I noticed the procession of tiny ducks crossing the kitchen towards the stinking pond.

Everything tickled my interest over there: the solitary wooden planks of an old fence, the black soil of the garden, the grey slime that once dry shone weakly, tomato plants lined up like soldiers, armed with vermilion bombs, *eggplants* shaped like clubs, shiny and voluptuous with their incredible purple brush stroke.

There was the swamp, at Aunt Uistiti's place, a compromised land where the stream mixed with the sewage of the hen house, the pigsty and the shed where turmoil bowels found some relief from the stench. Uncle Bizzarrone, Lory's father was always sweaty and tanned, just like the tourists, he was the self-proclaimed king of that world. A myriad of wonders besieged me. There were broken pans with no handles, pots with corncobs glued in the mud, rubber gloves with three fingers, a large rope for a wagon, abandoned in the mud. The portico housed the unique collection of broken handles, shovels, and other sacred objects such as the rusty sieve's grating and coils of barbed wire.

Objects I would have traded any day with the spacious attic on the fifth floor deprived of a lift, where I lived. I was investigating Lory's old house, the course new bride. I already knew the new one, the one at the back of the courtyard with no toilet. I compared it with other places, and I found it to be genuine, stinking of splendid aromas unknown to man, a marvellous wild village, lowered in the heat of primordial August. It was the house of spirits, according to Ennio, the bicycle messenger's sobbing tale. My magical eye had to indulge.

They take me to the dressmaker who had sewn the green-white satin dress with taffeta roses, and then to the florist where lilac leaves and trombone lilies were mashed into a sweet-scented pulp on the ground. There was a bark of stalks just over there, with their green mood dying to the ground.

Near the altar, other malevolent flowers languished, flowers embroidered with a nauseating miasma. Lory dragged me with her, distracted, introducing me to some and not to others, for no apparent reason. She laughed at nothing, causing the interlocutor to a faintly smile.

"This is my cousin, the one who stays in town," and then she crackled her laughing whip. This was the price if I wanted to stay in this wild paradise full of stinks.

Lory's erratic presentations broke the interlocutors' thoughts; my name was associated with that of another person, or to inconvenient events I had never been a part. For example, my name could have been Albino, whereas the events ... well those could have related to the relationship between the engaged couple or that which the pair entertained with those people.

So, the florist scrutinised me for good, quite sinister way too, releasing an annoying ambiguous smile. He was an accomplice of past subterfuges, perhaps, of something that only she, Lory, and maybe even Albino, were aware of.

The same feeling been then confirmed in front of the hairdresser, a well-shaped dwarf with a blouse unbuttoned over firm melons. *"Oh, but how nice is your cousin! If you have children, make them like your cousin!"* Discomfort, nothing more. Lory's laughter made the lily tips shiver and the delicate lace of her wedding veil vibrated like a sail in the wind. I would have willingly returned to the wild land of her father, whose yellowed incisors stood as tall as large beans among his gums. Only two days before the wedding, and in those two days, I managed to collect a series of disasters, which I remember to this day. I poured the cake's chocolate dough all over my shirt as I was bringing it to the village oven; that swiftly followed by me letting the big pig escape. All that teasing with a bamboo stick had made him nervous.

The beast and I immediately forged a connection; we understood each other. Its wild face had scanned me, to then return to its more natural attitude of sticking itself in the stinking pulp and rumble in a bid to reiterate its nature of a temperamental swine.

As I returned to my cousin's hairdresser and seamstress, I noticed some likeness, somehow, obscure similarities reconciled the pig's squinty eyes with Albino's, the seamstress' and the hairdresser's look. It is much easier to describe the chaotic pre-nuptial ceremonies than the pig's virtual kinship with all the guests and their oblique inclinations.

I heard her scream like crazy. The dressmaker was torturing her, forcing her hips into her wedding dress. I do not know where Aunt Luigina Uistiti had disappeared. Among all that madness, I thought of seeking out the cherry tree, the real protagonist in Ennio's terrifying story.

I was overlooking the staircase and the hatch connecting one floor to the other from a secluded position. The seamstress leaned on Lory's hips and jerked her dress down. Lory laughed.

"Well this is strange," said the seamstress.

"See? It does not come down!"

"Pull. Pull. Can't you see it is stuck? Careful, it will be scuffed. I cannot believe it, you've fattened up, it took you only two days to fatten up."

From time to time the seamstress' hand would go on its own expeditions, sometimes hiking on the breasts, other times galloping on the backside, all in a bid to convince the dress to give up its staunch refusal in clothing my cousin.

"Do you like it?"

"What now?"

"Do you like the dress?"

"Like I said the other night ... I like it." Laughter erupted from their wide smiling mouths.

"The dress? Pull again. Careful because it will break. Come on, come on, it will fit!"

"It fits, it fits! If you push a bit more it will fit!" I do not know why those two coarse women laughed.

"You will see, everything will change once you are married with your Albino"

What in devil's name had to change? I pictured Lory's naked body, with her shapely but short legs, proportionate hips; she was not exactly my type.

The seamstress's face was congested, after she had flattened the fabric on Lory's backside.

"Do not push like that."

"You do not like it if one pushes?"

"Turn around!" The seamstress' hands had to travel under Lory's skirt because the lining was unstitched. The seamstress now had a visibly reddened and sweaty face. Lory screeched: *"God look what messy hair I have, I need to go back to the hairdresser!"*

"Go back to her and she will fix you. You'll see, after your marriage... you will change too. Enlarge it here, shake it there, place the silk rose on the breast, there is still so much to do!

"You must also come with me to the hairdresser!" I spy the pair while she inspects the mirror.

There was no comparison between my current view and the visual memories of the shining siren towering in the basin and that of Cousin Olga, with her nun's blouse all prudishly buttoned up right up to her chin. Underpants and garters are stuck to Lory's figure, much like her seamstress' hands. All, including the *hair dresser*, would play their part with Albino, who would have held them ... by the hand, naked ... or so had I understood, without really knowing why. Holding their hands, deprived of clothes.

"Look at the little rascal!!! You never spy on the bride while she is trying on her wedding dress; it brings bad luck! Go play! Off you go!" The seamstress shouted, after spotting me.

I left, annoyed, confused while she said, *"Do you think he has understood?"*

"What did we say? We said nothing!"

"Albino has to like it," said the seamstress.

"As if my aunt would ever know!" Laughter showers down from the two accomplices.

I remembered those photos slipping out of the suitcase and the pig with its restless roach; I joined him to keep him company. Two days from now and there would be a marriage.

What I remember most vividly of that special event were baskets filled to the brim with drinks placed in front of the hangman's cherry tree and steel plates overflowing with salami, olives, mayonnaise and hard-boiled eggs, the ducks made sure to perpetuate their tradition of migrating through the kitchen, regardless of all the hustle and bustle around them. All these memories patched together by the thread of smells that corroborated the rural charm.

In the church, Albino winked at me twice, as he carried my bizarre cousin's arm through a hopping rain of rice.

The pig's pink face, great officer of the neighbourhood, and then, of course, hoes, spades, shovels, baskets, farmers' faces, florists and the hairdresser whose gaze remained glued to my cousin's backside throughout the whole wedding's liturgy. All of these things were worthy of remembrance.

* * *

Gilberta's sorrows and the first revelation

Azure fading to Celeste, I remember this, and in the end, a dark blue brush stroke. Along with lashes of radiant sunshine and chills, followed by black dotted with intermittent lights, stars and crosses.

All this colourful concoction happened inside my eye. Slaps of waves, more rarely, followed by goosebumps. I sunbathe, I dry myself, I chatter my teeth.

The terry towel wraps me up like a sail, like my mother's voice. It is salty in my mouth. Having a bite to eat is a requirement, the stomach needs food, immediately; but the shivers must first cease. I would find it hard to chew with my teeth rattling out a symphony to the cold. Nothing is visible, a darkness looms, sensational blue ceilings, vaults of immense sky. Then sand, and the scream of porcelain gulls. Gradually the temperature changes.

The warmth radiates life. *"Turn around!"*

The vision focuses on limbs of a dried-up mole cricket in the sand, one inch from my nose. *"Turn around to dry,"* fishers the maternal guardian. The eye fissure records the sky's vertigo. Salty wooden barriers, the perfect rendezvous point for fearful horseflies as large as pebbles.

The marina is flat, with a large dock made of imposing boulders and horrible concrete spiders incestuously stuck into each other breaking the winter waves with their confused tessellations.

A curtain of light falls inside the brain, the wakening wave of the waning sea, leaves the shoreline faded at each exhalation.

In August, the sea is a purple table of warmth and sand with flayed people strolling about, gnawing on watermelons. It is not a place for the wealthy, like the one Sostene and his first wife routinely visit, it is one for families, for children and the elderly. It is a place packed full of family-run pension houses, improvised verandas and faded dressing rooms. When the wind moans, the coast wakes, listening. Umbrellas fly away and the water thread of the fountain shines like a silvery horizontal rainfall. All around, faded buildings flock, and the waves foam.

You cannot expect much from an immense puddle pretending to be an inland sea, just as you cannot expect anything from Gilberta's mother's pension house.

After Lory's ambiguous wedding, I discover this low building's recesses, with gravel laid out like sprinkles on a cake. An electric mumble of cicadas fills the air, as these natural musicians orchestrate glued to the branches. Gilberta is very pleased by our arrival. *"You have arrived,"* she says, dark-faced; she has just fought with her mother.

"We come from the beach; he has already gone for a swim." My mother says.

"Go and rest then, Faustino! Cristina, Veronica! Where are you? They are never around when one needs them. Veronica give the keys to your room to these gentlemen. Veronicaaa! Do sit down for a little while, it is not late." She says.

The place would not look that bad if only Gilberta's dark face was not part of its decor. She has a large apron with yellow and blue flowers. She is strongly built and carries a large pile of terry towels tightened to her chest. In the dim light, I see two beard hairs protruding from under her chin.

She does not want to be a concierge anymore.

"What have I told you? I had to go away from the porter's lodge. I will leave it to her. I did not leave her a penny. So, you call this life do you?" She speaks standing straight, in the liquid half-shadow projected by the poplar tree.

"But you must rest. Go cool off. Cristinaaaa! They are never around when one needs them. I came here not to see him. My mother, what a joke of a woman! Can you imagine I am her daughter? Take a good look at me. My sister, oh yes, she is definitely her daughter. The favorite one. She does not come here to be a servant like me, not her, no, not the lady, the favorite!"

Gilberta places her hands on her hips after locking away the tower of towels. I was already half-stunned by the sun's first blows and called out to the Gods asking if any of them had plans to make a change in this whale's fortunes. She was not a bad woman, she was just cumbersome and pedantic, a victim designated by events and by herself. She had fallen prey of the trap of inferiority and persecution, reneged by her husband, "exploited" she said, by her mother who was a clear winner when it came to intelligence and resourcefulness. Thus, lived Gilberta, who had also brought onto her the shame of asking for her share of inheritance in advance. Another enraged soul, her furious father, Carlo the shoemaker, my august godfather.

79

"Veronicaa!!!! Faustino!! I will beat my children when I see them. I will beat them up! They are never around when one needs them. Blondy!" Exclaimed Gilberta while sniffing me like a bloodhound, *"go take a shower, the salt will peal your skin off. How very tall, your son has grown quite a stretch this past year! Did you understand what the situation is like? I will bring fresh water and fruit in the room, grapes, apricots, melon, maybe? Cristinaaa! What do you want to freshen up?"*

Then Gilberta disappears in the laundry, grumbling, always dark in the face, because she perceived her mother coming.

"Do you see her? Look how she pouts at me", the matron whispers in my mother's ear.

"She has always been like this. Jealous of everyone and everything. She's here, she even brought the kids. However, do they help her? They do nothing to help her. What more can she want? Those are mouths to feed too right?! Do you think she pays me for what I do?" She spoke calmly, smiling, making her golden tooth shine. Majestic, with a beautiful dark, elastic skin. She filled you with awe. She was the boss, the real boss. She ruled over daughters and grandchildren, porters and cooks. She managed a minute family pension, but it could have been a grand hotel, the mood was there, and that bothered Gilberta.

All that needed was the raising of eyelashes, or a whispered word, and all would go as planned. The matron was tired; she was planning to retire. *"She brought her kids here without bothering to tell me. They are my nephews and you cannot believe how much they eat! Do they help me? Never mind; she is a workaholic. That I can confirm. She never breaks a single dish at her place, no, she only breaks them here, I had to replace a whole pile of them. She comes here to break my plates, it's tradition now."*

She shakes her head and smiles; she is a z'dora too, just like the wife of the great tailor Salieri.

"What are you doing?"

"I am working, iiieieeh! Cannot you see I am busy shoeing flies away? I lack DDT for flies!" Says the nephew, Gilberta's son, sitting on the deck chair.

"He is like this all day every day" Says the grandmother, resigned, *"Doesn't even think about helping me."*

80

All this occurs while I scrutinize the great clouds looming on the marina's horizon. Freshness was in the air and perhaps it will rain. Maybe in the evening. The sky gets darker, electrifying the air, which shakes up the immobile poplar.

Bizzarrone's swamp is a preferred location, even with its stinks and solitary rummaging pig. I have no idea why, with all the possible places one could go to for a holiday, we had to come to the one which served us family embarrassment on a silver plate, the one in which one could clearly see the swamp between mother and daughter, forever destined to misunderstand each other.

"Dear pops, nothing has changed here; uncle Bizzarrone's ducks are still a better sight. After a while sand infiltrates everywhere. Gilberta's son is not mean; he goes hunting for ants. I played with him to make him happy.

Then I get bored.
He stays in the little garden all day and await if any of the customers require his help. He is also quite chubby. I do not want to play with him and his fly-shooing stick.
Why would I?
Furthermore, he likes to stay in the laundry room, but I don't."

This would have been the first page of a half-commenced letter I wanted to send my father, who had stayed behind in the city to work. A half-commenced letter, which has never sent.

* * *

The place of revelation

In the confused first hours of digestion, when some striplings are prey to gastric drowsiness, take a nap, and dream to dream, I learn disturbing news concerning my birth. Bewilderment and wonder emerge to greet my true origins and my esoteric inclinations, which I would later develop.

Sinking on the rocking chair, half-asleep already, I catch a glimpse of Gilberta's mother in conversation with my own. I struggle to connect the dots but then spasms of clarity assail me, and I comprehend everything. From half-sentences, I understand that I am the son of two mothers and that my name is Prophet of the

Past, I have been fed with the food of the Gods, prior to conception itself.

"Do you remember how much of it you ate?"

"I only ate the inside part, the white of the orange pulp, I went mad for it" answers my mother to the matron, manager of the pension.

"And what did the doctor tell you?"

"If I had a burning desire I had to find a way to control it or remove it entirely... but there was nothing for me to do. I woke up at night with the desire. I had to eat what the baby in my stomach wanted."

You have never seen a pregnant woman eat the inside of the peel, have you? I could have a gastritis! Gilberta's mother's sardonic smile follows as she caresses my mother's hands into hers and continues to ask sweetly: *"And what about the rest? They don't shock your head any, more do they?"*

"No, that stopped a while back, Rita Rambaudo, the neighbour, now goes to have her head shocked, and she goes in the same clinic I went to."

"And how are you now?"

"Better, yes, yes, at the very least I can sleep now." Such was the eye's power, as it scanned through the past. There was no need for anything anymore. I finally knew. I had nourished myself with orange peels even before I came into the world! The food of the Gods! The revelation shocked me. I could not even feel Gilberta's son tickling me with his ant-squashing pine sprig. *"Siehhshh!"* He screeched. *"Siehhhshh!"* As rivers of saliva frothed to the floor.

I was born from the pain of two mothers who had been treated with ECT in the basement of the same hospital, at different intervals; I had inherited the overwhelming experience.

My mother and Mrs. Rambaudo had resumed their investigative talks. Mrs. Rambaudo was the neighbour and my putative mother, to whom I have been submitted during my mother's meltdown. Even she had to undergo the treatment, which would see a pair of electrodes stuck in her head discharge and electrify her mind. This was all done in a bid to alleviate behavioural disorders. Only my mother, however, had eaten the sacred fruit's skin. From that moment onward, I had been gifted with the powers of a hindsight knowledge, I could see into the past, having been nourished with a divine fruit.

* * *

The advent of the Black Children

It smells of fried. A pestilent smell of fried. Whoever cooked had to come from Africa or from our deep South. Which after all is the same thing. Our nation is also plagued by food related problems. Polenta, adored by a Trentino, leaves a Sicilian abhorred, a Neapolitan's fried concoctions cause nausea in a Piedmontese, and so on... so much for unity.

This is why integration in our land proceeds with many hiccups. The stories of the Papacy, the Bourbons, of Aleramo and the Savoys still matter, but not as much. What matters now is the smell. The smells have a soul, the stinks emanating from food narrate stories of fish, onions, and tomatoes, stories of old women dressed in black, like hags bent over hot broths bubbling with leeks and carrots, of widowers in a tank top, while they fry.

While on the subject of food, let us leave aside for a moment the noble orange peel rind, the pestilent stench which cloaked the staircase of the condominium led to the top floor attic. *"If it gets any worse,"* Pezzuto had told me *"the smell will kill the turtledoves."*

We had just unpacked our suitcases, having come back from Gilberta's pension. We recriminated against my father because he could not find us at the platform, forcing us to waddle with bags and suitcases back to the house. With my mind already obfuscated by the smell, I set off to investigate.

Muller's son, a sculptor who constructed little balls of solidified mucus knew nothing about it. Pezzuto's sons had described a great hustle and bustle around mid-August but nothing more. My half-brothers, Rita Rambaudo's kids had gone so far as to say that Indians or Negroes had arrived, dressed in blue and red rags, a young woman, an elegant man and black children emitting monkey verses. They all crammed into the attic. Initial sorties around the upper floors confirmed that the smell came from there.

The woman barely showed herself, sporadic reports describe her as being thin, with very black hair, quite gracious in her own way, of non-domestic appearance. She barked; she kept her head down on the water dishes. You could not catch a glimpse of her without her catching a glimpse of you first.

She would then cower away even more; hidden by a closet, bent double to tuck a blanket.

The Black Children's advent was under way. They came from southern Italy, the stinking alien invaders. The husband looked like a banker, he was father to the horde of hungry creatures and descended the stairs with an air of great prestige about him. He seemed like a distinguished gentleman, momentarily living on the top floor, in the attic where the sun cooked brains and with it the hopes for better lives. He was the tribe's sovereign, and kept his wife segregated in that sheepfold, where, between tar and cement, basil and chili peppers grew. Nobody knew if he was in charge of an assembly line or if he was an inspector at the post office.

From the crack in the open door, one could perceive the opacity of objects, fabrics, and furniture, using a sort of visual touch.

A patina disheartened everything linked to those people, the skin, the hair, the clothes that looked like felted rags.

The squeaks coming from the open door were followed by dull thuds, the beating of cutlery, the flush, the din the table made when dragged on the grit. They expressed themselves in gestures and screams.

Madama Pezzuto's vain attempt failed miserably. *"I tried to give them candy, they're kids after all. She ran away, and the baby looked like he wanted to bite me,"* she said.

On the top floor, with no lift, wild people had landed with a female and her wary pups. Those were the facts. They had to urinate in some kind of non-conform recess because sometimes a stench diffused from the door crack, maybe it was the children who still could not properly lock in their toilet as a target, or just did not know where to hose and fired at will. We scrutinised them. We just could not get used to the smell that came from the den. Rita Rambaudo, my second mother, screamed at those two child scoundrels in desperation. Her nervousness had swollen her neck, and her husband, a pale cabinet maker, did not even know what she was on about.

The condominium gathered in front of the wet botch on the wall. It had extended its contours, until it assumed the dimensions of a continent. The wet stain was as much a totem as the Karson fridge, an object whose origins were unknown and would stay that way. It existed, like a relic from ancient times and that was enough, an invitation for everyone to reflect upon.

Its overflowing offshoots and inflorescences towered all those that passed in front of it. Iotti the doorkeeper said it was better to ignore the stain, otherwise it would have grown wider, eventually, as all things, it would have come to pass. As she said this her face got darker, and she became more silent, as the stain grew.

The totem, the wet stain on the wall, expanded its borders beneath the wall painting, fermented it in a hygroscopic drip; reporting events occurring in the condominium.

It had expanded when the doctor, Basovici's friend, committed suicide. It grew another branch as it heard someone talk about phosphorescence in conjunction with the death of beautiful Figheira's father. Even now, on the arrival of the Black Children, the spot seemed to have expanded, correlated with the events of the condominium; it signalled the alteration of the *status quo*.

"Right now," had said Dino Serra. *"Right now, what?"* *"No ... I... I... I w was was jus just sa saaaying."*

"Ah, but it does not matter," said the woman marshal. *"It does not matter at all. The stain is there, and we will keep it. Nobody has succeeded in making it vanish; the builders say that the internal material has yet to dry. They are having a laugh. What kind of a wall does not dry out after three whole years? They put crap in the walls that is how they built this house, with crappy plaster."* The marshal continued, frustrated, and Dino Serra nodded, perplexed.

I knew what others ignored. My second eye caught invisible events, the inexplicable ones, it scrutinised people's hearts in real time, skimmed through memories, scanned past and future lies and read of burning unspoken truths. I understood what others ignored, awake in a land where slothfulness reigned supreme and submission to the sleepy routine of appearances was the law. I was investigating, reflecting, pondering, finally remaining astonished, conscious of my all-encompassing ability.

Being born from two mothers' pains, I could see what others did not decipher.

The stain was the materialisation of my mother's nightmares, which were closely related to the fridge's incessant humming, which only she could hear.

How could I have told the condominium? They would have thrown us away. The stain summarised our family's moods, disappointments, tensions, oddities, discontent and my mother's precarious nervous balance, in that stain one could read the timely report.

Meanwhile the Black Children extended their domain on the landing. From my vantage points, I could spy them unseen. First came the largest one, barefoot, with snot drooping down to his lip, skinny, dark skinned, he half closed the door chased by his mother's bark bent over the sink. He held a half-bitten carrot, which had a predisposition to being one and all with the ground. I do not know how many times he picked it up and gnawed at it. Their barbaric appearance was intriguing. The female monkey went to the gas meter. She opened the door, glorying in the sickly exhalation of the leaking pipe. She squeaked, indecipherable so.

She looked towards the door, and out at the crack. She checked that nobody was around and followed his brother. Disheveled, of primitive beauty, with black lips, perfectly drawn on her visage, like her eyes, deep and shimmering like stars. She wore an opaque rag, with little flowers, and did not have any socks. The soles of her feet had disembarked on the landing. She looked like someone who had never seen a floor before. She followed her brother into the gas meter compartment, closing the door behind them. To tell you the

truth, the smell of piss was both present and absent; I would have half-expected to see them urinate against the wall, this would have explained the widening of the mysterious stain. The stench from their food had impregnated the walls, the ceiling, and the entire staircase, the family of wild beasts was growling, marking its territory in the process.

However, one observation remained incomprehensible to this day. Why was it that when the man abandoned his kingly court of fried smells his clothes released sylvan scents as he descended the staircase?

The stain on the wall and the smell of fried stuffs, were consequential to the advent of the Black Children! This was enough to convince my parents to look for a new home.

* * *

The new house and a poisonous letter

Pyramids of cement and sun baked tiles, skeletal apartment buildings and luminous houses grow in the city's outskirts. The new working-class and bourgeois city invaded the skies; it ate the earth, spreading its hasty forms in monotonous linearity.

Pretentious or decidedly poor, overcrowded with fireplaces, bathrooms, tubs, sparkling taps, kitchenettes, littered with tiny blue-green mosaic tiles, it widened into monstrosity. The new city: an omnivorous creature. My mother's brothers abhorred the gargantuan redbrick cubes and terraced houses. She complained: *"Let's go and look for another house, I cannot bear staying in this one much longer."*

My father indulged her with no intention of satisfying her. We had come to stay on the fifth floor without the lift upon the recommendation of a friend to her sister Antonia, whose photo dad kept in his wallet. Leaving might have offended the aunt.

"Offend who? For all the poison your mother and sisters spat on me? Do you think they did us a favour? You will either find the house or I will leave."

Sweating stairs, fresh walls, sand and bags of cement, beams, mezzanines, iron ramps, up and down, holes, crevices, kitchenettes, *"Oh no, not another attic no!"* Cooperative houses and luxurious houses, of the kind you waved past while pretending to play the part of a rich aristocrat.

Too small, too big, too luxurious, too high, too low, too dark, and then oh dear, so expensive, way too expensive! Too expensive, too much noise, too little space, too much wind, furthermore, it is isolated, it's cracking already, you can see the crevices on the walls and on the floor, like premature canyons ready to gobble you up in a couple of years when they mature.

"Where is the life you promised me? It would have been better if I stayed with my mother, at least I was breathing my air, it is disgusting here! You and your mechanics! And I believed you!"

The maternal thought slapped, mocked, and recriminated my poor father. Tears followed by hope which drowned in an ocean of tears again; destiny was playing games with us, the house she liked was available, and then all of a sudden it disappeared under a plethora of excuses best categorised under the banner of: *"Oh I am sorry, we misunderstood one another!"*

"What do you mean we cannot find the house?" The first of many neurotic arrows shot against my father's impassivity. *"Who is responsible for finding a home?"*

"I do not know sir, we already have waiting lists, and do you want us to include your name?"

The city was visibly changing, it filled up with heaps of houses, but ours was not there, it was not to been built yet, it was not compliant, maybe they still had to build it. A tired and phlegmatic father, an exhausted mother and a child far too conscious for his own good: this was my family. Towering over each misadventure: Tecumseh the refrigerator whose formidable buzzing filled our sleepless nights, while we daydreamed about the new house.

It arrived around a Saturday lunchtime. That is always the best time to ruin the weekend. On reading the missive, my natural mother becomes pale and tries to mimic a faint. This is what she just read:

Maybe you just did not think about it anymore. What? Oh, you will not play this game with me. Do you understand? Mario and I are waiting for you to remember the kindness you received from us when you first came here. Did you throw them away? I will have a lawyer write to you. I am sure you will find them if a lawyer writes to you. I know my daughter is visiting you, great, just great! If my daughter did not like to have me as a mother she could always choose to have someone like you, you get along so well. All the filth she did since she was a child is fine for you. I work, and I crack my back while you are 'the Lady', she who has a nervous breakdown and cannot work. The stuck-up Lady-like sister, who cannot even remember the four chairs I lent you when you and your husband were broke. You had better find those chairs, they belonged to our father… and if you happen to have thrown them away, I will send a lawyer, you had better find those chairs.

Your sister Prisca

I did not care about the letter sent with loving hatred from my mother's sister. I quickly searched for a diversion, but diversions don't come easy. Tecumseh's buzzing increased. I could have gone to see Ginetta's mother concealed in the grocery store, instead, I diverted my attention to the ant hunt, they had their nests right in the wall's inter space, under the window. Stun them with alcohol and massacre them with the hammer.

* * *

My mother's virtual lover

He lives in the house with crumbling concrete columns, his name is Nevio and his wife is overweight.

The pair are childhood friends with my mother. My mother occasionally wonders what her life would have been like next to another man. A man like Nevio, for example. Such thoughts had best remain thoughts, especially for that generation. My mother has arrived as far as destiny wanted her to. Discontent and bouts of nervous breakdown fomented harassing thoughts, which over the years have crept their way in her head.

Nevio is her friend's husband, the one she grew up with. He is a great guy. A hunter, a fisherman, a fornicator with sex constantly on his mind. He is the polar opposite to my phlegmatic and plush father, a mystic in love with mechanics, his only true love.

Nevio loves good food. He was scared stiff of heading to the front during the war, so, in a bid to save his skin, he hid in the attic. He was a kind coward, a deserter wrapped in a warm wave of erotic feelings; he held no malice towards his wife, of course. Nature is nature, and nobody can command it. This was his august thought, and he made sure to reiterate it in his wife's presence.

Women hid in his pockets, in crumpled pieces of paper concealing phrases, times and names. Women were in his shoes, under his jacket, in his trousers, he met them on the street, at bars, at balls and at work. Females wanted him, because he was pleasant and light.

My mother would have never received such gifts from her husband; however, had she received them she would not have been able to endure them for long.

The fog of perfidy that her two sisters-in-law had enveloped her with vanished when in the company of her friend's husband. Sometimes they would shake her off, allowing months to trickle by, because she was nosy and gave indigestible opinions about people and facts. Her happiness peaked when our family joined theirs; she frolicked in conjoint activities such as going to eat fried fish and ice cream, on Sundays. We sunbathed along the river and gathered dandelions for the salad.

On these occasions my father expressed his hedonistic irony: *"If they go there we can go there too. How are we any different?"*

"Nevio says we can. Nevio says we have to go, according to Nevio you have to trust …" On the third and last debut my father concluded with no irony and a smiling resignation: *"If he says so, then it will be so."* If Nevio said something, you had better believe it, Nevio was the gang's pillar.

"Why don't you tell us about the time when you were looking for a man under the bed?" his wife asked.

"You were furious. Greedy." Intruded my mother, the gossipy friend. *"You go around collecting women and your wife can not even have a sympathy. So? Is this your great skill?"*

When the diatribe degenerated into invective my father used to issue a: *"Sshhhss!"* to restore calm. With this peace-reconciling intervention, he halted his sorties into the world of friendly domestic worldliness, saved from the source of animated discussions and exhausting diatribes between old friends.

"I will find your house, I will make it, or I will not be called Nevio hereafter. I know someone in the City. In addition, we will build this house the way we want to be built. Not how they say."

"Good! Good man! Things should be done that way! Please help us Nevio, without you I do not know what we would do"

My mother's bleeding heart was healed, no cure could compare with that brought by his childhood friend, which brought with it social redemption, a nectar for her ears. Nevio the sympathetic, Nevio the storyteller, the braggart, the illusionist, Nevio the great hunter and amateur. Why doesn't my father ever speak like Nevio? He does not even echo any of his sentences.

"Oh, do be quiet, braggart," moans Nevio's wife.

"Was I not a mason? Don't I know how to lay out a floor? Pull up some walls?"

"Shut up, braggart. As if someone can build a home by themselves," says the wife.

"Do you want to see what an amazing house we will build? We will setup a cooperative. It will have a garden and a fountain, or don't call me Nevio."

"Really now? Where are you going to find electricians and plumbers? You were a mason," commented a quarter of the company.

"I can do it with my eyes clothes!" Nevio trivialised. *"The only thing we need is good weather, to let the walls dry out, you cannot go inside a damp house. For Heaven's sake, if I tell you it will be done. One just goes to register at the office, pays a certain amount and that's it! Don't you believe me? Tomorrow I will go to the town hall and you will see."*

In this very moment, Nevio replaced my father in my mother's mind. The substitution is complete, from the fascinating rhetoric, to the world of persuasion to the intention, which does not admit reproachful analysis. He will show us how to do it. Nevio, the backside caresser. The sincere braggart, and a woman-waster. Thus, does Nevio conquer my mother. And just like that, my father's credentials, tightened by six years of military service in Libya to repair engines, are discredited and forgotten. Tomorrow Nevio will setup the cooperative, the next day he will disband it if they say it will take more money and more permits. Its name will

91

be: Astra, like a star, as a hope of redemption for the inhabitants of all condominiums, it will be called: a better future, with a bathtub and radiators, and hot running water. Its meaning will be: a dream of a destiny that does not take off.

He puts a great deal of effort in this project. The great Nevio. Telephone calls, inspections, contacts with surveyors and masons. *"You cannot ... what don't you understand? You cannot register the cooperative under that name, because it's already taken. Astra is already registered, so I called it by another name."*

"Another name? ..."

"Sastra."

"Oh no, that is bad, Sastra, could you not have called it something different?"

Months pass, two, then three, and then that backside caresser goes to investigate why the reply is so delayed. He discovers a missive that says: *"Dear Sirs, the cooperative cannot be setup because funds for subsidised housing are no longer available."*

"So, nothing?" We are left with nothing?"

"Nothing at all ... it went like this. Yep, just like this."

My father triumphed over Nevio's failure with his gentle, smiling, unspeakable silence.

* * *

The divine food and the mermaid's escape

The discovery of the divine food which nourished me before I was born, followed by anchovies and butter, and the failure to setup a cooperative forced me to reflect. I summoned various characters to a virtual gathering. There was the plumber who had to replace the broken pipe on that lice-infested afternoon, there was Iotti the concierge, uncle Bizzarrone and Gilberta's mother, the pig was the guest of honour, inhabitant of the swamp which had swallowed up aunt Luigina Uistiti, God bless her soul.

I needed to understand.

Basovici was venting his innocence Iotti's way, he had been accused of stealing his friend's body. Dino Serra complained about bras dripping. My father's sisters appeared, with blood-red eyes ready to avenge my grandmother, who has been seen urinating in the same basin used by her daughter-in-law to wash her face. Another figure sat, disdainful and undaunted, at the center of the thought-invoked tribune, among all others summoned: the unattainable beautiful Figheira. All the virtual successive convocations confirmed the unfathomable cosmogony of the condominium and its surroundings. Moreover, how much power would the Prophet of the past (myself), have? A stripling whose power was concentrated in his different eye? What was the limit of my supernatural powers?

And where would my investigations lead to if not to a known landing? A place I already knew from the age of the first reason and feeling. However, my need to comprehend remained, insatiable. In vain. Had two women really granted me life? It was beyond any doubt that the ECT therapy they had been through produced some sort of osmosis between the two. I should concentrate my investigations around that drama.

The darkness in their minds had spawned parallel lives, existences tiptoeing along the borderline of nothingness and insanity, finally condensing into an eccentric psychic consistency: mine. My natural mother and Rita Rambaudo, our neighbour, were faceless creatures, deprived of provenance and destination.

I had to interrupt the investigation. A pressing call, like a cry for help, rang at around three o'clock in the afternoon: *"Hello? Ah it is you Erri. What do mean ... she escaped? ...why ... escaped? ...cries ... who cries? ... Ah Anselma and Fidelio cry, oh yes, well, why? when was it? Did she at least call? And where is she now? How do you not know? How do you not know where she is?"*

Vera, the siren I glimpsed splashing in the zinc tub through the keyhole, had chosen her path. She ran away. She left the house around nine, without a suitcase. She had whispered on the phone that she was going for a ride with a guy she got to know at the bar, and that the ride would last three days, or maybe more.

Then she hung up. Had I known that before! I would have promised her pearls of rain from desert lands, seas of happiness and palaces as titanic as the mountains in the distance; she only ever wanted that; flattery. I was irritated because I had to suppress my annoyance, and because men like myself were no food for the siren. She had her destiny written all over her, surely someone would had understood? Vera's eyes mirrored the desires, the temptations, the betrayals and fugues of many men. I could not forget her lust-promising gaze. She was like a modern pied-piper, she stirred up turbid desires and, through her woes, solicited deception. I used my special powers, I rummaged through the mind of the man Vera had fled with, and here is what I found:

"You're not bad, you know? with those tight-fitting shorts that could bring a dead man back to life. Go into the bakery and stay there for a while, wait, talk to the cashier, look through the window and if you can still see me, I will turn back. If you cannot see me, then you go out, you stop, you are amazed, you look at me sideways, as we take two steps round the corner, and I brush your arm; you just say you have to go home, you're almost scornful, you listen to me, shake your head, you're discouraging, but I will show you what could happen if you followed me to the sea, you do not hesitate; you do not say anything, I will add; if you are interested, I also have a job that could do for you, I touch your side, you do not say anything, you're cold, far away, you're silent, you look over my shoulder, I ask you if you want to? do you want to?

What? You say you're afraid they'll see you, but you're not doing anything wrong, I'm talking to you, and you look at me, so? shall we go? you say you have to think about it, I take you by the arm, you have a questioning look, but it's all fake, you already know that you'll come with me, you already know that you want to try the job I promised you, you mumble that you're tired, you've had a hard day, is that it? and what have you done? You did not do anything today, you're just tired, maybe you need a vacation, so what are you waiting for? I don't bite, we're in good company, there are other people, you look at me for the first time, I see what could convince you, you like what we are talking about, I try not to look at your breasts too much, my eyes have slipped down your neckline far too many times, I struggle to keep my distance, I lead you into the darkness of a door, I hold you, as you lay your head on my shoulder, and just like this, after I steal my mouth from yours, you tell me you want to try and be my bar's cashier, you say you're curious to know my friends and that if I am not too stupid you could become my friend and you just need a bit of time to tell your family that you're away for a while.

You want me to tell you one thing in particular, you want me to believe that Vera isn't a slut, and that she does not wonder off with the first man she sees. Vera is not of those who live on the street."

We hurried to Erri's house. Anselma turned into a convulsion of tears and jolts. Fidelio was in bed with a big headache; my search for Nicola's guitar was unsuccessful. Anselma's usually frenetic hospitality and the daughter-in-law's enveloping warmth are nowhere to be seen in that sunny afternoon. One world was on the verge of extinction, while another, plagued with unknowns concerning Vera's future, opened. As Vera's brother spoke, I searched for his usually calm irony, but that was gone too, like Vera.

"He wants to go to the Carabineers." Anselma sobbed.

"Who wants to go to the Carabineers?"

"Fidelio."

"But they cannot do anything."

"He's afraid she will get up to no good. He does not forgive her, and he is ashamed. He has a big headache. He is not himself. His daughter ran away from home, he no longer goes out because everyone is talking about this, he has aged some twenty years," sobbed Anselma.

The apartment had undergone changes in furniture and flooring, a white bowl illuminated the electric-yellow painted wall, the curtains had been changed as well, and the doorbell's electric *"din don"* constructed by Fidelio had changed tune.

The large painting in the living room, brought to life by Erri years before, now portrayed a dark toned marina, where the foam's icy white hues no longer softened the waves, quite on the contrary, they capped their peaks, suggesting underlying tensions, hinting at a collection of dangers concealed within the wave, just before the storm, ready for the foray. The water ramparts danced with the blue jaws of endless rip currents.

Dancers shaken by the smashing energy of the wind. It was a grandiose didactic picture, with sequences of purple sky floating above an almost indistinguishable boat languishing in the background, on the edge of the sea shore.

Spastic flashes of light, illuminating the soon to be flailed ground and the mighty mass of water hanging over it, not yet bursting in all its fury.

Colours rose to the sky in feverish breaths, in electric swirls, with nascent waves pushed by the sea's tumultuous energy and dying waves worn out by the water's gravity. In every surge of water to the Heavens a lifetime consumed itself.

In the bottom-left hand corner, a greenish wave rose up, brushing a bizarre, flowerless sunflower. The water no longer seemed to restrain itself, it wanted to overflow from the painting, stirred by the sky.

The clouds borrowed the sea's somber color, with occasional reflexes of rose and ivory; the brush stroke also captured the tiny cone of the approaching marine tornado. The same one which capsized my distant cousins' family. I stood with my mouth wide open in front of the large canvas, while everyone complained in the kitchen. Anselma's shrill voice, Fidelio's muffled muttering, the daughter-in-law's reassuring psalms. I could not find that joyous freshness which was so characteristic of the marina. The sky's water now complimented the sea's impetus and its immature swelling. The tiny boat was gone, swallowed up like Vera, the bad siren, in a zinc tub, before setting sail into the great sea of life.

The Neaopiltan friend uttered the last sentence, but nobody took heed as the phone rang. No, it was not Vera, it was someone looking for the Albricci pastry shop, where we used to buy pasta. Vera phoned the following day, all joyous and light-hearted, asking Anselma if she was well and if they could send her a bit of money and her swimsuits.

"Where are you?"

"I am moving with Eric, but what are you worrying about? I will come back once I finish my summer job."

"Who is Eric? What summer job? When are you coming back? ... Hello?! Hello?! ..." Vera hung up.

* * *

ACT III

My father's inventions and the Mauser caliber

My father worked through the night, to round off the salary. He laboured in the kitchen, on a retractable stand, equipped with a vice and a drill. Before going to bed the open window sighed heavily because of the miasma emanating from the manipulated materials. *"Let me smell them."* I said. *"I like smelling them."*

"No, that's poison." Inebriating and sulphurous gas exhalations emanated from the Arexon soldering paste, the liquefied tin thread as shiny and fluent as blobs of mercury, fantastic aromas, coming from the quench oil tin, as dense as tar. The mechanical piece had to be hardened so it was immersed in that bath of unnatural chemicals, which extinguished the red glow coming from Mars. He also managed to melt the aluminum to make a kind of crown with little feet.

"What's this?"

"A motor with no pistons, do not you see? The gases enter here and leave here, and here they are compressed, they move the crankshaft with a cam." I did not understand much, I had other interests, but I was attracted by his research, it was as fascinating as it was future less. My father's talent delivered two sets of inventions, those that were useless and those which had already been invented. A great deal of heat was needed to break down the metallic bonds keeping together atoms of iron, copper and aluminum. The kitchen oven was like the furnace on a train, opening its jaws to a furious heart of light; the pieces of wood from the closet were morphed in smoke, engulfed by the flames.

I imagined the great Native American shaman, head of the Tecumseh tribe, immobilised in his fridge's white coffin, watching us. Like the expanding mystery stain, the red-skin chief was the depository of objective truths, lying in his lap of time. Absorbed by post-work activities, my father fumbled with a copper umbrella stand, his conception was characterised by three tapered cones, welded together by tin wire. It was unappealing, dully beaming its brown leather-like hue.

"Careful it's sharp!" Too late, a purple star was already spreading on my index, making me shiver. *"Disinfect it immediately and place your*

finger under the cold water. It will get better, you have to be careful when you handle things, you should not mess around with metal."

My father was absorbed in his meditations as a mechanical adjuster; I was attracted by the deadly precision of his majestic Mauser caliber, a metaphysical tool that inspired respect, wrapped in its patina of protective oil. It was a gift from a German during the war, a sign of esteem, an exchange between two men with the same passion wearing different boots.

The Mauser caliber with its blue scabbard, the tachometer, the thickness gauge and a hand-made metal compass, are the symbolic objects I inherited when he drew his last breath. They are part of the mechanical adjuster's armoury and represent an archaic skill that faded with his breath. The skill of the first factory workers, juggling feedback plans, logarithms, spindles, inch-to-millimetre conversion tables. Masters in Withworth threading and surface hardening, they performed tensile tests that would smash your temple with a big bang whenever the test tube exploded, leaving a cloud of smoke hanging from the jaw.

He showed me his world and

did not expect me to fall involve with it.

In addition to the umbrella stand, which revealed itself to be unsuitable because the cloth constantly tangled up against the metal, he built flagpoles, but these were so dangerous they were immediately made to disappear. An era of clocks and cardboard sewing machines began. Maybe one day he might figure out a way to make money from his contraptions, like the real industry pioneers did before him. The methodology was simple; make a million copies of the object and reach economies of scale, enriching us all and making us abandon the attic on the fifth floor without a lift. Simple.

The handsome long-haired German shepherd often looked out from the neighbouring house's balcony. For father, this was an incentive to invent. The prototype would be tested on the animal's fur, who unknowingly sniffed scents from a time before oil and iron drove the world. An aluminum comb with hollow teeth and a built-in pump to that would sprinkle the strands of hair with flea powder or talc. According to him, such an invention would have immediately been awarded a patent and would have cascaded us all with fame and wealth. And instead: *"Dear father with a failure infested talent ... please stop trying, you need other things in order to succeed."* But I did not tell him, he would have felt terrible.

My father listened to his internal voice, it overcame time and space and failure. It made him forget the feeling of those buboes full of psychosomatic pus which flourished inside his wrists.
His brilliant creations were destined to fail.
Always.
But he did not want to admit it.

* * *

Tiles and chimneys, as far as the eye can see

The torrid expanse of shingles, resembling the red stone flakes of the African desert, with their steep descents, spires cloaked with steaming heat, concrete walkways, eaves ready to crumble under the murderous sun, all collapsed on us. The tar, which some idiotic surveyor insisted on randomly spreading here and there in every corner of the expanse between the dormers, mad the situation worse, because it was a fetid cover, which cracked during the winter and softened during the summer, it breathed, stifling everyone and everything else.

Roofs, more roofs, an array of shingle ridges and smouldering pots that a bit of cement had the presumption to hold together, extended as far as the eye could see. A clear, assailing geometry sometimes rendered invisible by winter and summer mists, which melted contours, obfuscated architecture, and faded into nothingness the dormer windows, the parapets, the walls and window frames that opened and closed cones of shadow in an unorganised choreography.

The hills were as dark as the forest and extended into a never-ending green carpet. When the light shone brightest the hills were the clear winner towering over the crumbling roofs, the already-corroded new houses, some of them elegant, like that of the great tailor Salieri. The whole place suffered the sky's immanence, it was intent on threatening the inhabitants of the top floors. That

100

panorama must have had calamitous effects which have never really been taken into account.

Rita Rambaudo, Basovici, Gilberta's husband, Dino Serra and the young Fiorillo: they had all been compromised by the magnetic turquoise of the stones encrusted in a cursed Aztec crown. That was often the color of the sky under which we had taken refuge.

Returning to the paternal insignia I came to think: *"dear man cub, misunderstood husband and father, afflicted by a childish engineering voluptuousness, with what strength would you have stolen your wife from the basement of the psychiatric ward?"*

Having realised I was the Prophet of the Past, I finally managed to enter the paternal mind; it appeared to me like a long, curved tunnel. At the end of which I finally understood what my father occasionally brought to light from his past.

* * *

1925. From my father's memory

A child throws a ball of rags against a large wall. The year is 1925, an insidious era for a nation which is only 64 years old. The red wall has faded after the great blow suffered at Caporetto, prelude to the glory of the Piave. The child kicks the ball wearing boots three sizes too large, boots without strings. The outside of the house is bare, there is a row of distant poplars, the large heads of newly pruned willows border the canal.

The cry comes from inside the house, towards the child who continues to play, unperturbed. The light leaves the farmyard and the cottage. Darkness looms.

We are still in the farmyard, in front of the dark mouths of the portico's three arches. A second cry cuts the October air. The child picks up the precious ball of rags.

The mother wears her black apron all the way down to her feet, her hair is pulled on the back of her head. The two daughters watch the brother enter. The older one says: *"Give me that stuff."* The boy hesitates, then obeys. The onion soup grumbles in the hanging cauldron. The mother looks at her three children. The husband will arrive later, to find his dish already prepared. One hears a rasping noise at the door. The younger sister utters a cry. The dog whines and stops.

Silence is the table's true food. The child asks if he can have more bread, the sister looks at mother and brother. The second sister beckons him to pull the other hand out of his pocket. He obeys. He will be able to play with the ball of rags as much as he pleases, after his sister has given it to him.

A year later

Village party on a Carnival afternoon. The sun rips through the pungent air. The big puppet, a woman composed of rags, was burned the night before, on the woodpile in the center of the square. The child's sisters laugh as do their shoes without laces. One of the sister's gypsy dress was borrowed, it had very long cuffs and six mother-of-pearl buttons. The dress' skirt turned like a wheel inside the child's head who, twenty-seven years later, will become my father. He now smiles as the skirt immediately drops to cover the older sister's legs.

Four years later

In the background you can see the great faded wall at an angle to the portico. There is a smell of dung. The indolent steps of the priest tread the road; he came for the extreme unction. The dog's eye fixes the door. Nothing stirs, as the horse collects lice as she rolls around in the barn. The sisters sit in their room. Mother and father are bent on themselves, side by side. They make the sign of the cross while the priest arrives holding a small bottle. The dog rasps the door. Nobody chases after him. The wooden coffin is resting on the kitchen cupboard. It was ordered two days after the doctor gave his judgement. Death revolved around the feverish sickly body covered by large purple spots that flailed the skin. Spanish or soldiers' fever, the doctor said it was because of too many grapes, too much corn and too little joy.

Shoes deprived of their laces lay like offerings by the patient's bedside, the ball of rags was in the fireplace. The blame surely lies with the putrid grapes which knot the intestines. This is what the party confabulates, before remembering that the soup included small floating spheres of rabbit poop, before realising that the blame can also lie with the naughty witch who farts on the patient's face. The priest prepares for extreme unction.

But the wine-coloured mask mocks the party present and the witch's farts mess up the solemn event. The witch's feverish farts kill the disease and heal the child. A Gentleman with a top hat firmly stands by the side of the coffin. *"Look look here, saved you'll be, look look down death's not in town, up, down, down and around, the disease in you is no longer found"*. The tarot card drawn is that of luck.

The child, my future father will not die, the tarots have spoken.

1946 and beyond

My future aunts are confined to the house. They have to redeem their lives, and someone will have to pay for them to get started. Who will be the victim? Faded wall, with two cracks at the top. The house is silent in that shining morning, a piece of sky looms, with chasms of light and the earth that radiates above the shimmering canals. Hemp and grapes are spread to dry on the straw grates. My future father is restless. He is a young man with tumid lips. The dog has been missing for a few years now. The window opens and closes. Three women await at home; my future father stays on the farmyard pretending to be busy.

The mother is hiding in the dark corner of the kitchen and occasionally directs her ear in the general direction of a sound.

The younger sister mixes the cards from the Tarot deck. But she cannot read what she wants. The brother has tidied himself up in honour of the guest.

Here they come. It's her, it's them. The cloud of dust at the end of the road widens, staining the blue; the carriage is driven by Sostene, elder brother of the bride-to-be. He wants to see who he is about to leave his sister to. It is a day of presentations.

"She was not the one he had to marry, she is not suitable, she is from another country, she is spoilt and cannot do anything, she always has something to nag about, what does she want from our brother? He had to pick Mena who has a pot of land at the periphery of the town, and then our brother did not have to

leave our mother. He had to stay with us. He lacked nothing. Our mother loses her only son, because of that strange woman."

This do my aunts, all of them Erinyes, think of their future sister in law, as they conceal themselves within the house, their territory.

The unwelcome host arrives. The hem of her dress gets caught on an iron stirrup as she descends from the buggy. Is it an omen? Three glances are fixed on the graceful creature, but only one of them is imbued with love.

"You're alone?" Insinuates the falsely naive bride, turning to the promised groom.

"No, they're all inside the house. Come. ... come ... go ... enter, please. You too Sostene too, do come in ..."

"But didn't your sisters hear us? ..."

"How? ... There's also my mother," he says. *"Now they will come out."* The son's voice begs. *"We are here. They have arrived!"*

"They will come out when they feel like it." says my future mother. Three furtive shadows appear, framed by the great fireplace's mouth, motionless. Three dark Erinyes hissing imperceptibly.

"And your father? When does he come?"

"Come on everyone, do sit down..." my future father says.

"I need air," his future wife whispers and he accompanies her outside. A chair falls to the ground as the couple in their flight hit it. Sostene observes and considers. That gypsy of my grandmother tightens her lips, satisfied. Her nefarious daughters imitate her ... She thinks: *"Why is this person even here?"*

I left my father's mind, perplexed, a little depressed, had my life had a different prelude would my existence have changed its way?

* * *

First Communion

The copulating fanatics are coming out from their cove; the room without a toilet, spied by the Black Children and myself. The couple is empowered by their sacred bond of marriage. They can go ahead and do it for as many times as they want; they have their badge of approval.

They are at my party. Pictures have been taken to celebrate my first Holy Communion. Pictures taken in front of the tram stop; behind which is the Hag coffee advert. I moved, and I love all of them. The acquired relative places his hand on my shoulder and smiles at the camera. Even Lory grins and then bursts into one of her famous laughs simply because my father tells her to look inside the lens. *"Uncle, I have to look inside a hole? Ahhhh haaah!"*

I need male figures to emulate; father cannot be my inspiration. Dog combs with pumps, prototypes of piston-less engines, umbrella stands, copper spearheads are disseminated on a battlefield of broken dreams. He strolls through his graves of greatness in his cemetery of surrender.

"And what happened to the lice?" Asks my cousin. I ignore her.

"Aunt? Did you know that Albino and I are going to go on our honeymoon?"

I thought: *"All of us have been waiting for this amazing piece of news."*

Cousin hadn't had enough of the multiple carnal gatherings with her Albino Purusa, the primordial Hindu male, in the enclosure of the railing room.

However, this is my day.

Letters, postcards, fine Bavarian porcelain saucers, my blue band encrusted with a golden cross and the plastic cup of the Redeemer are laid out on tables, chairs and sideboards. The sun illuminates Nevio's gifts, the fountain pen and the useless ivory-coloured diary that will never be opened let alone be blessed by ink.

The candies sparkle like spheres of RIV SKF pads, the cake supports the breaded silhouette of the Prophet of the Past, standing tall on his alter of sweet prophecies. It looks like me, sinking, exhausted on the sofa. They made us gather in church, all ready to take a black and white picture with all the classmates even those who had once kicked a ball on my mom's neck, fuelling perpetual ire towards the oratory and the bruise on her skin.

In this moment, hostilities have ceased. There are intermittent skirmishes here and there, but nothing that would bring the Heavens down. Between the stone roofs of an expanding working city, lava-like overflows of overturned skies and threatening blood-bonds, lives the prophet of the past.

For me there are no more secrets. Am I or I am not the Prophet? I tell myself nothing is new. My paternal grandmother was a gypsy, the younger daughter, a fortune-teller, helped in her monumental struggle to get past her days by a sip of red wine during mealtimes. My father, an aviator destined for the surveillance of the Libyan deserts, the last swathes of land stretching across the empire of rocks and sand. First to see and first one to be seen. In addition, his wife refuses to come to terms with the buzz of the Tecumseh refrigerator. What can I do?

Throughout this most special day I only nibbled cream cakes, I rushed to the toilet approximately ten times; my gaze waned from the mysterious skies to my palms as I prayed to Jesus. I then returned to the sofa that looked like a raft billowing here and there at the waves' mercy.

"Are you okay?" He speaks in a low voice, puts his hand on my shoulder, and immediately retracts it, as if burnt. *"Good little man. Keep it up."* He says with his solid grey-tinted tie, the kind you wear at parties. He is the cosmic cobbler, sent by Shiva; a great blasphemer, husband of Gilberta's mother. He would like to say more, but he does not really know what. I remove my mask of sufficiency.

"Keep up the grades?"

"Yes, just that. Keep it up, study a lot, you know," he has a lump in his throat; he does not know what else to say. His heart spoke for a moment. By way of farewell, the cobbler mutters: *"Be good, for your mum and dad's sake. I remember seeing you when you were so young, your mother was sick on the day of your Baptism, she was always very nervous… I was your godfather and your dad's sister were your godmother."*

The masterful manipulator of uppers now appears under a new light, one that makes him shine as the most important person in my life. The cobbler added: *"You never know how it turns out that women are whores ... and then children grow up as they please those stinks."* It's almost a rally. Then, without adding anything else, he drinks a glass of Muscat and leaves without looking back.

He is a messenger of love in disguise, that unparalleled blasphemer, who cursed saints and *madonnas*, I will never see him again.

This headache will end up splitting me into two. I'll still have to double check the ant nests. You never know. Around me is a continuous buzz of *"hello, hello, hello"* and *"behave"*.

My mind wanders to the Black Children, who was probably been intoxicated by the leaking gas pipe, suffocated by their green snot; they will have heard the clamour during the party. However, today, I do not have time for them; ... I therefore abandon myself on the sofa's lifeboat. In time to assimilate the story being narrated by the surprisingly loquacious doorkeeper, Iotti. Her protagonist, or target, is Madama Giglio, who lives on the first floor and behaves strangely.

* * *

Madama Giglio loves Bran Mallon

Giglio eats pistachios and candies as her eyes devour the television. Her socks rolled up mid-calf. The film begins like this:

Checked jacket, and work trousers. He is arrogant. Quite a handsome face. The phone rings. Madama Giglio does not answer. ... The view from the port: ships with great towering smokestacks. A garden adorned with benches a church with a priest with a big potato-like nose. Ship workers with lout faces, they smoke, the criminals smoke too and stand in a small wooden house minding their own business. Then the film continues like this:

One falls from the roof. *"Joey!"* People know. Did someone push him down? Malefactors hover around the port. Dead Joey's sister does not look like Greta Garbo; but she is beautiful anyway. That blonde one is really in love, the priest sees it too, he's happy that the two love each other. They killed Bran Mallon's brother, strangled the pigeons, and they want to take his skin.

"Uuhhh!" Madama Giglio's pistachios trickle away as does the movie's last scene: fistfight on the quay and a big thud in the water. Who would have thought? Sometimes the bad people lose.

Water splashes everywhere, even in Madama Giglio's quarters. She has been stuck to TV for two months now.

"If you look at her feet," says Iotti, *"you will see that she does not wash herself anymore. She is convinced that her son is coming to get her; poor soul, she does not know he died two days ago.*

I told her," says Iotti. *"Can you stop throwing wrappers in the yard? They are gross. She did not even answer me. One day I will call the Carabineers. Do you know what she did? She started singing."*

The water does not give way, it overflows from the impromptu doormat dam, it floods the landing's floor and cascades down the stairs. It walks down the steps.

"Open Giglio. Madama Giglio, please, open!" Punches on the door, *"open the door Giglio! Do you hear me ?!"*

The broth boils, it is past two o'clock and sweets are scattered everywhere, the pistachio shells float in the sink like small arks traversing the vast blue with no passengers on board. Madama Giglio is lying on the kitchen's sofa, with her socks all rolled up. It is really peaceful, the food cooking and the stash of menthol sweets.

"Lily open, you are flooding the lower floors!"

"Hmmhh. Huu?"

"Let us check, maybe something has broken. It is flooding. Open, ... Knock louder," says the carpenter in the yard, he is already reached by the water armies. *"Open, stupid!"* Bangs on the door.

"Hmmh?" Giglio opens the door. She peeks from the crack. *"What's up?"*

"What? Can't you see? All the water!"

"What's up?" She asks. *"There is no water,"* say her soaked slippers.

"And when was this?"

"On Friday, her daughter-in-law arrived on Saturday to take her away, and she still does not know her son is gone." Says Iotti.

All this happened on the day of my First Holy Communion.

* * *

The Black Children's exodus

They left, just as they had come, with stealth. Maybe it was during the night, or at the first light of day. The advent of the Black Children passed without a trace exception being for the squeaks, the trail of stench, the clinging onto doors like koalas on tree trunks, the silvery burrs marking where they licked the stairs' iron railings and in some witness' testimony, the handles.

The marshal said they were not that annoying after all even if the mother did occasionally lurch. So, they too had to be swallowed into nothingness, pursued by the condominium's silence.

Their stench loomed for a while on the top floors, as is usually the case with wild ones. In the end, I was feeling quite sad, also because their sudden disappearance deprived us of self-appraising ontological confrontations.

Like that time when one of the boys in the building had said: *"Come out from behind your brother you are stinking monkey."* Both brother and sister looked without understanding. This is what I remember about them.

The segregating measures softened adopted against them, such as being locked up in the gas-meter compartment, via the lie of there being a carnival party inside or threatening them with arrowheads, only led to the collection of lethargic looks.
The boy really made me want to pinch him. You could have fed him to a dog and he would not show any sign of expression.

Their existence's daily events occurred on the bed. They slept there, ate there, dressed there.

If you were unfortunate enough to venture deeper into their den you would have found their fetid dishes, a half-naked child sitting on the edge of the bed, clinging to the breath of sleep, the tasseled braids and the perfect parting that ran down her head.
Bright Alhambra, with lips more perfect than freesia petals where lilac fades imperceptibly into violet.

This did the Black Children leave behind.
An indecipherable and bitter insert, they will never curse us again with their barking, or their stench, nor will they ever bless us with their wild beauty.

* * *

My first love: Angela, the Tunisian angel

An angel had come to fill the void left by the Black children in the little inferno. Ugly enough was adorable and dressed in white. She had emigrated with her peasant parents, first to France then to Tunisia. Her nose was tap-shaped, and it had been driven away by floods of successive migrations and the expanding desert which engulfed her father's stale fields.

"Life was good there."

"What about the scorpions?"

"No, just goats and some lizards," says Angela, the mature virgin, as candid as milk. Was she perhaps desired by some Arabs from the former colonies?

"Not a chance!" She exclaims smiling. Angela now belongs to the condominium and its besieging stares; she has replaced the Black Children and must be studied. Finally, the condominium has found its goddess. Not a bad zouave, but a beautiful French immigrant, a fashionable ethereal gypsy.

Angela painted her cell's walls of a pale azure, making it look like a ship's cabin, a radiant lighthouse, it secreted the pleasant narcotic smell of white spirit and washable enamel.

We are invited to her palace on a gasping July Sunday afternoon. She is with her parents, a pair of kind and luminous souls, like precious diamonds from Gabon. We sipped mint flavoured tea, sweetened by cubes we had to put under our tongue, the Arab way! This does the angel explain, all the while showcasing her dark gums more than decency would allow.

Her metaphysical qualities of joy and dedication to the family are touching. We sit on the sofa, (yet another flowered sofa!) rumbling and gargling with boiling tea, as we sweat heavily. This is how it should be sipped when in the desert, to give a feeling of freshness. The delicious African creature has polished her sink with Max Meyer, mounted a shelf, on which she placed a radio and a postcard of Tunis.

She also polished faucets, painted the grilles, waxed the varnish on the parquet which had great canyon-like cracks, and finally she turned her window sill into a miniature Versailles. I already love her! Whenever she speaks of Tunis, her eyes are encrusted with jewels of tears. She considers it as a second homeland and I already fall in love with the thousand suns that dance on the medina.

Maybe she does not remember she has already introduced her parents to us, so she represents her father, a leather covered mammoth, who smiles wide and is finds it hard to control a thread of crystalline saliva.

A St. Barnard of the desert. And her mother? A barrel with width surpassing its height. The barrel routinely asks: *'Wuuaat?'* She is as ignorant as a boot, calm and composed in her slow-thinking ways, she is adorable.

"I'll show you what I wore back there," says my beloved, opening the closet door of that former mortuary.

"So light? But it is almost see-through Miss Angela!" Says my mother's tongue.

"Because of the heat! There is no winter over there."

"Did you make your own clothes Miss Angela?"

"Mais non, pourquoi? The Market, and by the way, just call me Angela, only Angela," says my beloved. Her parents shake their heads and then shake them again when they show my nosy mother a pair of yellow leather slippers with tiny mirrors and a tip so sharp it could pierce a sparrow.

"Oh but with these ... with these ... If you kick someone…" My silvery Angela bursts into an uproarious laughter and says: *"If you kick someone you would sting them!"* What a treasure of love!

"When I could, I would go barefoot, mais non pourquoi?"

"Barefoot? What about the snakes?" More laughter, another palate-scourging tea. Another layer of love that sediments on my heart. Meanwhile, my eye catches glimpse of the French exercise notebook, it is riddled with red corrections. What if I … learned ...

The courtyard looks different as well; those are not doves but birds that glide in a clearing, overlooking the Tunisian port, it heralds the beginning of a new era. My father jumps in narrating his six years of war, spent defending the homeland's southern border, in the photos he is posing with his helmet and anti-sand goggles, in front of the massive propellers of his Caproni reconnaissance airplane; he would like to finish his story but is interrupted with:

"You and your Africa, you had to stay in Africa if you liked it so much!"

There is also a typewriter with a sign on button number nine.

"That key does not work," says the fragrant fairy. *"Feel free to write, her is some paper."*

"Papier?"

"Yes, papier, good!"

In the renewed apse the Tunisian approaches me and in a large movement of her arm I see the bluish hair of the underarms, not perfectly shaved. Angela sits near me, about to introduce the sheet of paper in the old Olivetti. What will happen? Meanwhile, an embarrassing and unequivocal whiff approaches, straight from stairway's toilet and it sits next to Angela, and her gauze dress.

Dung is always embarrassing even when one pretends not to notice the smell. I do not know if this giraffe does it on purpose: she sits, gets up, comes and goes, the fact is that, the living room is very narrow, and some strands of hair come touching my face.

"Oh pardon, pas du tout. Très bien." .... The sewage smell fades, but she does not.

I love her.

God of the sea and deserts: her bra's cups share the sky's tint. Blessed giraffe, I graze around my wishes. I am starting to think that a second language, possibly French, can propel me in my career become a fundamental asset to the Prophet of the Past.

I decide to marry my Samarkand there and then, this way, she will teach me Balzac's language. We would be entwined for life, until the end of time. Angela, a sarcophagus of delights with purple gums, now associated with the vile odor coming from the stairwell toilet. What a pity! But what is my insipid parent telling my hearts' sovereign? She seems to have noticed a red spot on her face, a spot which was not there before, how did it suddenly appear? My beautiful desert rose scarred by imaginary maternal neuroses?

"If I were you, I would visit a dermatologist, Miss Angela"

"Oh fine, bien," she says, vaguely displeased; I want to sink underground.

One must be wary of sunstroke, insists mother,

"Peut-etre, but yes, we will check. It is nothing n'est-ce pas? Bon, allez. A bientôt."

I think the red stain dreamed of by my mother is the result of her chilling fantasies. Angela shakes my hand and adds: *"Mais oui, pourquois pas? French lessons. Very useful, aujourd'hui for a kid like you. You can start right away. Très bien. You'll see that you will soon learn the language."* She called me a kid! I will soon learn your language and you will learn mine: that of passion. I think. The die was cast, I would have my French lessons with Fatima, my sovereign.

* * *

Let's hear Uncle Sostene's news

These are days of waiting, if they had to be identified by a color it would be a pearl grey, the opaque skies close in. There is no sugar, so one has to go to Ginetta's mother. Here I am to beg for kindness among her jute bags. The store's therapeutic fragrances will calm my voluptuous love. Fatima turns my head and her hair enters my mouth, this is how intimate we have become. She would like to teach me Diderot's language!

I have time to see the unloading of tuna crates while Ginetta's mother beckons me to be patient, quite a crowd is gathering. I peek through the Double Stock Star Cubes advertising window and notice Salvatore, the great barber, resting by his shop's windowsill, home to the village gossip. Next to it is the chasm of an underground garage, which smells of tires and engine oil dung.

The guardian, a great entertainer of females had a surly air about him. He waits, leaning, ready to throw his baits of love. One such fish was the long-haired German Shepherd, the very same one that had inspired the creation of the anti-flea comb. In the same block one could find: a carpenter, the hardware store and the dairy. In the former's dungeons one could find candid inflorescences of yogurt and cheeses, and wade through a forest of rocket and basil. The components of that portentous little family, whose life seemed to revolve around the church, the churchyard and the shop included; the pale mother, the pale mother-in-law, the pale husband, almost as much as the deceased grandfather, and the children who had a cerulean look about them.

They inspired disgust, probably due to the fact that a while back the grandfather had been seen squirting mozzarella cheese after having meticulously explored the insides of his nostrils.

But let's focus back onto Ginetta's mother, she is telling me: "...
Mom has been here before and told me to tell you to go home right away, sweetheart. Your uncle has arrived..."

My affectionate nurse smiled.

Uncle Sostene at our house! I liked my uncle, because I alone, among the ranks of nephews, managed to get onto him and snatch a smile, hugging him.

"I know lawyers," I hear him say. I'm behind him and he did not hear me coming.

"Your brother does not mention how he has already done the things that came into his head. And who am I? Because he certainly does not tell me. Is he you ashamed, perhaps? We are not his servants. First he does things, then he tells us that he was forced to do them. Where I am from, this is called being smart.

He is still mad at me because I got the motorcycle and the carriage; he spent seven years in war and I did not, and when he came back from the war he expected to find more of the inheritance. Well, he might have gone to war, but we were under the bombs.

You tell me not to make a fuss so as to not hurt mother … honest? …. So why earth did he write you this letter?

I know the law. Ah no, my dear chum, this is a step too far. Last time I was standing by the door. It was also very hot. He kept me at the door like a stranger. Do you want me to just forget how his villainous wife lays her wet laundry on our mother's head?"

My mother shakes her head.

"Even if he was to invite us I will not go. Do I need to ask to be seated? I will bring my own chair from home. That way, I will not ask for anything."

I cannot resist much longer, so I attack and embrace his whole great bulk.

"You have become so tall and thin!" He exclaims looking at me. *"Are you eating, uh?"* I extend my arms and lay myself in a corner to look at him.

He has a big fresh beautiful face, quite well-shaven, the dark-silver hair, marvellously waving in a sumptuous hairdo.

"Had I hanged my mother in my house, I would not have touched a single bit of inheritance, and I could leave without shame."

I would have preferred hearing other stuff. It turned out that her grandmother, who always smelled a bit like urine, was being neglected, her head was wet because of dripping linen, she was besieged by her hungry uncles. Jackals searched for remnants of her heredity. In short, all these worries about money, the anxiety towards grandmother, the uncles who did not speak to each other and the "misdeeds" of the "villain" sister-in-law, disturbed me.

I looked at Uncle Sostene, he was massive, his vest adhered to his shoulders' cold fat, his stomach suggested he was calmly sluggish. He was the spitting image of a bovine figure, weak, by his incessant reflections on money and this ungrateful destiny. Uncle Sostene no longer had a purpose, although one should check and see if he ever had one. He was living frugally with quite a lump sum hidden in the bank, so everyone wanted to hear from him.

A great melancholy, relegated to the closet-room with the creaky parquet, disappointed by life, and by the two sons who did not really want to follow his trader's footsteps.

Before abandoning Uncle Sostene to his predictable destiny, composed of silences and melancholy, I heard him say *"I do not have that much time left, I have already written the will. And we'll see to who all my stuff goes to. I want to be buried near my first wife, I want to depart with poor Yole, when I will not be here anymore ..."*

I did not let him continue, I gave him a big kiss on the base of his chin. I do not think I've ever seen him again. Besides, I had other things to take care of.

***

A cave of decayed teeth

They brought me to Dr. Aselta, a well-known dentist who had his own name engraved in a plaque. We missed the waiting room, stood in the wrong queue, and I eventually found myself on another doctor's chair, in the wrong studio, adjacent to the right one.

"But it's not here, madam, you have to go to my colleague, look, right next door. .... Not to worry at all ...." said the other doctor.

I fell into a chasm of shame as I entered the new studio. Silence followed by a long wait greeted my fall. The inspection proclaims its verdict before I have a chance to justify the disaster. A disaster caused by my diet's tormenting scarcity of calcium.

There was nothing to be happy about. Regular controls were not enough; drastic interventions were needed. The apocalypse knocked at my door. From that moment onward, my gum disorders were rummaged, controlled, sterilised. I swallowed potions which should have turned me into an eternal being, my teeth were sure to last past my due by date.

The French window gave onto a large courtyard; some writing was vaguely decipherable on the opposite wall. No doubt a test to see if I was literate, or perhaps one to check if the effects of the anaesthetic had worn off. *"What can you read from over there?"* He asked. There was some kind of yellow writing on the wall. I said what I thought I saw. *"You are wrong!"* Exclaimed the dentist with joy. *"Read, go on, try again."*

The arbitrator's judgment was not infallible, it was INDISPUTABLE. Who would have thought? Reading is an exact science. You have to be careful. I knew that word: in its finality it was a sentence above all men and events. INDISPUTABLE. The wall had a death decree written onto it.

"... Open a little wider good lad, come on..." All the while the torture continued. I was tied to the dentist's chair with rusty chains, I was shaking, I knew my teeth had that blackness about them, all the evidence required to usher forth the INDISPUTABLE sentence.

The dentists, hag-like nurses and myself played hide and seek did not give a damn about my teeth, they were just training. The whole matter started to intrigue me, the initial sense of fear dissipated as the plot thickened, and my tolerance to pain grew.
The hypnotic mixture of nitrogenous oxides granted entry to a parallel world. My gaping mouth was an open cave through which devils and hallucinations galloped to the inferno concealed within. Sometimes, a mist hung low, clouding the referee's judgment, which remained unperturbed, INDISPUTABLE.

The anaesthesia introduced me to those dreaded underground worlds, whose existence was occasionally rumoured, but whose access always remained hidden.

Hidden to all but myself and the dentist.

I could not wait to go to the doctor's office, I wanted to face the grim nurse, the praying mantis, and shamelessly return her suspicious look.

The synthetic fumes I often inhaled, the wide array of gauze and bandages, the horrible instruments of torture which chimed against each other, all resided in the anteroom to the chamber in which unquestionable secrets lay.

"How is it going?" Asks my mother.

"The boy behaves well, madam. At first, he was very scared. Good lad, it almost looks like he is pleased to pay us a visit."

"How strange. And what about the teeth?"

"We will be at it for a while longer, not too long."

The news froze me. I had to hurry up, time had to flow faster, I had to access the cellar in which further knowledge resides.

I was supposed to reach that place; for only there would I find the key with which to discern my vocation.

Who could I rely on? I invoked Tecumseh, the native Indian, but he lays in his cold white coffin, silent. Yet again, I was not ready to understand. I reluctantly gave up trying to understand what had happened in the underground world of the dead where my two mothers had suffered an eternity of electric shocks. Enlightenment would only come when many more events would come to pass.

* * *

Afternoon of a dog day

She put the pot on the stove but realised that the fire was spent, and the water had been poured into the sink. Silence, it was almost noon. She looked for her mother, who was submerged under her wardrobe's clothes. She opened the window, clasped the curtain and went to the toilet. On her way back, the window was closed, and both curtains removed.

"It is past midday," said but she did not receive any answer, and returned to the toilet. She spread the washing powder and began to rub the sink while looking out into the courtyard; nobody was on the balconies. The sponge glided on the bidet's opaque enamel.

"Why are you wasting water?" Those were the first words of a Summer's Saturday morning. *"And the water you threw away?"*

"Which water?"

"The water for the pasta." The mother did not reply, giving her a harsh look.

"You dumped the water, it was meant to cook the pasta. Why?" She had dared challenge her.

"Spaghetti? ..." No answer. *"For the spaghetti or what far?"*

"Whatever you want. I am not going to eat…"

"Why?"

"We eat too much here. I have not finished tidying the wardrobes."

The day dragged on like this, but it could have been much worse. *"I eat nothing, but does anyone worry about me?"* The girl said nothing, rinsed the towel and flushed the toilet. A few drops danced out, promptly dried. A cry came from the courtyard. The greengrocer's van had entered. It was a quarter to one.

She cooked spaghetti for two, in case her mother changed her mind. A few drops jumped out of the pot ... *"Like in the toilet,"* she thought. She took the sponge, dried it, and threw it away. It was in tatters. She went to the closet to get a new one. There was no sponge. *"Where are the sponges?"*

"Hm?"

"Sponges for the kitchen. Where are they?"

"You are the one who put them away." She stayed silent, returned to the kitchen and rummaged the trash to retrieve the sponge she had just thrown out. *"Eventually the sponges will want to make their presence known."*

She picked up an onion and a can of chopped tomatoes as her mother opened and closed the wardrobe doors. The smell of mothballs fluttered its way to her. She could not stand it. Quite a while had passed, but every day, the mother diligently went to polish the tomb's red marble. The stepfather was more present in death than in life.

"Are you going to go to the cemetery today as well?"

"Is it any of your business?"

She will probably tell the dead man he is dead because of me, thought the girl.

She drained the spaghetti. The steam slipped away. She laid the table for two. They often ate together in the evening, in silence. Her mother fixed her plate while she furtively gazed her. *"What have you got to look at?"*

She had postponed her wedding day twice already.

The mother used to say: *"Too young, too soon, scoundrels everywhere. One disgraced soul is enough for this family."*

To which her daughter replied: *"Even the mother-in-law wanted to get to know you, but you told her that southerners had better burn as soon as they are born."* Of course, she did not only reply to her mother.

"Who did you tell this to? You mule. Now they laugh. But they laugh at me, not at you. Who did you tell that I do not want you to marry? You mule!"

The girl had fallen in love. Even though the man drank too much. Sometimes her stepfather defended her, treating her like a real daughter, maybe there had been too much care from the man …

"If you want to come it's ready to eat," she told her mother while covering the plate. No one answered.

A Dog day, without any doubt.

The girl goes towards the bedroom. *"I'll finish,"* she says.

"It's about time." Answered the mother, placing the wax and rag on the floor. *"There is dust under your bed as well."* as she collects it with the other humid rag.

"The pasta is getting cold."

"I'm going out."

"But you went yesterday as well."

"Is it any of your concern?"

"Shall I throw the pasta away?"

"Go ahead and throw it, we have lots of money, don't we?"

The door clicks shut, the mother fits her shoes on, outside, on the stone stairs. The girl leaves the house shortly after. A whole world can be seen through the hazy windows of the number sixteen tram. A world composed of beautiful houses, ugly houses, dormers, gates and rows of magnolias on the river.

That was the same water which her mother had threatened to throw herself in, out of daughter-induced despair.

The sadness rises. The tram stops in front of the Hag coffee advert; the girl enters a doorway, goes up the stairs and rings the bell. In the sun-drenched kitchen, on a hot summer day, comes the fateful request: *"Aunt ... please, if you know, could you tell me my real father's name? Please, aunt!?"*

My cousin Olga sits on our kitchen's flowered sofa. Exhausted. My mother prepares her a fresh lemonade, but not even she knows her granddaughter's father's name. The heat forces Olga to unbutton her blouse's first button.

* * *

Te Pe Tee di Fonza

Alive and blossoming in her third age. Indulgent, with lavish toothless smiles giving her a fun and friendly appearance. Te Pe Tee Di Fonza lived in a sort of green gut, facing my girlfriend's lair. Angela, my beautiful angel, my dreamy Tunisian.

Te Pe Tee was part of a large tribe of southern Indians, who settled even before we did on the top floor of the building with no elevator. She was the most discreet and kind creature ever appeared on earth.

The long, bizarrely dislocated mansard was located between that of Basovici and that which had once been inhabited by the Black Children. When inside, it appeared as though light lingered before disappearing. From within, galloping fragrances of basil, mint and oregano, rode to the senses. Te Pe Tee Di Fonza never quite stopped smiling at you. This was also the case after the unfortunate incident, which compromised her and her family's honour.

Assunta Maria and Nello Giovanni, known as Nino, were her nephews, Carmelina's offspring. Carmelina was a trouser-maker and was often commissioned by the great tailor Salieri himself. Assunta Maria was the most affectionate of the two siblings, her love for her grandmother was total.

The shell which contained her was not very suitable for a female; it was too tall for her age, rigid and with a hoarse voice. Saliva stretched between her teeth and lips and produced bubbles on every sentence ushered. She was a great talker, with a slightly scuffed masculine voice.

Her physique resembled that of a wiry boy, to whom in jest nature had given a pair of rough tits. Assunta Maria and femininity were poles apart, except perhaps when it came to character inclination, that which she had probably inherited from her grandmother, making her available and understanding. She was held in high regard by all the boys as she was quite competent in football player figurines.

"There's Assunta Maria, won't you go play with her?" So, I had to put up with her long preambles; the girl likes to explain, in detail, everything that has occurred to her in recent weeks.

The Pezzuto crew and Rita Rambaudo's offspring were also introduced in the sheer precipice of going up and down the stairs. Within a few minutes there was a lot of chaos until Dino Serra's cross-eyed mother appeared, lashing shivering horrors our way.

Silence fell and then everything started again. Assunta Maria was second to none in spitting down the stairwell. She nodded, quite content at the result.

Assunta Maria and Nino never traveled together. He was bigger and came to see his grandmother on Saturday afternoon when he was free from work. Nino was an acknowledged authority; his merits were so great and of such importance as to be utterly unknown. He was the staircase's role-model. He descends precipitously, like a madman flying over us. Athletic, virile, a handsome boy who certainly did not waste his time on figurines and toy soldiers.

Even Giglio, who was half mad and slobbered for Bran Mallon as he struts on screen, seeing him dash the fifty-thousand steps down onto the road said: *"Nice kid, he will go far."*

During a hot autumn-like summer, it happened.

A frightening upheaval explodes on the staircase. It feels like an army in tumbling retreat down the stairs. In reality, two individuals, with raised collars and handkerchiefs covering their mouths jettison out of Te Pe Tee Di Fonza's shelter, who in that instant was absent.

The thundering door slam is followed by a descent, similar to an avalanche, provoked by the two frantic thieves. Te Pe Tee Di Fonza's door slams, the lock is not that ruined after all. My mother, who all the while was leaning her chin on the stair's railings shouts: *"I saw you, you know. I saw you Nino! It is useless to escape! It was you, you and your friend, and when your grandmother comes I'll tell her. What a vandal!"*

Why on Earth would Nino force the lock? My deadbeat spying mother had heard noises, and although she did not see his face, she imagined it really was her nephew, because the body-type matched.

The two petty thieves were condemned in absentia by my mother's enmeshed voice which like a broken record-player repeated: *"I will tell your grandmother everything Nino! I will tell her ... that it was you and your friend. Oh well done! Shame on you! Why would you!?"*

They had stolen two thousand lire from their grandmother's kitchen drawer.

For many months after these events, Te Pe Tee Di Fonza, looked at you in a questioning, almost fearful way before saying goodbye. Nino had disappeared. Assunta Maria reappeared after a whole year; she had transformed into a boy with a bra, with scabs on her knees and perceptible hairs on her lip. Of her brother's daring past not one word was spoken, as a matter of fact, she began exchanging figurine packs with Rita Rambaudo's sons, as though nothing had ever happened.

Her grandmother leaned out and smiled but no longer ushered her complacent *"Teee, te pe teeeh"*. The shame was lurking, and she was afraid that the old story of the thousand lira would come out.

* * *

Dancing afternoon

"Me? Dancing? Are you insane?" One like me, who had gypsy ancestors and who could squeeze into the psyche of others? How could I ever dance? Never! *"Oh yes you will,"* confirmed my mother. *"Claudio Muller and his grandmother are also coming, the tickets are free, his mother is giving them to us, it's not that big of a deal if you are not that friendly to each other."* I had to give up.

"Useless gatherings." I thought to myself, *"nothing good ever comes of them."* This is not how I wanted to make my entrance in society's higher echelons.

When I learned I would have to wear the bullfighter's dress with a great cape and the typical headdress, I was flooded by shame.

Flowers, music, applause, spotlights, the precursor to all the world's play boys had to wear fake embroidery on his thighs on fake trousers belonging to a fake bullfighter. Just like mine. A Carnival parties? Good news at last! My appearance would be disguised, maybe enough for no one to understand that the Prophet of the Past was there in that ridiculous costume.

Was I, or was I not, an advocate for a united Italy? I was a friend of the Carbonari, the Zouaves and of those valorous men at Sevastopol, a sworn enemy to the Austro-Hungarian. These were my exploits as Prophet of the Past, and now, they were forcing me to be a dancing puppet. What torment! Music vibrated in my stomach, the children's party was sponsored by Zanadu, the publishing house which gave kids their encyclopaedia.

A limited number of tickets had been provided by Mrs. Muller, the rigid widow with oxygenated hair. I was actually in my natural environment, despite my initial fierce aversions. Suddenly the music and social life flooded my veins.

For a moment I believed the microphone was blathering my name, had I become famous already? The low notes bellowed inside my stomach, the contralto ones pinched my eardrums, all in a universe of frenetic rhythms. Then came the slows, and I latched onto a gypsy with a smoke-black coat. She was dusky and had fleshy sides. During the presentation the Zanadu publishing house showed historical notebooks, scientific dictionaries, adventure books: a real boon for the cultural spirit.

I saw Muller's son dig his heels in for a long time, like a sullen tawny, glued to a column. His breathless blue-haired grandmother begged him to dance at least once. *"Come on,"* she said, *"Claudio, if your mother comes to know you were sulking she will punish you."* I hovered beside him, close to a lady wearing a lemon-yellow dress. Confidently my moves spoke: *"See how good I am?"* During the interval, a beautiful lady, no longer in her prime, spoke of the value of the publishing house's books and of how appointments could be scheduled to eventually buy some volumes. What a great commercial gimmick.

Claudio Muller's grandmother tries to drag her nephew to the wardrobe, but, just as I had discovered moments before, he too felt good in that surreal pagan atmosphere. The weirdo did not want to leave. But it was time to go home. It was in this period that a technician from the Stipel agency came to install a black contraption in a corner of our attic, he called it a telephone. This nefarious herald was the gateway through which faceless people spawned, like Zanadu's agent, and many more thereafter.

So, spoke the black box: *"The president of the praiseworthy publishing house, placed a comprehensive and easy to use tool within the reach of all families, educating children who overlooked the fascinating world of knowledge."* The publishing house's agent called after dinner asking: *"I hope I am not intruding?"*

My father was in bed because of the buboes on his wrists. "I live nearby, we will get in touch soon, thank you and I wish you a speedy recovery. Said the agent, as he sniffed my family's spent climate.

* * *

Letters from the African front

Dear all,

I am off to see the women around here, together with the boys from my squad. They are all really black as they go and get water from the well. They are not exactly like ours, but they are very dark. Our team's commander is from Bologna, when he came to know that I come from the same region he said he will keep an eye on me. He then burst out laughing and mentioned how he had never seen someone from our land look so much like an Arab. The sand is never ending. The other day, an aviation General came and said that our country needs us. That may be, but we have not fired a single shot here yet.

I hope it does not happen either. This is paradise for me, for my work. I keep learning about airplane engines, some of them are so big that they would not fit through our stable's door! They are stellar engines and they are mounted on the Caproni reconnaissance plane.

I take care of their maintenance along with the other mechanics.

Please sisters, do tell our father and mother to not worry about me. Just the other day a companion found a scorpion next to his bed and squished him with his cardboard boot, it has a poisonous sting to it, and I dread to think what would happen if I was on the other side of it.

The food is what it is, however there is still more meat here than at home. Sometimes we scavenge the village, although calling four houses a village is pushing it a bit. The people here are as poor as we are, they pretend not to see us, but they are not evil, and a small kid even gave us a date branch.

Greetings from your brother

Letter from the front. Libya 1942

Dear sisters,

I do not feel that bad here at all, if only I wasn't here because of the War, which is never a good thing, but we try to do our duty. I managed to get some pictures taken, and I will bring them to you when all this will be over. I cannot even tell you where our camp is because of the censorship that the generals have imposed.

The other day we were on a reconnaissance mission, and we saw a plane come to us like an eagle diving for a dove.

I tell you, I found my heart in my gut because we knew we had to shoot, but, just before the pulling the trigger, the plane turned itself and we realised it was one of ours. We even waved at each other, I cannot describe the relief we had. I also have a helmet and glasses, not so much to fight against the foe, more so to fight against the ghibli (a wind which we do not have back home, but here it comes and stirs up a thick fog, almost preventing you from breathing).

Dearest sisters, now you know that I am well and that I am about the come back to the woman that you know, if she has never worked a day in her life, she will learn to. Anyhow, I hope she will calm down a bit, she is too nervous, and this is not good, because just as I hope I will come home, I would like to marry her, and I would love to have a family, with you being a central part of it.

This is what I want, dearest sisters, I have noticed that mother does not like to see her.

She asks me if she will be welcome in the family. But mother really does not like her.

Your brother is fine and wishes to be back with you all.

Letter from the front. Libya 1942

Dear …

I am doing fine here, and I hope you are too back home.

As I told you before leaving for the war, you are free, and you should do what you think is best. War is war.

You'll see, when I come back, everything will all right, even with my sisters, even with my mother, who perhaps is a bit jealous. When she will see you make pancakes for her, her mood and ways towards you will change. I told her I could not get engaged with Jolanda or Mena; I love you, not them, even though they liked her. You will see, everything will fix itself. Anyway, I have nothing else to say, apart from; please stay calm, because there have been no bombs, and no shots have been fired, and I am in good company, the commander jokes with us as well.

See you soon.

Letter from the front.

Libya 1942

What high hopes could I have for my buboes - mortified father? In those letters, found in an old drawer somewhere in the attic, there were the preceding symptoms of meagre and bitter lives. Everything had been postponed. My engagement with Angela the beautiful angel, the visit from the agent of the publishing house, the descent in the electric realm of the dead, located in the underground clinic where electroshock was practiced, all had been suspended.

How could I think of new adventures? My father was the fretting mouse in a pot of cream which did not go hard, forever tormented in the diatribe between his wife, sisters and mother. When I entered into my father's thoughts, I found scorpions, pistons, stellar engine connecting rods, black women taking water, wings of shabby aircrafts, disappointment, and even a daunting naiveté. My father had not moved from there.

His buboes were the outlet for a life led on the fifth floor without a lift, in the company of his perpetually nervous wife.

He was father to an eccentric son, a son who, according to the Tarots, would not follow his footsteps in the world of industrial fires and spinning rotors. The inability to find a home, let alone one with the bathtub his demanding wife wanted, must have added to his resentment.

We placed the paper bags used for carrying bread around the light bulbs, the intense light bothered her. It was necessary to conform to the precarious atmosphere induced by maternal mood swings. It started to feel that in the warm and diffused bread-bag-filtered light, life was taking a turn.

I felt this even though my mother's phobias outburst like a thundercloud. *"Close the water, close the gas, open the gas, have you closed the gas? Go check again. Like this it is closed, like this it is open, check the phone's handset, and the window handle, we do not want thieves to come inside, check the fridge door, it was open yesterday."*

The catafalque phone remained silent. We had no number to dial, except that of the doctor, the plumber and Nevio, my mother's and his wife's virtual lover. They had been lost-lasting friends of hers.

* * *

How the black phone begins to change our lives

The first taste of disruptive technology took place at twelve o five around the end of May 1959.

"Trin Trin" the ringing rings, *"Trin Trin"* it repeats peremptorily, *"trin trin"* the trill repeats like a broken disk, *"Trin Trin"* the drilling noise savagely echoes, *"Trin Trin can somebody please answer? Can't you see I am draining the dough? Is everyone deaf in this house? Hello .... Ah? Who? ... Oh, it is you? .... But who is speaking? What do you want? No, I'm not deaf. No, this is the number ...If you do not tell me who you are ... Oh is it you Fidelio? ....?! Oh, good God! I did not recognise you!"* I think to myself; they had already phoned once before.

Agitation near the precarious telephone station. I wonder if answering the phone will always be so will be so traumatic... *"And Anselma? .... Vera ... She's back! I knew she was going to come back. And she wants to get married! ... Ah not with that one ... another one ...understood ... maybe you put some sense into her.... eh, we are all here ... do you hear me well? Goodness your voice on the phone ... It really does change... Well what a surprise, sure…sure we will come and visit. Can I have your phone number? What a surprise!"*

"Here," says the breathless mother, as she turns to me, *"take a piece of paper, wait I will… take the pencil … here, tell me …. what? Wait it does not write… what? Give me a pencil that always writes, right? and a piece of paper … sorry Fidelio? and who is he? ah it's a surprise. You want to surprise me … yes … I'm excited, … and yes, I am happy, yes … I would have called you; I still have to get used to the phone. In short, everything is fine. Wait till I repeat the number … yes, thank you."*

"Fidelio is so strange, he gives me a phone number and tells me to guess who it belongs to.

Who knows whose it is?"

Curiosity rhymes with voluptuousness, perplexity, but also with evil, excitability, and blindness, and, if we want, with falsehood.

Curiosity also rhymes with: *"now you're going to see what me roll over the floor in laughter, ignoring that the person whose phone number I just gave you is on the black list of people who you should NEVER call. Never!"*

* * *

Lost chairs

"… Hello, hmm? ah … it is you?! and who gave you my phone number? … Ah! … Fidelio … and if you knew it was mine you would not have called … You have no shame at all… To surprise you…. Oh look! …. Because he does not know what kind of person you are, that's why … Oh now you are telling me not to start again? As you're on the phone, we can end this right here right now, I'm still waiting for you to answer my letter… There will be a God for you too … Oh I must not talk like that now? I lent you some chairs that belonged to our father and you never gave them back to me! … And then what does my daughter want to know from you? She wants to get married with that southerner … who will immediately leave her for someone else? What does she want to know? … What name? … There is no name. I do not even remember her father's name anymore. That scumbag. And what's it for? That mule has not said a word in three days… She must have come to complain at your place three days ago, isn't that so? Yes, I will go to the cemetery, at least there nobody will bother me … Yes, yes, feel free to hang up, you little nobody"

So, she hung up, and thus ended the phone call between my mother and Prisca, my mother's sister, parent to the unfortunate Olga.

We started checking the gas and water taps, the handles and the telephone handset which had to dangle. *"Unplug the phone! I do not want to hear anybody anymore."* Said a broken mother, whose honour had been trampled on. The *"toot toot"* characteristic of a busy line could be heard in the distance, in its endless conversation with the void. Anguished, repetitive, yet soothing: no one could call us if the cornet was dangling like a hung man.

Then it was time to go to bed, but first there was the natural series of curses and cries directed to Fidelio, Prisca, Olga and on the latter's ancestral right to know: who was her father and what was his name.

We inspected taps, handles and the telephone handset one more, this time the cornet was cautiously returned to its seating place.

That night, yellow and green glances penetrated the attic, peered into our windows. That night, assassins knocked on the windows, overlooking the desert of roofs. So much agitation, so much anxiety and offence suffered by my mother's soul.

* * *

ACT IV

The talking refrigerator
and the first step toward the unification of Italy

A long crack formed on the stretch of ceiling just above my bed and, through its progressive lacerations, the sky's vault appeared.

A thousand sudden black suns, framed by a crown of flames, at the center of as many galaxies scattered throughout the universe revealed themselves in my investigation.

The maps of time and space were engraved there, on that starry vault, clearly visible, towering above all things. They spoke of the thousand stories, of clamorous betrayals, of the appearance of the Black Children and the progressive defeat of the Mechanic King, my father, a martyr who had no way to escape his wife's madness. They spoke of the appearance of my cousin Lory's husband, the stellar fornicator reminiscent of Bizzarrone's pig, grunting in the garden. And of course, they spoke of the unity of the Italian nation.

Everything was clear to me: the past, the future, interpolated to the present as grim and bumpy as the life lead in the condominium.

The shimmering suns began to beat inside of me, pulsating, fabulous, apocalyptic. Which alien energy could animate them so? I had no words, that gash, that authentic open window on the universe revealed what burdens came with my clairvoyance; suffering and responsibility.

Lulled by the stars, sucked into the metaphysical orbit in which everything is corrupted and healed, I floated like an astronaut lost in the cosmic void.

Friends and strangers gravitated in the huge basin of the sky. But the place was nothing more than the fictitious representation of time and space. I was free from the wails of relatives, I regulated the pressure of their demands, and their troubles, so that Lory would not tear my ears apart and Olga's laments would not disturb me, so in that huge room with a starry ceiling, the Black Children would return to their lair, Dino Serra would finally find the courage to answer back to his mother, and my father would become the universal leader of all mechanics, inventor of the water-powered engine and of the powder pump for dogs. Even Uncle Bizzarrone and Carlo, the mystic cobbler, Gilberta and mother Eugenia would find rest there.

No place seemed worthier and more promising than that one, it was able to accommodate people's reconciliation and diatribes: the sky at night, observed from within the attic through its slanted, cracked ceiling. I had to change my mind, because that stillness turned into trouble.

The titanic starry vault was covered by chills, I gurgled stupor and vertigo. What had appeared to be within reach; the reconciliation between relatives and the building's inhabitants, was definitively compromised.

The negative electricity which resulted from the phone call between my mother and her sister, Prisca, was still in the air. She had revived their resentment. I perceived the dripping of a roaming drop diving into the sink, shoes rubbing onto the doormat, the warning launched by Rita Rambaudo to her rowdy sons, the silvery voice of my beautiful girlfriend Angela.

Then there was nothing but a longing for silence and the wait for something huge that was just about to happen.

From the bowels of silence came the voice of Kit Karson, the Apache refrigerator. His hiss surmounted what remained of the pile of firewood, neatly placed in the closet near the window and the light bulbs wrapped in yellow paper. He dictated his armistice and soothed troubled spirits; a shy snore could be heard from the other room.

The buzz had dispelled the whispering between curtains and windows, the bickering between toothpaste and

toothbrushes, the jingling between the chain holding the sink's plug and the white marble. The only voice: that of the Tecumseh refrigerator. Still, barely perceptible.

Something unusual was about to happen. Something I would not forget in my next hundred lives. Vivid images began to overlap, then faded, others returned to permanently disappear. But something and someone stayed. I dreamed of dreaming, but how much truth was in the dream?

A palace, a staircase, a figure that rushed down the steps with a piece of cloth in his hand, crumpled. A boy, a little man, with a lapel which appeared to be glued to a decidedly old-fashioned dress.

My imagination was dictating this and more. The image faded suddenly to then return more defined. There was a deafening silence along the stairs, the figure now walked close to the wall. When he saw me, he froze and lay his eyes on my face like daggers.

"Who are you? What do you want?" He hissed. I showed I did not understand. The individual, seemed to calm down, but never once dropped his gaze. He tightened the scrap of cloth that he had hidden under his cloak more tightly to his chest. I had to look surprised and not at all threatening. So, I let him speak.

"If you are" he said defiantly, *"... if you are the one who has been following my footsteps for days, the one who spies on me, and investigates, well, know that it is too late for you and for those who have commissioned you. Tell your instigators and torturers that the people of Emilia have confederated and that today, December 27, 1796, the Cisalpine Republic is born. The united cities are ready to bleed to defend their newfound unity. With the help of God and the enlightened support of Napoleon Bonaparte we will fight against the stranger. Our patriots will become martyrs and will break the oppressor's yoke. The fire of Italian virtues and of its proud identity awakes in our hearts and will chase the usurper. From this day forth we will live and die under one banner, our vindicated declaration of freedom will not go unnoticed.*

Reggio Emilia is finally free"

With those last words he unrolled the rag in my face, that cloth he had been clutching tightly to his chest.

Then, to my great amazement he continued with what looked like his rally. He seemed grateful towards me, grateful because I gave him a reason to declaim:

"... The yoke of the oppressor has broken; the free Italian identity unites hearts and minds which in unison fight for the conferral of freedom and equality within their governments. Viva Napoleone, Viva France, Viva the Cousins of Italy, live San Teobaldo, Viva Milan and the revolution! Long live the congress of Reggio Emilia" he waved the tricolor and began to sing: *"Already the Samnite and the Bruzio shake their oppressed bones. And united to the Tosco and the Insubre fly with their weapons to Rome."* On these words the

individual started to run precipitously down the stairs. And after having descended three more ramps, he stopped, addressing me like this: *"I do not know who you are, sir and I also appear outdated but anyway I invite you, in the square, tomorrow, at this hour, together with the Cousins, the patriots, and the free citizens, the Republicans of Emilia! Long live the Cisalpine Republic! Long live the revolution!"*

He was not alone. Other people with banners and flags were now calling and swelling the streets of Reggio Emilia. It was very cold and I, numb and confused, decided not to leave the street, at least for the moment. I crossed a door that gave onto a kind of storage room along the stairs. It was less cold there. I curled up against the wall and in that position, I finally slept, or so I believed.

Who was that guy? Where was I? What was happening and what I was doing in that remote time. I would have investigated but I did not know from where to commence.

Was I or was not the Prophet of the Past?!

***

At the communal pool

Two cans of tuna, three packets of biscuits, the omelet pressed between two slices of bread in a box, a plate of cold rice with olives, anchovies, a can of mackerel and a larger one of canned meat. A sandwich with a breaded cutlet, two hard-boiled eggs, a tube of mayonnaise; in the glass pan there were two peaches and twenty cherries, in the white bag, a packet of vanilla wafers. All the food was contained in a paper bag, usually used for bread, inside there were also ten paper napkins that then became twenty.

Two more boiled eggs were added to the rice and half a pepper, cut into small pieces. A second one was added to the bread-crumbed cutlet. A box of dizzy cheese was added to the big bag at the very last moment, followed by a packet of small jam, the same Gilberta distributed in his mother's pension.

At first, three eggplant slices, impregnated with oil were also added to the happy food committee, but it was later decided to leave them behind, the blistering heat recommended they rest within Kit Karson, the Apache fridge.

The bag was bursting with food. The oozing bread was wrapped in waterproof paper. No vegetables were invited, but we could do without.

A separate sachet was then added containing a comb, sun cream, three handkerchiefs, eight tram tickets, sunglasses, two hairpins, a second bag with a string closure, a diving mask, a pair of fins, a bathing suit, and a rubber cap that pinched your hair. This last sachet was introduced into a smaller bag, which could still hold the terry towel, two pairs of slippers and rubber sandals.

Around ten past ten on a July morning the party set off with all their bags and sachets. We were all there of course, Rita Rambaudo and her children with a cousin, Basovici's son with his mother, and last of all, Claudio Muller was also scheduled to come, in a bid to make up for his abysmal performance at the dancing gala. He fortunately could not come, as his grandmother's skin was too sensitive for the sun's rays and would become irritated. Other voices said that Muller was too much of an aristocrat to join the company.

The Pezzuto tribe did not come. The reason became clear some time later, namely, their mother did not have a proper bathing suit and her husband found it unseemly that his wife showed herself "half naked" while sunbathing, especially with all those rascals that went to the swimming pool expressly to see and dream about women in costume. Stones, cement curbs, sand of uncertain origin, intermittently working showers, plane trees, horse chestnuts and dry leaves, still pebbles, and yellow meadows, all this was waiting for us.

But first we had to suffer the journey on the number four tram. The tower blocks of the horizon piercing periphery were in plain sight. They bit the sky with their uncertain offshoots from the countryside.

Barracks, houses, pillars, bulk cement ships, subjugated the sky with their interminable sequence of hives and dormitories. The leaves tumbled along the tracks and the sun illuminated clouds of dust through the sloping avenues.

The tram reaches the second periphery, populated by lower houses, swallowed by the city's giant teeth, and what appears the first of the three rivers crossing it. The bridge arches onto a chasm studded with piles of gravel, collapsed concrete walls serving as a bank dotted with pools.

I am quiet as I contemplate the city's broken teeth as it smiles at us. All the while, the mothers' chatter increases.

Rita Rambaudo, my second mother, cannot take it anymore; her two sons turn her crazy with exhaustion as they constantly fight against each other. Basovici's son suffers from bouts of nausea because the tram waves left and right; *"It would have been better if we had stayed home"* says his mother, who puts a hand on his forehead to see if he is gripped with fever. Backpacks with sandwiches, desserts, fizzy water. We dream of refreshment in July's heat wave.

Finally, we behold the greenish oasis, on the outskirts of the city, it is dotted with a curtain of disembodied plane trees and robust horse chestnuts.

Glares from young rascals' loom. Was Pezzuto right? Will the locals threaten us? I think this as I sharpen my thumb on my penknife, which is as long my little finger, but too short, to sing as it cuts the air.

Rita Rambaudo's headache promptly arrives, and shortly after, Basovici's son is plagued by bouts of nausea. He will remain dazed, under the protection of a large linden, leaning on backpacks full of food. The thorny, sharp grass sneaks into the sandal worn by one of Rita Rambaudo's sons and torments him.

People appear and disappear behind the hills. The kiosks, the oranges and sparkling Coca Cola housed in strong wicker baskets resting under the shade. The fridge overflows with icicles and ice cream cones. Our party's decimated encamp in a depression. We will refresh ourselves before assaulting the muddy waters. You become leather coloured at the pool, your body turns into a David. However, our troops seem to be returning from the clash at Custoza against the Austrians, they languish among debris of backpacks, bags, and fins scattered across the field. I pretend not to belong to this company of metropolitan guinea pigs whose knees tremble because of the journey on the number four tram.

After having properly sniffed the bullies decrease the frequency of their visits, and after a last piercing look over both Rita Rambaudo and Basovici's mother's shoulders, they disappear. We will find them later on, muscle against cement, warlike and shameless as they dive from vertiginous trampolines.

We are disheartened because of the dispersed rubbish, the ice cream cones that dot the hilltops, the fluttering pizza cardboard boxes, which asphyxiate the pool's filtering net. We are looking at a graceful creature, which melts, like a yellow flower as she jumps around, hip hopping, behind her tennis ball, on the crushed brick field. Further on there is no-man's land, a place where weeds grow, void of function save that of being a parasite. There you can find corpses, stolen objects, crime scenes or burglary tools.

It is a sinister area frequented by people who have nothing to do with the pool, and Rambaudo's sons who are promptly chastised by their ever-watchful breathless mother.

"You must not go there!" She screams. The water reaches my groin, and I wonder why the pool party does not take off, why is it becoming entangled in a series of bans, dirty looks, stolen food and where did the backpack withholding all the apparatus required for a picnic go? Basovici's son was resting on it just a few moments ago. The first thing Rambaudo's children do is go beyond the forbidden zone, in search of the backpack, pursued by their mother's cries.

I reach out into the stinking water and the lifeguard shrills his whistle because I cannot use a diving mask in a swimming pool. I sink into a pool of shame; after all, I am not fishing in the Red Sea but in a pool of sewage. Silvery droplets of pee shine in the air. An enterprising little kid adds some more to the mix, as he smirks in my general direction. I get up suddenly. This is not for me. I would rather cook in the sun than swim in piss.

Our expedition resembles the retreat of a handful of Neapolitan insurgents during the revolts of 1820. The light shoots straight into your retina, making you bleed tears, nobody, except my mother thought of wearing sunglasses. The sun gradually diminishes its hammering blows, the atmosphere changes, Basovici's son points to the forbidden zone, where boys raise broken baskets and armless dolls with their sticks. The remnants left behind in that macabre soil as the troops marched on.

Midday coaxes the stomach. In addition, with a *"pinf"* and a *"ponf"*, the calcined yellow figurine, continues to follow the tennis ball. We move under the shade of the great lime tree, trying not to perish. We find the lost backpack, we soldier are celebrating, the admirals too, the day is unblocked, there are those who propose a walk and those who, hunger-driven, swallow the last cutlet. I remember the young man from Reggio Emilia, who in my half-sleep shouts: *"Long live Napoleon, long live the revolution!"* Who was he and what did he represent? I will need to investigate. I am the witness to a bizarre exchange of foodstuffs between mothers. *"I want Federico's chocolate, I want Marco's wafers, and I want Pinuccio's toffee ... and I want to slap your face, if you do not stop, let's go and never come back here"* my mother's word is sacred.

Rita Rambaudo is afflicted by shadows which consume her, it is clear to all that she suffers from the intense sun. She has already undergone two sessions with the electroshock in the clinic's basement, where my mother had also gone. In addition, she does not know what to do and where to go.

You charge back with carbonated water and a new form of ammunition: Hydrolithine and bottles of fizzy orange juice with cork caps. Then the skin starts having its own say, its language speaks in dozens of sores and white stains on shoulders, necks, noses. The day made those accustomed to the shadow of the condominiums pay a heavy toll.

Our troops retreat, leaving the field to the leather-coloured boys, undeterred assault divers, who had spotted Rita Rambaudo's white shoulders. We turn their backs on them. Exhausted, we leave behind the debris of a very fancy afternoon and nameless regrets.

* * *

The book agent calls again. Food is within sight

She should sell us the books from the Zanadu publishing company. We are waiting for her, anxiously. The encyclopaedic volumes of Universal Knowledge would be a springboard for my wisdom, wisdom seeking the truth behind the revolutionary ongoing steps in Reggio Emilia.

Increase your knowledge, so said the advert, *and become your era's own protagonist the past has no more secrets.*

It was necessary to satisfy my insatiable curiosity concerning the oppressed peoples of the early 1800s. I required manuals of historical analysis, the maintenance booklets for the Karson refrigerator, special cards on how to identify women in the Libyan oasis, the ones cherished by my father. One of a prophet's utmost interests is to touch knowledge. Agent Giulietta Libretti is about to arrive. *"When did she say she was coming?"*

"Maybe tomorrow."

"No no, she will come today."

"... How should we address ourselves to you? ... Miss? Mrs? Madam? Will we have to pay in cash? Will they send alerts? How should we address the female vendor? Seared pinzimonio? Algido risotto di mare, or undergrowth sylph? If a person comes, we need to buy what they sell, how can we say no?"

"I hope it won't just be an encyclopaedia for kids who won't look at it anymore after a while." My mother said.

I risked seeing my investigations on phosphorus balls, on beautiful Figheira's psychology and on Rita Rambaudo's crossed destinies vanish. So I hissed: *"Alternatively there is always that new bike you promised me,"* and with this sentence, they forgot their qualms.

The bell rang at sixteen past eight. I was ashamed as I greeted her with a "good evening", as it was a meagre greeting for one who had just climbed five floors and was short of breath.

"Oh, a little motion is always good," she anticipated, and I immediately thought that we would have come across much better had we not inhabited that cave among the roofs.

I studied her. She was neither beautiful, nor ugly, she was not thin, nor was she flourishing. She was what she was not. She stood on the attic's doorway with her hand outstretched, hand whose duty, was to communicate sympathy. She was dressed as a hostess with her leaf-coloured suit. Her shoulder bag reminded me of a train conductor and her hair formed a honeycomb of laborious bees, like her.

The girl illustrated the advantages of owning an encyclopaedia; after all, do not you want to know about the moth's sucking apparatus? Alternatively, the jet engine's propulsion system? *"Oh look!"* My father murmurs, *"I know that, but ... during the war, I mean ... the engines were different, with cylinders, of course, I guess this is progress. Jet engines are completely different."* I would like my father to continue, this way he vents what keeps him alive, but at the same time, I would like him to keep quiet because he sounds pathetic and inappropriate.

"A drink, a coffee, a tea?" Maybe she has not eaten yet. *"Do you want a sandwich Madame? A piece of omelet or a half steak maybe?"*

"Oh no!! Thanks."

"Coffee it is then".

I scrutinised her while the girl titillated the ashtray, smoothing its beveled edges; she was a little woody, reticent. Was she selling kid's encyclopaedia as a second job in a bid to round off her salary and prepare for a wedding? Alternatively, did she have other secrets? She was uneasy and finding it hard smiling. Do you think she judged us? What did she think?

Could we have seen ourselves as the happy island in life's stormy sea? Let us not joke for now. *"Oh! ... Are you feeling well? You went quite pale! Another coffee maybe? Would you like to rest? ..."*

"No, no, ... tha ... thank you." She says visibly pale.

This was just what I was waiting for. A breach in her armour through which I would probe her life's recesses.

While she was illustrating the importance of the noble icons of the Italian Resurgence, of course all available in the notebooks, she hesitates, her cheeks fade. She becomes a pale rag. Was she also in contact with the revolutionaries from Naples and Reggio Emilia? My special eye comes into action. I am now investigating. *"Take off your jacket, if you are hot,"* says my mother. *"Does it often happen? For you to get so sick? And so pale?"*

"N ... no. Not often ... no." She unbuttons her suit's jacket. Lovely woman! *"It could just be her low pressure, or something similar. Promise me that tomorrow you will immediately go to your doctor,"* says my mother. *"You*

gave me quite a fright. I saw you become completely gaunt ... You don't suppose it could be..."

I am as ashamed as a dog. The unknown woman was just about to show us the illustrated breathing system of whales and the expeditions of the Piedmontese in Crimea. What was my mother going to tell her now? With that face turned into a worn-out rag, poor child she had suffered enough.

"... maybe, just maybe ... your faintness has come ... because maybe you are pregnant? That is why, you are about to get married. I understood, you know." *"That's enough!"* I think, furious. Mother just had no restraint whatsoever.

Guardian angels in heaven, please prevent my mother's tongue from plunging us all into shame! I do not even know if the encyclopaedia vendor has finished drinking her second coffee loaded with three teaspoons of sugar. Returning to the volumes, are we sure that everything is in the encyclopaedia? What about the methodology behind the preparation of hellebore poison. Is that there? In addition, how much current passes from the electrodes to my mother's and Mrs. Rambaudo's heads in their ECT treatments? Before buying a closed box, I would like to know on which page I may find Vera, as a mermaid, foaming orgasms and soap. Prophet of the Past has to understand.

"Why not?" my father says. *"And how much is it?"*

"A trifle and you can pay it in convenient monthly instalments."

"If we pay in cash, is there a discount?" We played the part of the rich, although it was obvious we were not.

* * *

In the cellar of horrors, the descent to the underworld

There are nightmares you carry within you for who knows how long, without even realising it. Floods in the metabolism of feelings, metastases that refer to sick and gloomy mindsets. These shadows require but a whisper to awaken. Once alive and treading on the horrid paths of decomposing thoughts, they force you into a subterranean, custodian of a thorny truth. This happened to me as I descended the stairway, with a trash bag in my hand. You hoped your infancy lay dormant; but my fate is without a shred of meaning. The fingertips linger on the light switch, the soles pound rubble as you descend the first steps. The sour smell immediately attacks you.

"Where are you going? ... Does your mother know?" Where was I going with a filthy bag in my hand? Madama Pezzuto, to whom I clarify, comments my first descent into the underworld, in the basement of the condominium: *"I am not doing this by own initiative."*

".... Yes, my mother knows, she sent me."

"Do not close the door, leave it open."

"Yes, of course, open."

There is light on the ground floor, where the stairwell's geometry ends. Five floors with no lift, with a large hole in the middle and light that swarms in the entrance hall, as glazed and shiny as a clinic, Iotti made sure of that.

A second door leads into a closet full of brooms and buckets, where a stretch of wall reconciles one end of the room and the hungry mouths of letterboxes. Another door, with an iron grate and knurled glass; and in the atrium the wall blackens. Some strange hieroglyphs adorn the walls.

I do not want to enter. I would rather paint a line of blood on the wall with my self-amputated fingers.

Yes, I would rather do that. In the damp and calm antrum, where the association of stinks hovers, a light goes out, and other flickers on, as though receiving a baton from a spent athlete. Antique memories speak of their insane nature as the light snakes its way in the tunnel, leaving no monstrosity in the dark. I would rather throw the garbage down the stairs than venture in the lair of unspeakable leviathans. In the cellar, valleys of infected land open their bowels, granite ridges bar the pass. They say there is nothing to fear, that it is just like any other cellar. Fantasy causes these things to blow out of proportion, leaving the dreamer frightened and disgusted.

They also say that the hung corpse is still oscillating, enunciating the passage of time, one, swing, at a time. They say many things. If a pregnant woman walks down the stairs she will abort, if a young woman walks down the stairs, then if she rises, she will rise with white hair and be in menopause, refusing to describe what her horrified eyes beheld. All lies!

That door hides pure horror. Sacks of crushed bodies are nothing in comparison. The endless spiral forces you towards the bottom like a corkscrew. Blind jellyfish dwell there; some have my gypsy grandmother's face, ready to suck the blood from gaping holes in ankles.

How can one not see the unclean swamps, alternating with the slurping quicksand? I know they are there. I can feel it. Not for nothing, I am the Prophet of the Past.

A mountain rises from those depths, bordered by a river. On it float the drenched letters my sisters sent my father both during and after the war, sentences read out by doctors who had taken care of my mother and Rita Rambaudo, letters written in the clinic of the mentally diseased. Their hospital records also re-surface.

On that dark waterway, madness floats, a Styx of broken aborted virtues. Black Second World War seaplanes glide by, with their immense engines, and my father waits on the riverbank with his Mauser caliber and his not yet degraded hopes.

I have lost myself again, and suddenly I hear my mother and Rita Rambaudo talking, their suffocated voices coming from one of the ravines. There grows the tree of vengeance. The same tree onto which both my two aunts and my grandmother, with her black apron perch. Bizzarrone's cherry tree, with its candelabra-like branches, the pus plant, that of cold spaghetti, pigment -voided worms, entwined on branches, moving, the same worms which hunted the colonizing flea from my head. Moreover, this is just the beginning.

After a small opening, the cellar floor slides ever more steeply; you feel like a ball, inexorably rolling downwards. The light comes from syncopating neon lights, like those in old cinemas, looming above the semi-bald person with standard jacket, standard grey face and standard lack of aspirations, sitting there asking for your standard money if you wish to urinate your expensive piss. Everything has a price. You slip on the earth's soft frame on which the filth's zinc blade is sticking. Do you really want to know why I do not want to go down there? Do you want to know why I would rather cross ten burning Styx? Do you?

Because I was born there.

* * *

The second stage towards the unification of Italy

"Mistico Rosolino, that's how they call you .... What do you think not talking will accomplish? You are confused, they will not come to save you, you know. Your companions! What will we tell the Prince of Canosa? That you were confused? Or that you didn't want to tell us the names of your cronies? Or maybe you want to be in the revolution? What will a revolution accomplish? You dirty your mouth with such a word.

How old are you anyway? Fifteen?

Do you think Murat will come and save you? He is already neck-deep in trouble. Don't you know that Gioachino will soon be hanging from the noose or better still get some lead in his belly? You want to be a hero. They lie to you. Do they even know that Mistico Rosolino is languishing in a jail, ready to hang? What use do Mazzini's friends have of you? You go back to helping your father run his tavern. You see, we know everything about you. Now you pray to San Teobaldo and not to San Gennaro?

Where it is written that you are a masonic? They do not know you are here; those guys chop you up before the police get their hands on you. The game that is being played is on a chessboard far too big for you to understand. The tricked you Rosoli'! And we caught you. The police do their duty, but we are Neapolitans.

You don't think of your mother? No? Are you so heartless? Oh, come on, what country? What homeland? There is only one country, that which fills your belly. Talk!'"

I looked through the windows, it was very early. There were people on the street, I had fallen into a deep slumber, I only remember a great chill. A staircase where the boy rushed downstairs waving the tricolour.

146

But this was surely another city. Could it be? Recent events had triggered riots and bloodied the peninsula from Palermo to Naples, from the Marche to Lombardy. Only Piedmont remained quiet, but there, under the ashes, things brooded. I went down into the alley. A woman bumped into me with her basket. Other people swelled the line. Some brandished hoes and sticks. *"Where are you going?"*

I went into a kiosk and took a piece of bread. I arrived in a wide space. They stood in a semicircle, crammed onto the steps and on the wagons. Soldiers with white jackets. The condemned. The gallows. Among the condemned, one name; Mistico Rosolino. Immediately I thought of the boy I met in Reggio Emilia, and the proclamation of the Cisalpine Republic.

Those facts were surely connected.

I kept my eyes glued to the tightening noose. Petrified with horror, I remained in the square for duration of the executions. Naples 1820, blood and repression following the uprisings. My special eye had reawakened those events, so distant in time. They took me away, someone gave me water, a woman said I had the same white face as the bodies one could find in hospital, not a drop of blood in my body, all had vanished, like the life of Mistico Rosolino and others, vanished patriots, all hung. The road for the redemption of the Italian peninsula and for freedom and liberation from the oppressor was cobbled with heads kept together by ropes. Darker days still were set to befall those who tread the path of liberty.

All this was written on page eighty-four, in the great encyclopaedia of knowledge published by Zanadu, purchased in cash.

* * *

The misfortune of having a black telephone

It always looked like it wanted to tell you something. It was about to put you in touch with who knows who, from who knows where? Maybe, someone buried deep in the building's basement. Black made of a ferrous and opaque plastic. Under the telephone was a triangle of cut glass with a green border, an unstable triangular shelf that tended to fall at one's glance, and an agenda which struggled to fill itself with numbers and names. The virtual lover's wife told my mother:

"If you're on the toilet and the phone rings, you either answer it or you don't, if you don't you get a cystitis." It had happened to her, cystitis or not.

"Hello, who's talking? ... Who?"

"I have to put you in contact with... long distance for ..." My heart skipped a beat, and my mouth dried up. This happened every time they called. She could not take it anymore. This was abuse. But it was not so, this time.

"Who do you want to talk to?" My mother's virtual lover starts with: *"Hello, beautiful! I propose to go and eat fried fish next Sunday, in a place where you will spend close to nothing, and you can stay all the afternoon watching people fish."*

The phone introduced a torrid anxiety. I look for a diversion and set off to explore the cubic meter of wood in the closet, under the window, from which bizarre olive-tinted worms emerge. The handset is raised and lowered several times, but no one answers, yet, someone is still calling. I reach the bathroom closet where one cannot sit.

The tension is intolerable. I want to bury myself under the woodpile. The deluge of rings begins again.

I emerge from my life's pressurised void, while my mother leans against the wall. We have come to it at last, what else is there to do?

"... And when was it again? Okay ... Sunday. Thank and my deepest condolences. I will tell him. Then he will call. Yes."

The phone call also carried with it talk of mourning-infused invites. That old woman's skeleton had farted, and then returned to her coffin, pulling her skirt down beyond her feet. She lived with her two daughters who had come from the metropolitan necropolis immediately after the war, insulted by fate, concussed by death. The black grandmother had been seen urinating in the basin my mother used to wash her face, her utmost disdain for the woman fuelling this most grotesque act. The black gypsy then disappeared.

She remains embedded in history, like a diamond deprived of light, she, who could neither read nor write. The black grandmother left, enshrouded by her rancorous silence.

"Let me be clear, you will go alone. The cemetery is always cold and he (me) will get sick and have a throat ache. Furthermore, a funeral is not a show fit for a child. Go? What for? She is dead anyhow." My father is as rigid as a stick of butter and promises to go alone.

Too bad, I would have used the funeral as an excuse to put my nose between documents enclosed in a patched suitcase, the one I caught a glimpse of in my aunts' cellar. That was an aseptic cellar, there was not a single shadow of evil, not like that of our condominium. Old letters from the front, greeting cards from Rivabella who lived in Rimini, certificates of my father's good health as he was looking for work. All this stuff cooped there.

* * *

To paradise, to heaven!

Rosa and Secondo Cavallotti lived in a salty cave with their daughter. Few other places are as close to my heart as that salty grotto. They lived deep inside Liguria, a region imbued with a repertoire of phantasmagorical smells. We paid them a visit every summer, and every summer Rosa Cavallotti would joke about how I looked like a German and how my hair resembled like their old broom's fibres.

The embarrassment of choosing one aspect over another, one expression over another, one mask over another, was mine to bear. I had to choose. Choose between the eunuchs' dumb looks and the family of vintners' barbaric salute. The latter stayed at the ground floor, flooding it with vines.

Memory demands the existence of precedents, but here, everything is important, everything has no past and no future, everything is present.

The sour smell of vine mush and the decaying scent of leaves washed against the corner of the road accompany us on our way to the beach where a peddler sold his flowers in a small shed amidst the sands.

In the distance; flashes of light. In the evening, dazed by the great sun; the homely worldliness of elegant sweaters, streets filled with lavender, strawberry ice creams and never-ending yawns.

We shared the kitchen and the living room with the Cavallotti spouses and often ate with them. The toilet on the stairs was shared with an apartment occupied by the eunuch's son and his mother. There too, like many a stairway toilet, hovered wild smells.

Access to our bedroom is only granted on tiptoeing. This is due to the fragile fossils scattered here and there, enveloped in a fog of memories. A nothing is enough to desecrate them. The walls are a work of art, a mixture of periwinkle colours, they conceal hidden whispers, whispers which are in no way related to the enclosing Adriatic Sea, that same sea in which Gilberta's mother drowned.

One has to witness events unfolding in the landing's narrow theatre. A closing peephole, the ants' solemn procession, the fly which crashes against the glass, the acidic breath of wine barrels located close to the entrance which bland the aspidistra.

We have just climbed up the razor-sharp stairs; we are greeted by a flash of immersing light as we stand contrite, as though this was our first Mass, as though we were hovering around a young girl's lips. In there, lies the sea. The sea, and my parents, who tried in vain to be a couple like many others. Rosa Cavallotti's voice echoes, her daughter's difficult silences deafen. Her daughter is an elementary school teacher, she wears petal-patterned skirts, tightened with soft leather belts, she is quite adorable.

Swollen mattresses, bundles of cloud, old golden chenille bedspreads, they were all there as well. Pillows and sea-tasting blankets, and then a childhood of objects, suspended over the flickering lagoon of regret.

The waxed blood-red floor supports plaster statues of Jesus and his Mother, the former has a ragged nose. They rest on the large alabaster shelf which sleeps on the tin chest. The master bedroom is a circular maze, with two adjacent entrances. The sea is omnipresent, it floods the street every night, it drowns who lingers in their sleep, it diminishes cats, drunks and lovers into nothingness in its embrace. The coastal villages suffer every night from its assaults.

They gasp until the first light of day, then succumb, then emerge again, with sparkling gardens and fountains spotting forth rainbows from a blaze of fiery drops. Liguria is so unique, just like its grim indigenous people. There is a hustle and bustle of slippers and life jackets that come unstuck from forearms. Other holiday-makers ascend as the iridescent vintners descend into their burrows, engulfed by the darkness of the stairs. Apollo has no power in that antrum, it is an uncharted place, one his fiery chariots have never trod on.

"Say hello to the lady. This is not your home … you are so rude."

"Aren't you the cheeky one?" Says Rosa Cavallotti as she pinches my neck.

Calm and wise she governs her realm under a veil of mould. Antonia, her daughter, stays silent. My mother adds: *"Love, love. If it won't come on a Saturday it will come knocking on a Sunday. Love!"*

Rosa Cavallotti smiles, her daughter shrugs and smiles at the thought of her boyfriend crossing the Turchino pass in his Lambretta. Antonia does not drink, she does not eat, she lacks the creative *furore* to come up with extravagant ideas. When she does eat, the meal is comprised of a couple of apples and a yogurt. She keeps her distance from me, she saw me grow older and ruder. Our communication is reduced to a muffled whisper; we are afraid of disturbing Mr. Cavallotti, who lies exhausted after his rail shifts.

All Ligurians have been railway men, dug wells for water, founded cities, and fought on galleys against half of the known world. All Ligurians have planted their warehouses in the far East to exchange precious spices, fabrics and subterfuges. And now all Ligurians complain about their bad luck, about how tourists invade their coast.

They are not entirely wrong, it must be hard to go from world-power to nation-state to region, with Genoa and Savona admiring their spent, dull reflections in the calm sea.

Now they possess a small piece of paradise in the countryside leading to the sea. Cavallotti is content with what he has too. He is

Charlie Chaplin's double, and wears a soft, baggy tank top even at the dinner table. Today's Ligurians are vulgar and perennially grumble, they have no glory or future ahead of them.

Her mother says: *"You are not eating yet? Come on!! On!"* Antonia snorts. Her new blue belt tightens her hips. An adorable wasp's waistline. Adorable Antonia. *"I will go out mom, see if there is any mail"* She will undoubtedly stay out with a female friend.

I remain alone in the holiday home. My eye has found a sight to feast on. Three steps of chipped cement leading to the paradise glued to a window. The light showers blue and green particulates in the room's darkness, it is a gateway to a new world.

"See where they end up? Shall I kill them? Shall I kill them? Tell me! What do I have to do! Look how many there are. Follooooow theeem!" Cackled my mother. *"They are all going in the sugar bags, they come from there. Lemon try with lemon not the insecticide! Insecticide next to the sugar? Nooo!"* The peace is disturbed. The ants must be stopped or else they will conquer the jam jars and sugar bags. The ears are filled with the thumping of hooves on the landing and the cries of tourists staying at widow Emma's place, tourists submerged already by their load of towels, fins and already inflated lifebuoys, you never know, one might sink in the sea of light.

Cavallotti's bedroom lies in total darkness. I cannot resist its call, and with curiosity-backed courage I give in to the call of danger. I sneak into the cave in which Antonia was conceived. I feel like a thief. Already I am like a fly in the middle of the room, my eyes are getting used to this new-found darkness. I am profaning this homely shrine.

"Do you need anything?" Antonia's voice suddenly whips me. She was behind me. For how long? I do not know. I cannot see anything anymore. The darkness is darker now. I would like to sink. Will Antonia divulge I was spying in her parents' bedroom? Does she want me to throw myself at her feet? To jump from the rock and beat my head to a pulp?

"Forgive me Antonia! I only wanted to see, to understand"

Her wide bell-like skirt brushes against my legs, it will go away, forever. I immediately abandon the door handle because it now burns. I am a worm, I know, and there is nothing to add to a worm's shame.

I found an excuse not to go to the beach that day. I wanted to show you what profound penance I am capable of. She did not show up for two whole consecutive days. She had her mother say she was suffering from heartburn, in reality, she was punishing me. *"Antonia, forgive me!"*

* * *

The treasure of Cantalupo

If you looked out into the horizon, you could see the marina's haze, steaming above the great blue. In the opposite direction were the hills furrowed by tortuous groves through which powerful fig trees stood out.

We climbed with my father; and it was a breathtaking sight, up to the peak. He still felt troubled by the albeit not manifest, but very much recurring aversion of his sisters towards my mother.

After the hard climb we progressed through blackberry bushes, passing near the Dancing Nautilus, which overlooked the sea, and finally returned to the houses scattered on the slopes.

"Let's stop for a moment," he says, *"let's take a breath, there's no hurry, you know, your mother is alone for a while, and will not get agitated ... you know how she is."*

I had my doubts about her not getting agitated, after all, a couple of ants had made her reverberate like a tuning fork. The ants are not only in the sugar bags, they are also marching on the dead-mother-in-law's dry skin and in her head. Her sisters-in-law had asked: "Why didn't she come to her mother-in-law's funeral? She took away our brother and our mother died of a broken heart" These words were like termites, gnawing at my mother's mind.

The top of the hill awaits us, as it juts out of this magnificent blue. The uncertain stone road returns and disappears. We take pictures with a Certrix camera, the ones with the self-timer, allowing all the family to fit in the picture. And just like that we are immortalised one meter from the summit. We contemplate the mind-boggling beauty of the sea on which a hundred breezes blow, tearing their lungs apart. This is one of those rare moments which see my father and I united in the contemplation of beauty. This windy chorus rips away at distant horizons, to the glittering eras of blood and conquest. Moors, Pisans and Genovese. Romans, Phoenicians, and pirates. And still the wind blows, sail lingering in the wake, sanding the water, to then get lost. There is nothing else to see, let us proceed. Our eyes forever glued to that deep blue. *"Do you want some water? Are you hungry? Do you want to go back? There is nothing left to see here, it is getting late and mother will be getting worried. Let's go back."*

Back in the village, there is not a single hole, or door, or fake pearl encrusted on showcases that I am not aware of. The scattered houses the stage onto which a myriad of actors play their parts. In order of appearance; first we have Margherita's breasts. Margherita is a shapely kitchen-maid who bathes in the evenings and her breasts wobble now here now there, without any malice, wrapped in her red costume.

Then we have the angry attendant lifeguard; he has to make sure swimmers on the free beach do not usurp the frontier leading to the fee-paying beach. Next up is the pedophile poet; parents tolerate his presence, he wears soft half-leg black-wool trousers, and undermines children with his sugary sonnets and poetic lust.

Chilled polyps slip on the steel plate in the fridge box. There are posters announcing that old circuses are camped nearby full of their ravenous jugglers and sleeping donkeys.

Just how much time has passed? I do not appreciate the thought of starting my walk again through the long sea of calla begonia and lavender flowers without first knowing where my final destination lies.

The inexorable passage of clings onto the room where blue and green molecules of light jettison from the sky.
Time, ever clandestine in its dealings with humans, immortalises me, a young vain man with no muscles, lazily busy in the act of admiring himself in the bus stop's tarnished windows, already the first Kent decaying between his lips.

Once I get back to the city, I will have to see a dentist.
He will check the fillings, and I will know whether my sentence has

changed. *"Are you OK?"* The dentist will ask. I will nod, as a disturbing oppression ripens inside my gut, something unquestionable, like the judge's judgement, written in large letters on the great wall, in front of his study.

* * *

The electric current will heal you

On closer inspection, other events also deserved to be labelled as *"unquestionable"*, however, memory is evasive, their identification proves difficult.

Some events took a deep dive into a pit of ridicule, where they swam side by side with aunt Prisca's strident chair-demanding phone call. Others decided to race against the terrible phosphorous spheres in Bizzarrone's swamp. The mind wandered but always returned, where to? A mystery.

Consulting the encyclopaedia of Universal Knowledge would serve no purpose in this fog of confusion. Where was this place I was looking for? And did unspeakable mean inevitable and unidentifiable?

One of Professor Ugo Cerletti's epigones whispers something about electric discharges:

"These reactions are induced by violent stimuli, convulsions…of the electric kind… epileptic." I slowly sank in a swamp of medical records. Around me were decaying trees on whose broken barks were engraved illustrious and contrasting diagnoses. Runes which whispered of neurone vegetative illuminations, of blood transfusions infused with equivocal substances.

I had to return to my mother's psychic collapse to find answers, an alarming thought. For now, however, I was sitting with my mouth wide open in the killer dentist's chair. Caries… cellar…clinic…. catatonic…. There was very little to joke about. After all, crisis chaos and catalepsy also began with the letter C.

I would start by taking care of my molars. This first step will lead me to understanding the complete working of the defensive system, which kicks in after the convulsive therapies.

So spoke Professor Cerletti's assistant while looking at his shoes' shining extremities.

The professor dismantled any walls I had raised to defend my ignorance. Do I have the right to not know what happened in the clinic's basement?

"The rate of production of enzymes has sped up. These enzymes are responsible for the reduction in the concentration neuro-transmitters in the synapse. We can now confirm there has been an increase in the release of endorphins, vasopressin and…"

"Please stop professor, I don't understand any of this stuff."

"I'm sorry," says the doctor *"but we are obliged to inform the patient and his family about the possible side effects …"*

"What are the side effects, doctor? And after all this, how will the parent feel? Once the electric current has flown through her head will it all be all right?"

"Alright? it will be much better than alright! It is a well-known fact that in fifty-five percent of the cases …"

"Excuse me doctor. Better in what sense? And what about the other forty-five percent?"

"The variation in cerebral blood flow is ascertained. And she will feel better after this."

"Will the fridge still bother her? Will she go pale again and shake like a withering leaf on a branch when her sister-in-law calls? And what about Rita Rambaudo? Will she be better too? You know, I would like to have some more details, this stuff is important to me you know? Rita Rambaudo cannot stand the color white, nor can she stand light in general, or the radio. Did you know all this?"

"What she needs is the shock-box!" Says the doctor.

"But, where do you want to go with this? With this shock-box?"

"Well we certainly cannot perform the treatment in the clinic, now can we?"

"Perform what?"

"You know, make her feel better. You do understand?"

Less than an hour ago, I was walking under the palm trees of the Kursaal Margherita asking Antonia for forgiveness, now here I am talking about Metrazol and hypodermic needles as an alternative to electrical discharges.

"What is it, doctor? Would you care to explain all this calmly from the start?"

"Electrodes are sprinkled with gel to not allow the electricity to burn the patient's skin. We then discharge 70 to 400 volts of electricity at a current of 1.6 Amps. The law asks us to inform one family member at the very least. ECT treatment heals biological and unknown abnormalities in fifty-five percent of cases."

"And what about the remaining forty-five percent of cases?"

"... The worst part of ECT is brain failure, which incidentally is the title of a book by Norman or Sutherland. I quote: There are many reports of patients comparing the atmosphere in the hospital on the day of their treatment to that experienced during an execution."

"But what are the contraindications?"

"Electroshock works by damaging the brain. Some say that this damage is negligible and transitory. ... like a hammer hit on the head, sometimes you can lose your sense of orientation."

"And what does Karl Pribman say?"

".. He suggests having a small lobotomy rather than a series of ECT shocks."

"Doctor, I don't understand any of it, what happens to the patient?"

"Dr. Sidney Samet says that this type of therapy can be succinctly defined as a: "type of controlled damage the brain suffers when it undergoes electrical stimulation. The electric shock reactive the pool of norepinephrine and increases the rate of release of endorphins and vasopressin."

157

"Did I understand this correctly? At the very least, this process will reduce Rita Rambaudo's desire to throw herself from the balcony. And where are they taking her now?"

"Why don't you understand? Everything is white! The face, the balcony, the children, the stairs, everything is white!" Says the woman.

"What is white, Madam?" Ask the doctors.

"All of it!" Says Rita Rambaudo. "Do you not see it too?"

"Get a hold of her wrists, otherwise she might escape."

"Everything is white I tell you!" The woman grinds her teeth.

The sea scent, Antonia is rustling clothes, the onion buns, the smell of a sea country are still all within me. And here I am with these people in white coats talking to me about hammering heads and brain damage.

"It's white!" shouts Rita Rambaudo, our neighbour, my mother is crying as she is taken over by a *"synergistic mood swing fuelled by an uncontrollable involuntary emulation."* That is what the doctor would say.

Rita Rambaudo is still shouting, she has beautiful white shoulders not even my first mother can distinguish between colours anymore. *"My kids, my husband and the stairs are all white. They are all… white,"* she mutters.

"The color white," explains the doctor, *"is the visual materialisation of anguish, or, it is the optical translation of a patient's pains. We will need to modify this perception through the treatment."*

"Is there any hope?" I ask.

"Let's try," say the doctors. *"Fifty-five percent of the cases … prove its validity."*

White is the nightmare that crawls at night and throws itself like a killer onto my parents' bed. White is the assassin's escape and white are the soles of his shoes while escaping capture, running away on the roofs, after trampling on my belly. White is my mother's face and her bed sheets.

"How are their eyes doctor?"

"As white as the straps fixing their heads into place"

Do I have to tell my father about the great hustle and bustle that has occurred? He will breathe a sigh of relief and calmly measure the whole event with his Mauser caliber.

When I woke, there was not a more involved and alarmed face than mine. A curious event took place during my anaesthesia, Fergallo's apprehensive face came into view, he was the new official family tooth-extractor.

"Hey young man, are you alright?"

I do not know what had happened, but I did know I had rummaged in the affairs of other people's lives.

"Don't you worry now, it will come to pass."

I wanted to run away from these nightmares. Doctors say that some kinds of anaesthesia induce hallucinations. I was slowly regaining the gifts I had lost. *"Unspeakable."* I blame this word for unleashing the nightmare. It is synonymous with *"Be careful of what you say,"* or *"dig your grave with your own hands."*

Fergallo the dentist was the cheapest most merciful of dentists ever to walk this Earth. He was a friend to tram-drivers, retirees and even to some quite rich women. Word spread from mouth to mouth and his list of customers grew because of his crackling sympathy, rather than his skill.

During my virtual journey through underground psychiatric clinics, Fergallo must have worried about the dopamine and norepinephrine levels I had invoked aloud.

The new tooth-extractor probably blessed my resurrection. He would not have known what else to do. What if I felt down stone dead? What if I suffocated by the mere thought of unexpected electric shocks? He looks at me now with gigantic eyes, surrounded by veins of bizarre serpentine capillaries. He had a good soul but was naive with women, who promptly took advantage of him.

* * *

159

From shop assistant to becoming the dentist's wife

Fergallo, the new dentist, became a cuckold shortly after he became a husband. When the extraction of a molar was imminent, he sent you to one of his many acquaintances; a real dentist proudly highlighting a shiny plaque with the inscription: *Prof. Dr. Dental Practice. Visits by appointment only.* Fergallo held no such office. He held his door ajar, ready to flee with his inscription-less cardboard plaque whenever clients were there. He always had a reason, or an excuse to be interested in you, when that reason did not revolve around his profession.

Mind you, this was not the same sneaky interest Salvatore the barber had; this was a good-natured interest, the kind of which would be displayed by his hands patting his thighs, highlighting his participation to your misfortune, alleviating it a little bit in the process.

His error was to have conceived a child, and after this most unfortunate event, the couple slept in separate rooms. The son was now struggling at school and lacked respect for his father. The latter's paternity was uncertain, if one lent an ear to the tittle-tattle hovering around the mother. She was a former pastry shop assistant, wore periwinkle-coloured sweaters and now walked cloaked with a veil of superiority, carefully choosing her lexis.

Once, the woman has been seen with her arms tightly folded, as though she was a zipper, concealing her true self, while displaying her newly found posh upper-class mannerisms. Her new status naturally made her ashamed of her husband; he was half man, half a good ogre, wandering around life in his pair of ragged slippers because his "feverish" feet swelled at every step. Fergallo symbolised an almost accomplished social ascension to the villager's modest and humble inhabitants, he was a half-shaped dream, a malformed desire.

I could smell his liquorice breath, it faded into puffs of aromatic eucalyptus, hah puff had an odor to it, which reflected the degree of annoyance his wife had had with him. I learnt to know him by the way he held the spatula, by his trembling *moustache* and by the rhythm of his breathing. I was symbiotic with him and I could read his state of mind as he amalgamated waxes inside his mortar, ready to spread on diseased teeth, covering their grotesqueness, but to me he was as easy to see as a lone tree in a desert.

Sometimes he would say: *"Hello my dear,"* other times, he would not acknowledge your presence at all, and you had to guess where his tongue hid itself as his eyes scouted your mouth's ravines. The infamous writing on the wall resided in another part of the village. As far as Fergallo was concerned, the unappealable judgement was a sentence, which accepted no contest. One afternoon, when Fergallo's mood was particularly sour, I managed to get into his thoughts using my qualities as Prophet of the Past.

I was curious. I had identified a woman's silhouette, she was with her back to me, but her entertaining attitude towards a man was very visible. It was Fergallo's wife of course, wearing a white coat with a collar and the pink striped cuffs from the pastry shop she had worked in before the wedding. She approached, put her arms around the man's neck and kissed him unabashedly. An avalanche of warnings, insults and threats came crashing down Fergallo's mind's slippery slopes. He was asking his wife to give him her version of the story, but she simply denied the story there and then. She would said: *"If you believe all the nonsense people say… My life does not change just like that, you have nothing to reproach me. This is what it is, whether you like it or not, the choice is yours. He was here before you were."*

Now I could feel Fergallo's blood pressure increase, it was almost choking him. This was an unappealable situation, much like his marriage. He had given her two pairs of pink silk sheets. He had given her that fur coat as a present. He had accompanied her on the cruise she desired, and she looked satisfied then, for a while.

What was wrong now? Was it because he was ugly? Were his bad teeth putting his wife to shame? What about the son? Was he his or was he the offspring of a host of men which were here before he was? The marriage was a complicated affair, pacts never clarified, trailing nets dredged the bottom of the relationship, trapping old lovers and their vices disguised as virtues. Fergallo's smiles froze, as the soulless teeth lined up like toy soldiers on the shelves, with their cold and obscene smiles. Fergallo and his twelve hours of daily work.

Maybe one-day Fergallo's practice will go to his son… however, for the time being that scoundrel did not even want to go to school. He spoke of his son to his patients too. *"He treats me badly and my wife says nothing… Sorry could you please open your mouth a bit more… yes that is good.*" I was his patient. I was on the receiving end of Fergallo's waterfall of insults. I was an innocent victim caught between the couple's crossfire. His invectives aimed at the mischievous ex-confectioner, the one who had taken advantage of his good nature without firing a single shot of betrayal, after all, she had not promised him anything, before or after the marriage. Fergallo felt his wife's infidelities were like mountain peaks smashing onto his head and mood. His dreams spoke of her neck adorned with a necklace of pearls, of her visage with no make-up; this is what he was imagining… she would hold his hands gently to say: "*I love you… and I always will…*" His heart spoke of a growing empty warmth, he knew everything was false; his life's dream was to see his wife in love with him.

He murmurs and can no longer hold back the torrent of insults; he is both orator and public: "*Never get married my son. Run away if you have to.*" His wife says that she wants to take part in a string of conferences. Another excuse to meet her many admirers. "*Who does she think I am fooling?*" Thinks Fergallo, without having the strength to reproach her of anything. "*They are all alike,*" he says as he sniffs the tip of the sharp speculum. "*Oh, but you are young still, and you cannot understand.*" I think to myself; the cuckold's crown is bare and laden with lies. "*In the end, the last one is no better than the first one.*"

He thinks about his wife. "*They're just superior. They are women. In the blink of an eye. Zac! They take advantage of you and you find yourself married, with a ball and chain at your foot, and a son who… Ah forget it… he cannot get any worse.*"

Suddenly I remember the painting hanging in the waiting room. It has a shabby wooden frame, which has impressed a large dark stain on the wall. It portrays the garden of knowledge, where nudes hosted in the eternal primordial forests. Thick carpets of trees with drooping yellow fruits and dark red berries. This is the ancient paradise in which curtains of distant mountains drop onto endless green stages. Your eye spots a multitude of tiny herds gathering in the pastures dotted across the forest, your black mouth's reflection slowly approaches the mountain, the trunk, the heart of the forest which slowly secretes naked figurines and their delicious breasts, their calves tense in the act of gathering berries for the table. These are timeless women, forest nymphs, owners of the dew, which constitutes the forest's epidermal defence. Their behinds are like silk petals, a touch darker near the parting of the buttocks. The painting has been hanging there for years now, indecipherable, dusty. Because of that, I respect it. Handmaids gather under the light rays, which splinter through cracks in the vigorous tree trunks. What are they looking for? Noon's unadorned hour? Nectar secreted from paradisiac flowers. Now the virgins open their smiles, like certain berries with vermilion teeth, lips of vegetable flesh.

"Whores... do you understand?" Blurts Fergallo at the end of his sermon against women. *"You are still young. They will make a fool of you, right under your very nose. Whores! Do not get married, dear... Here we go; we are done now, now it should not hurt anymore. Spit and rinse your mouth. So... Is Wednesday at three good for you? Great, see you then my dear."*

In the waiting room, the big stain on the wall protects the virgins of the forest. The neon light, which usually importunes them, is spent. They are certainly resting.

* * *

The fridge has a crack

One of the biggest misfortunes ever to have occurred in those years was the ruinous breakage of the refrigerator handle. Yes, the same fridge that contained the beating engine from Tecumseh Ltd. This tragic event sits alongside our family's great misfortunes.

The event itself instigated shouts of *"Betrayal!"* It demolished certainties; it put into question previously unquestionable truths and brought discredit to the apparatus' supreme quality. It also caused the maternal mind to plunge back into the clinic's basement, where another series of ECT treatments would continue. My father scooped up the remains of this most criminal wreckage and said; *"Oh look here, the handle has broken."* He stood with the metallic pieces in his hand, fascinated by the brilliant badly forged lump of alloyed aluminum and nickel.

The mother cried rivers of tears, which bled, through her visage; she was a modern day Anticlea. Kit Karson's honor was forever tarnished. His defeat was of an atomic nature, the very fabric of matter had torn, large voids in the certainties of science screamed at their precious four-dimensional membrane's perforation. Faith and optimism vanished. In addition, as these were already scarce in our abode, his error left an indelible absence. The unfortunate relic laid for a long time in the kitchen cabinet, so people could contemplate it, like a statue in a museum, where curious visitors could relive the dramatic moments of its sudden rupture.

My mother accused me of opening the fridge door with no regard. In short, we had mistreated him, and the refrigerator behaved accordingly, as though he had a soul. I always knew he had a soul, and now that soul was ashamed, affronted, derelict, unless…

"Unless what?" Unless one could make a new better handle from the previous one. My father's projects were inspired by a utopian creative fervor, and this fervor would invigorate the fridge door.

"Keep the broken piece, let's show it to Nevio, show that braggart you were able to make a new handle," said the proud motherly voice. She wanted to show Nevio, the braggart who had not even able to set up a cooperative to build their house of dreams. She wanted to show him both handles.

My father told me:

"It is the carbon that really screws you over. You must be very careful with the carbon composition. Cast iron and steel are not the same thing, what makes them different is the percentage of carbon you add to the iron. Do you get it?"

The handle's parthenogenesis took weeks. In the meantime, we had to force the fridge to open with pincers.

"I have already told everyone you are making a new handle. Do you have any idea how much shame will fall on me if you do not succeed?" Said my mother, the aspiring suicidal martyr.

The leading representatives of the condominium's families routinely came to verify my father's progress. *"You are so good."* Said Muller the widow. *"My husband was good too, you know? He was as good as you, but he is no longer here."* She said with her liquid look. Te Pe Tee Di Fonza and Basovici's wife also came, only Rita Rambaudo did not contribute to the condominium's curiosity, however, she did let everyone know that once she was cured she would come and see the handle.

I was half asleep, and in this hazy state of confused absence, my thoughts started to converge. The breaking of the handle was a precursor to a host of events which lack any rational explanation even unto this day.

Nevio had not been invited to see the handle; mother was afraid he would start making fun of my father. The heavy coffin door confirmed its sealing with a tranquilliser *"Clack"*. The fridge had been given new life.

Its reparation temporarily restored bonds of respect between myself and my family, I decided to postpone my escape plans.

The miracle of the handle was followed by sleepless nights in which I would dream of a purple cat, of the reappearance of Tecumseh the Indian and of a host of episodes linked to the Italian Risorgimento. One such episode described the persecution of patriots at the Spielberg. This information was found in the encyclopaedia of knowledge we had acquired in cash.

* * *

A cat is a cat

"Where shall we put it? Look at that cute little nose! Check if it is a male or a female. What shall we call it? What shall we feed it? What if it dies? Look at its little paw. Careful, it will bite. So, do we keep it? What if it does not get used to us? With all those strays out there. What a lucky little guy. And where will it pee? We have to teach it."

A cat is a cat. You will always get to know it less than it knows you. It is absent half the time, and is capricious the other half, reservedly docile, ambiguous and effusive when it needs to be.

All cats are purple. It is their color, purple, purple and yellow, electricity's invisible colors. These animals don't die, they are earth spirits, companions to witches, alembics and jesters. There are no innocuous or innocent cats; the ones we are about to stab, because we have grown tired of their company, will haunt you forever. This was probably Vera's cat's story. One of her suitors had given her a cat, which later turned out to be too much for her to handle. She had been warned to: *"let it go, let it take care of itself."*

165

When in the right state of mind, one can see cats everywhere. There are doorkeeper cats and cats bearing the milkman's and greengrocer's faces.

Cats disguised as men, as women, as armchairs, fridge cats, handle cats and electric discharge cats.

There is the great tailor-cat, then there is the one who borrowed barber Salvatore's lineaments, and they are followed by a delirium of felines; master inventors of siesta and ambush.

This specific cat rolls around the forearm, it plays, meows, nibbles your thumb to then escape, for fear of reprisals. This is a cat which participates in my mother's obsessions. It jumps out of a holed cardboard box my father brought home. The cat simultaneously pees, plays and eats. He is immaculate, with a black spray on his face, always on top of the pile of firewood. *"Must we keep it?"* The creepy, cold-hearted question. Mother understands she should not ask any sillier questions; after all, she would be the one to suffer from the cat's absence the most. A cat is a cat. And a cat is the law. It rolls up into your hand, it is so tiny, it rubs its rough tongue on your forearm's skin. It is restless because it is in deep conversation with your subconscious, it reminds you how little difference there is between your seemingly separate natures.

China is the first female to arouse a sense of sincere affection in mother since her brother's, Sostene's wife, the now deceased sister-in-law.

We baptised her around five o' clock on a Saturday afternoon as she stands on the edge of a chair, staring at a wooden thread. She will be called China. Mind you, the Ch is hard Ch, like that for Chemical, kiss, or Queen. China, synonymous with the downhill road leading to all the world's cellars.

China, the extraordinary event which could forever change my distressed family's precarious equilibrium.

You place her on your stomach and soon find her nibbling away at your chin. Put her on your knees and she will sneak off to sniff your ear. You don't get it, you don't know how to get it, you with your fridges and broken handles, you with your battles and attempts at restoring a Nation's identity. You are not a cat. A cat understands everything, from a housewife's manias to the diatribes between Olga and her mother, from the erotic eagerness of Purusa, the primeval male married to my nymphomaniac cousin Lory, to the apparent death of Gilberta, who lived and died confined to the fourth floor of a house with no stairs.

China stands motionless, like a tiny Egyptian statue, intent on contemplating nothingness, the wall, the ladle. She looks at you, with her false air of disinterest, but swiftly turns her gaze to the fissure between the cupboard's doors. She fixates the windows, overlooking the jungle of roofs and tar. April's flies are passionate about her presence, they crash into each other from opposite extremities of the window panes.

China had no references, she was like many a bastard cat vagabonding around the village, yet she represented the final stage in her species' exceptional psychic evolution. She was the final iteration of an experiment whose goal was to create an elaborate affectionate character. My mother took her seriously, and in doing so slipped into her trap. A trap made of tender honeyed meows and fake ambushes around her ankles, she built a privileged relationship with her, one built on a resonance of the psyches.

China acted as a surrogate of affection, she was able to saturate the gaps that neither son nor husband were able to fill. My father and I were by the window, waiting for her bouts of madness to vanish.

The cat was special: she spoke and vibrated. They got along just fine, her and my mother, one looked for the other, and they both kept an eye on each other. It is very likely that China was a sponge intent on absorbing her master's overwhelming emotions, reshaping them in the process, but she would have never let her own mood reach such an azimuth, only my mother had such talent, and China was a cat after all.

Her world was made from the cardboard box, from the pile of wood in the attic, from the legs of the kitchen table. China suffered no mood swings, her concern was limited to hunting, to the state of her fur, to the daily ration of boiled lung, to the appearance of a flea in her throat's undercoat and to the puddles of pee she showered under the beds. She was a glorious concentration of nerves, muscles, nails, and good moods, plus, she was shrewd enough. If you had to describe her in one word, that word would be: *"evolved."* She was at least two evolutionary stages ahead of her adopters.

167

She seemed to treasure our teachings, placing herself as a privileged interlocutor between us and the world. She knew how to be appreciated by rare visitors who asked: *"Where is the cat? Where is China? She hasn't disappeared, right?!"*

They were all happy, exception being for Pezzuto's doves, they were terrified in their aviary, as China had turned it into her hunting grounds.

There was no connection between Iotti and China, not even a geographical one. One lived in the vast noble spaces near dorms and large windows, projected towards heaven, the other was secluded in her humid corner in the courtyard.
In short, they were poles apart, both dedicated to hunting, one for rats, the other for Spring's flies. And their affinities ended there.

* * *

Iotti the concierge has something to say

"If I see that hag again, I will crush her." mumbled Iotti the concierge as she swept cigarette butts and litter. *"Do those dirty people make such a mess at their own place? I am talking about the butts"*

Iotti slams doors and makes a big fuss. Nobody ever dares tell her: *"sweep here, clean up there."* She knows what to do. Her daughter's premature death affected her every thought. She was a young widow, and she repaid life back with the scraps it had given her. Whoever asked her for any information was a scoundrel. My aunt, who had asked to see her brother alone, also fell under the same denomination. Time was a scoundrel too, as was the wine, which helped her live through boredom and menopause. Scoundrel too was the disgusting type of life she was living, the great Venetian with a balcony for a bosom. She leaned on her broom, put her hands on her hips and inspected the row of baths.

Someone had dared to say: *"Go clean there."*

"Why don't you go clean up that crap? Stinker. I already have my own things to clean. With what audacity do you come to me and tell me to go clean? To me? You go and clean those Southerner's toilets. They shower the floor. Why don't

you go and clean the piss and crap and other delightful presents they leave behind?"

Both the priest and the milkman were cheeky. The former had stopped blessing the concierge and the mailman who had invited her at the bar. *"What coffee? What on Earth did he think? The cheek."* Iotti thought, with or without the wine, her sorrow burdened by the defunct. The house administrator had asked her to inquire about the bizarre people who lived on the first floor. Parsley, two sacks of potatoes, one of red onions, and a Southerner who went to the market to buy fruits and vegetables for her, discreetly courting her in the process.

The prosperous and still pleasant Iotti, with her iron-coloured eyes. She got mad at anyone strolling in front of her with the wolfhound, my father's source of inspiration for his flea comb. *"If she struts around here once more I will swipe its feet."*

"But why Iotti? Why?" Had asked Madama Pezzuto. *"Because she is a whore, I do not want her. My daughter never had such friends. And she must not mention she was my daughter's friend."*

The Sun sinks and the fog rises. The street loses itself into the nothingness of the woman's hairdresser, the cove of profitable gossip. The morning is gloomy, the shutters still lowered, and the dirty opaque glass of garage doors mirror their grime onto the streets. Iotti is furious about what happened in the garage.

The garage door opens in the guardian's face. He was sleeping on a mattress resembling a dog's kennel. The man gets up, meticulously explores his nostrils and disembarks a sumptuous yawn; he passes the palm of his hand on his bristly cheek and negligently folds the checkered blankets on the cot. His companions are a telephone and dust, old diaries, and rent receipts scattered on the creaking desk. The garage is voluminous, with penetrating scents of rubber, cement and motor oil, ready to infect the lungs. An ominous faded yellow color dominates the interior, a color of bones and teeth and the whitish cream of a two-day old beard. The guardian observes his crumpled face. There goes the first honk. *"Oh, go fuck yourself. Here comes the first stinker for his car."* He thinks and presses the button to open the garage door with a great sloth about his action.

"Shhhhtt. Idiot go fuck yourself," he moves his chin up in a sign of false greeting. *"… This is for your sister… fuck you… cuckold…"* The car

trudges on the climb. The lights flash. The poisonous smell of the exhaust pipe invades all; an invisible toxic cloud dissolves in the sticky air. Neon lights flicker; it is six o'clock in the morning. *"Already on the road, hu?"* The greengrocer starts the van and leaves. *"And there we go! Asshole ... mhhhhm."* The old paramour smiles.

Had he bothered Iotti? The scruffy playboy whispers compliments to the young woman as she fondles the wolf dog. Maybe it is the dog's sympathy combined with November's mist that makes the woman rethink about the guardian's impudence; he had asked her to visit him by night in his garage... wolfhound permitting. A blue light filter from the skylight onto old cigarette papers, on leaves entangled in the grating and on those tessellating onto heaps of tires.

"What if someone sees us?" There is no mattress and no bed sheet on the cot. Nothing to see at all.

"Will you stop by?"

"What?"

"Will you stop by? There is nothing to wait for. You no longer want to stop by. Hey, make up your mind! When? Whenever you want: but the dog..."

The guard's velvet undergarment and trousers already lowered, like a flag in mourning. Grey turns to black, covering the lovers' rags.

"Who can see you during the night? We are together. Are you afraid of the air pump? Does it make you uneasy? Come on, come here I like you... mhhhh! Yes, that's it, come on!" A rough beard, caresses and other blandishments. Soft underpants and away they go. In the garage's alcove, there is a passage with a ladder-leading straight into the underground car park. *"Who can see us there?"*

The black hours of eleven, midnight and one o'clock are set onto the symphony of grey and yellow. A gash of yellow from the hanging lamp cleaves the black into two. The road has a hundred sleepless eyes.

"Look at that whore keeping that Scoundrel Company, you would not find me dead by his side, such is the disgust I feel for him". Thinks Iotti the doorkeeper, framing her thoughts with stares she slingshots towards

the garage, its small door closes, shielding the cheeky couple. Madame Iotti's sleepless eye wants to see for how long that bitch is going to walk her urinating dog into the night.

"She must not even dream of saying that my poor daughter was her friend. My daughter was no friend to that cow and her flea-infested dog."

* * *

This is true love

The buy two get one free offer available from the village's first mini market was not a great success. Apart from the occasional visit, we continued to shop at Ginetta's mother's store. One could not ask for better.

When one went to Ginetta, one met the whole village, including its gossip. Iotti was still in turmoil because of what she thought she had seen in the garage, and promptly talked about it in the grocery store. After all, you cannot stop a grumbling pot of beans unless you turn the fire down, but Iotti's stove's handle was malfunctioning to say the least.

Around that time, I was wandering about my business homing in on the source of my desires: my Tunisian giraffe. *"Check if Angela still has that mark on her neck, it must be a skin disease,"* reminded me my malicious mother. I am brushing up my knowledge of Racine's language. My fantastic creature is a cornucopia of treasures, a bandage of love on red-hot mouths. Angela's lips maybe. In my imagination.

One day I see her coming out of the grocery store with a bag in her hand. What a coincidence! I follow her, greet her and smile. My eyes devour her. I offer to help her bring the package home, knowing that it is as light as a feather.

I love her with a voluptuous love that makes me drool. I also love her gums. It is time we faced one another, after mother mammoth cleared the table and daddy mammoth licked the last drop of coffee. It is time we exchanged warm tokens of love through the language of poets. Angela will be my love card, my viaticum in learning the French language.

You don't need to show me anything else, I think, while her gazelle-like thighs cling to the seat, I swallow, suffocated with pleasure, while she takes an eternity of ten years to sit down; showcasing all her forms as my passion spreads.

The Tunisian gypsy has become my teacher! How can I put all of these words together?

Après, matin, je suis etonné, Pourqui ? Pourquoi pas ? Et alors je t'embrasse et je t'embrasse"

I love you, divine. I will sail with you on ivory vessels with masts of translucent alabaster towards islands of unattainable destinies. Now she closes the door because the fatherly mammoth snores. *"Alors: Le couple s'en va par la route"*

"What? Who is going par la route?"

"Le couple, les amoureux."

"The lovers walk down the street."

"Repeat, please."

I am not even listening, the French lessons fade away, useless, they are only an excuse to see her, and to make her fall in love, in love. The smell of pancakes is replaced with her neck's scent and her skin's folds. She is everywhere and everything.

Effiges of desire adhere onto my skin. *"Les amoureux. sont…"* and then change the subject *"… Alors…. Le Palais du roi"* I am paler in the face than the king on his throne. The king is pale. But, what am I saying? *"Les jeux sort faits."* I love her birch wood breasts. *"A bit of attention, n'est-ce pas? L'espace du matin…"*

I have to pay attention to her hocks, they are so thin they risk breaking at the slightest touch. My love wants you with its floppy raised arms. I love you, my silvery star with a tap-shaped nose. Ecuba concealing a mature but not yet expired virginity. *"Alors, you look distracted today!"*

Give me at least one kiss.

"Qu'est-ce que tu as ?"

"Rien."

"Bien sur." And what might this be? The minestrone's effluvium frames our passion. Flatulence haunts us.

"Qu'est-ce que tu as ?"

"Rien du tout."

"Oh, Good and clever boy!" Exclaims the succubus.

"Bravo!"

I am comforted by this mature receptacle of unabashed passion.

What has she got on her finger? A freshly healed vermilion wound? She removes the tip of her finger from her green mouth and smiles at me. It is only a cut. *"Try to say it in French: It is only a cut"*. I need to save her; the infection could kill her. We will save her finger, together.

"Ce n'est rien, n'est-ce pas? A scratch caused by the cheese-grater, as I was scraping an apple" She says with her accent originating from the depths of La Goulette.

"I wanted to…"

"… Qu-est-ce que tu dis ?"

I will suck your finger! Where were we? Oh yes, marry me! What do I say to that duchess?

I want your bristling shoulders, your brushing eyelashes, your mane's bush concealing lizards and topazes, the moist grace of your dripping nose, and I seem to faint whenever I think of your hips.

This lesson will end with the ignoble stink of cabbage and onion dissolved in the minestrone. We are two hopeless virgins, with hearts living in separate and alien deserts. I take advantage of my alibi: a good pronunciation to burst forth with a: *"Je t'aime"*

"Good boy!" Sings the naive angel.

"Good boy! Je t'aime" She repeats.

Have my ears fallen foul of some curse? Have we just said that we love each other? Her eyes are suddenly liquid. No detail escapes me. As I leave her, I hold her hand's wounded finger for a moment. I ask her for: *"Pardon. Pardon moi mademoiselle Angela."*

"Clever boy!" Responds the tremulous giraffe.

* * *

The dead talk

Something atrocious is engraved in the Risorgimento's blood drenched pages. The Universal Encyclopaedia read:

"They came at three. I was afraid they wanted to kill us in the dark. They brought torches but did not say anything. They pushed us, forcing us to move. I helped Oroboni get up, he could not stand on his own two feet because of how weak he was. They unwound the mattresses' padding, they rummaged them. They were looking for tools designed for escape. This is not the first time I see them. Thy stripped us of our clothes. The cold immediately chastised our limbs. Many of us complained. Oroboni and Grindati began to cough. There were other guards in the fort's courtyard, sentinels checking we dig the cemetery and emptied the latrines. They overturned our jackets, rummaged in the lapels, in the pockets, they rummaged like mice, looking for files, irons and so on. We were made to stand in line against the wall. Naked. Oroboni could not stand straight. I raised his chain, he could not do it alone. He was trembling in the cold. He was not well... Yesterday they added nails to a new companion's chain. He is a handsome young lad, tall and muscular. He reminds me of my first day here, they day where I had not given up hope. He looks at you and does not speak. I do not know where he comes from. I come from the Po valley, and will no longer see the light of day, this is my bride, these are my dear parents who still cry for me. They will throw my body on the cart. There it will be in the company of murderers and criminals. You can hear it pass, it treads the pavement with its wooden wheels... if I lean against the window I can see it pass, the wobbly wagon of limbs. I will end my journey there, on top of that pile... I am about to become dust.

Antonio Villa

Brunn – Moravia, December 1825

I rushed in a bid to resurrect documents from the Encyclopaedia of Universal Knowledge, which stood, monolithic on the attic's single shelf. Who was Antonio Villa? Why had he written those distressing things? I had to investigate the Italian people's redemption process. I reread the dramatic pages written by Mr. Vannucci, the excommunicated priest, in his Opus Magna: *"The martyrs of Italian freedom."* His writings mysteriously coincided with the document I found in my father's sisters' suitcase. Such coincidences ceased to amaze me. This is what the Encyclopaedia of Universal Knowledge said about Antonio Villa;

"Martyr, carbonaro, imprisoned in 1819 together with other patriots and General Arnaud. Firstly, at the prison on the Island of San Michele in Murano, subsequently at the Piombi in Venice. He was recognised guilty of conspiring against the Austrian Empire, by the Trentine inquisitor Antonio Salvotti, bitter enemy of the Carbonari, who were finally locked up at Spielberg fortress.

Initially sentenced to death, his sentence was commuted by the emperor's decree to twenty years forced labor in prison…"

The riots in Reggio Emilia and Mistico Rosolino's hanging, to which I was a witness, had been nothing but the beginning. If I wanted to see clearly into this, I had to examine faces, edicts and battles placed in that dark tapestry narrating Italy's reunification. The announced sentence released its infamy:

"Italian mothers cry bitter tears for their children, children which the Austrian stranger's anger snatched from their breasts and throws into a chasm, where they die of pain and hunger…their only sin is to have thought about driving away the Austrian chiefs from Italy. Glory, freedom and the Italian independence crown their every desire, and this is why the Austrian Emperor buries them alive in the pits of the Spielberg prison."

I rummage for documents in my aunt's cellar, and find papers referring to Villa. These came from Rovigo, the city in which my father had attended the mechanical adjustment course.

Atto Vannucci read doctor Felice Foresti was the inquisitor for the government of Romagna, and in turn he was investigated due to one of his disciples' long tongue.

He fascinated the wealthy youngster Antonio Villa, infusing patriotism in him, and convinced him to join the Carbonari in

1817. In the end, he was betrayed after having been dragged into ruin by Villa, that excellent disciple of his, who diffused names and events, revealing the conspiracy.

"The young Villa spread names, signals, papers and the Carbonari's statutes... He was being spied on by the police, who already suspected him of illicit political activity, during a dinner, he let slip his enthusiasm for Napoleon, freedom and Italy."

Baron Salvotti's face is also freshly imprinted in my historical memory. He was a hungry inquisitor, a faithful servant of Austria, owner of wooden amphitheaters extending from *monte Baldo* all the way to the Adige river. He was the founder of a noble dynasty, and was buried in the cemetery of More, together with his son Scipione, who had denied his father as he considered himself a liberal and a supporter to the Italian cause, and his granddaughter, who died aged eighty as the ink sets on these pages. This was the same woman who my future father-in-law had bought acres of land some forty odd years ago.

Aldo Vannucci writes:

"When they took Villa, he confessed, then retracts, then confesses again, the names and surnames are laid out, he then asks for mercy, he gets mad, he lies crumpled up... When they read that the death sentence has been commuted to twenty years forced works in a dungeon, he almost dies. Then he bursts forward with an incandescent anger. The charge is: High treason on the basis of a law which was standing before his arrest. His accuser, Magistrate Baron Salvotti, coldly said: "He will calm down. He will calm down. Twenty years hard labor ahead of him, will calm him down."

Poor Villa effectively did calm down, in the company of another three hundred thieves and killers, his health degenerating as fast as his hope and faith... His cadaver was loaded like an unclean animal on the cart with creaking wooden wheels, to then be thrown in the pit he had dug just a few days prior. It was not over yet, Pellico and Confalonieri were already knocking on their prison cell doors.

I struggled to sleep that night. China the cat restlessly wandered on the woodpile, and then the refrigerator buzz filled the attic. Perhaps Baron Salvotti's thugs were already on my trail.

* * *

Jack Lo Cascio has gone far

One cannot say they had not told Iotti to be careful. What could she have done? Keep the whole street under control? She was content to sweep, spy, mumble and square you with her iron eyes.

A whole month came to pass before people got to know the bizarre little character who had replaced the shoemaker. He wore high-necked sweaters, tight jackets and pointy English shoes. He drove a lacquered red Ford Anglia, with yellow pudding inserts. A small beard came and went on his triangular visage, and there he stood, with an open smile and a colloquial air hovering around those who know how show business works. Iotti would have had to tell the administrator about a guy like that.

The *"philosopher"* and his ring promptly placed on his little finger had replaced the shoemaker. The shoes druid gave way to this musical and theatrical impresario, one who had attended Sinatra, Nilla Pizzi, Mike Bongiorno and the Platters. He was the show's magician, slightly lame, as thin as a stick and with an elegant mole under his cheekbone.

His Anglia, model De Luxe was parked in front of Ginetta's mother's grocery shop, shining in that stretch of road, conquering the village which was populated by gypsies with tight jeans, aspiring singers, infatuated with the idea of success.

Lo Cascio organised singing groups, auditions in recording rooms and competitions for Celentano emulators.

His luxury began and ended with his Ford Anglia, his tight jackets and his pants, similar to the ones worn by Elvis Presley.

His desk was glued to a piece of mouse-grey carpet, full of ash trays, butts, clasps, letter openers, suggestive photos of housewives who transformed into queens of song. There was also a lacquer-red horn with a golden chaplet, an image of a saint, empty cups of cappuccino, occasionally filled with burnt stubs or charcoaled matches.

A second desk opened under the emerald green crystal table. Here lay the impresario philosopher's treasure. Photos and postcards of singers with curled hair posing infant of Vesuvius, your eyes redirect to Carmela and her lacquered red lips. A dedication read: *"Thanks Pino, a hug from... Vincenzo Pappafico, Salvatore Casa, and Mimmo Rosella. From the Tammuriata band, greetings and a kiss to mom."*

Pictures of guitars, golden uvulas, crowds and stages. Short-lasted success stories filled by roses and applause. All professional fortunes to which the great Jo Lo Cascio had in some way contributed to. Newspaper cut-outs portraying him and his green jacket with pink decorations could not go unnoticed.

He told Madama Iotti: *"This is the photo with Gino Latilla and Giacomo Rondinella,"* but she just replied with a: *"Mmhhhmm?"* And let it go. She shrugged and went on ranting about how the guys from the furniture factory had left sawdust all over the laundry bags in the yard. She stuck the postcard Jack Lo Cascio gifted her under the box of rat poison in the cellar of despair.

"Hey, let me see, we can give it a try. I will talk to them. They will immediately see if you have talent. Those guys know me. If you are wearing Elvis trousers there is a higher chance, I will schedule the meeting. Go relaxed and if they like you, well, you made it!" This is what he always said to all those aspiring Sinatras.

A mouse, an interpreter of the southern song and a manager, collector of young talents, those which the post-war city fomented.

Jack, the mouse, had spotted me. *"If you want, we can talk about it,"* he said. And I turned away.

At home they told me to stay away from him and from the world he represented. *"furthermore, you cannot sing,"* added my mother. *"But I do know how to act..."* I thought to myself.

Nothing came of it. *"Don't you dare talk to him. That stuff is not for you."* That was the sentence. I don't know if they thought I had an aviation mechanic's career ahead of me.

* * *

China behaves crazy

The cat started behaving furiously. It was not out of malice, we always came for five minutes to calm her down, nobody thought she could be in heat. This had occurred before we went to visit Erri and his band of castaways. China was abandoned to the deluge of roofs and gutters, a forest for her to explore in our absence.

She went to spy on the dormer's damp, where she pounced onto unsuspecting ants and cockroaches. It is quite likely that she cried every now and again. It appeared as though she wanted to let you know about the epic events that occurred on the roofs, events she played a key part in. One could not simply ignore her, you imagined her under some tin sheet, spying on an ant busy carrying a seed, or composed, standing guard to Pezzuto's turtledoves, who once came and told us:

"Keep a close eye on her, she scares our doves"

"What on earth is she going to do to your doves? They also stink. It might be a good idea to remove your turtledoves from up there. Too too tooo all day long" said my mother. China looks at you sideways, stern, her white outline with her black facial stain introducing her nostril's tiny pink triangle.

"Open the window, she wants to go, can't you see?" Said her owner. On the way back she would rest quietly, iconic her being a feline and would look at you with wide-open insolent eyes. She was bewilderingly commonly beautiful, with her polished hair, leaden paws and warm furry sides.

Whether it is your leg or the table's does not make a difference to her. For her it is just some other stuff to explore with her nails. She is always alert. Always. Does she sleep, or does she pretend to sleep? Her eyes progress from being half-closed to hermetically tight. It is quiet. My breath calls its name, *"China…"* Her defences are down, a drop of saliva snails its way down her mouth. She does that when she is satisfied and satiated.

Things are in their proper place, including the boiled lung she is now digesting. She is a snoring ornament resting on a shelf. A tiny totem of knowledge.

I am still sorry about the incident, but she had little done to with it, it was her nature. She had developed this mania of running out far and wide towards the evenings. She ended up on furniture, bumped into chairs, banged on all sides, we stood there, spectators to that apocalypse, thinking she would eventually calm down.

We put the cat in the box and away we go, dragging her with a rope along the floor, she happily sits on the cardboard ship and dives onto the floor whenever it hits icebergs made from table legs or the fridge. She wants endless rides on this rollercoaster. She is tired and is getting nervous.

She is almost an adult, with a great desire to play without restraint. Her sharp claws have planted themselves in my forearm's skin, bothering me quite a bit because now the cat is literally hanging onto my skin by its own curved meat-hooks. I shake it off, freeing myself from the murderer's weight. She falls, slamming her lower lip against the bowl's edge, cutting herself. The saliva is now reddened, it falls onto her hair, a few red drops stain her chin. A wounded cat is not a good show.

China has not reacted, quite on the contrary, she would like to continue with the game. I feel guilty, I will have to explain what happened. I hurt her for no reason. China understood it was a mistake and that I did not mean it. Her owner, who stays up all night, was the one to convince.

"Why don't you try?" I told my mother, *"Why don't you try to have a cat hanging from your forearm?"* The following day I tried to justify myself, mortified and in vain.

* * *

One Sunday afternoon

A picnic with my mother's friend, his wife and their friends had been months in the making. My mother began arguing about what clothes to wear more than a week ago, as well as Nevio's wife's refusal to ride in tiny cars whose seats almost touched the road, cars like ours. This she said, and this had offended my mother. So, my father's proud second-hand motorised truck was not so good for such cumbersome individuals.

180

"With the backside she finds herself with! I felt so bad when she criticised our car. She is only capable of offending! ... Had we not invited her husband (Nevio) over to sleep in our mansard after the war they would still be there in the countryside, both of them, working the hemp."

The rage ended there, their friendship was still tenaciously longstanding. I had a headache, my father's buboes grew again, while we were choosing the route. Mountain slopes? Healthy lake areas? Sparkling hilly landscapes? Or maybe the canyon's narrow gorges where we could take baskets, seats and sandwiches? Triumphant uncertainty. I proposed to go to a city of Art. They looked at me horrified. *"What clothes do I have to wear?"* It is just a picnic! *"And if it rains, we will stay home and dance!"*

"I will take care of it all" he said, *"you just come with me"* and with that, the party followed the great Nevio, the pastor, the objector, who never once saw the front, because if he had he would have pissed his pants.

"I will take care of it all" the Great Nevio repeats, in his elegant blue shirt onto which a scarlet tie shine. He strolls up and down the field looking for a place only he remembers but cannot pinpoint with certainty. With a couple of unknown friends, we all mount a Fiat 1200 Granluce model, my parents have to drag me to it because I have no desire to get drunk under the sun.

What was I doing there with my nightmarish totems made of cats, wet spots on walls Tecumseh engines and the bursts of tragedies from the Risorgimento? We are huffing and puffing on the huffing and puffing jalopy towards Sunday's abyss, when the headache kicks in. I am perched on the backseat, where cushions and bags overflow all kinds of comfort, and I feel it come, the migraine, deadly. Insistent indictments resound in Sunday's miscellany.

"Don't stay so bent over yourself, you will start vomiting, don't put your head in the magazines: tell him something, you are his father" All the while the pain grows, it is serious now, as we huff and puff down the road. The headache covers my forehead with a crown of spasms, finally here is the large meadow, glowing with dew. I have the miraculous drops of Diidergot Sandoz to save me. A gallon of its bitter tasting drops would make my migraine vanish instantly.

Nevio says: *"here we are. We have to go over here, we will need to walk a bit, just to get hungry"* As I can read Nevio's mind I understand what he is that we are not: optimistic. Nevio is the frisky messenger of good moods, towering like a pole bearing the flag of hope, while my relatives are the lifeless bushes at his feet. However, why should we feel any shame? He is perennially happy banqueting with porters, Totip fans, baristas and dives from one bed to the other. He knows no anxiety, discomfort, rush, I am sure the fog of sloth has never hung around him. He receives and gives favours to the barber, the baker and his tram driver friend. This is why my mother is attracted to him. This is why she would support him, by virtue of a fraternal friendship, as one would seek protection sympathy and well-being in a tree. My father lacks these gifts. However, to live with Nevio means to live with lies and deceit. His wife knows this all too well. Great Nevio *"hunts"*. He recounts one of the many episodes of his illustrious career:

"I tell Gianni to keep the dogs away, they had already exhausted the beast, but it is not an easy task" says Nevio, as if he spoke to a single spectator, *"hunting on the mountains is not the same thing as hunting in the planes. You break a sweat and your resolve. Then, you have to be lucky. We had it right in front of our very eyes since the morning, nice and ready, and he let it go away! If it comes out, it will run, it will not just stroll out. I almost feel it come out of the bushes. As a matter of fact, there it goes, it almost stumbles on the undergrowth. Oh no, a boar cannot hurt its neck no. What a beast! And what does he do? He stares the clouds! But! Where on Earth are you looking? It fled right under your nose. What a beast! What are you doing shooting after it? You cannot see a wild boar? You would not see a whale!"*

We entered the pizza house adjoined to a small fishing lake. A jumble of voices, laughter and smoke, fries with mounds of sizzling little fish which pass under our nose inducing stellar nausea. A quagmire of voices, screams, stinks and rotten brown water where pikes, trouts, salamanders and whales splash about. The fresh catch is expediently dropped in the rancid water. Sweaty waiters, chefs who become one with their creations as they mess around in the dining room's botched atmosphere.

The story is about to end: *"I shoot at the boar's head as it rampages towards me. What a beast! Ah no, he definitely did not escape me. No! I do not let wild boars escape!"*

Fried fish platters are followed by skewered chickens, liquefied sausages, pork ribs, boiled meats, with cigarette butts and telephone rings flooding the air, preludes to the arrival of married couples dazed by the altar-church-restaurant route. *"Sit over there!"* They shout to the spouse and to the congregation of relatives. We are isolated near the windows, at the very least, our strategic position will allow us to breathe some fresh air.

"And then do you know what we do? We jump on it, all three of us" this is what the Great Nevio says as he ends his hunting song. *"You can see straight through the hole, Paaam! One shot and the dogs jump on it"*

"Mah!" Says the mother. *"I never even saw a steak from your large boar. Is this even true?"* Great Nevio yells in desperation, mentioning how she is always the same, and justifying his actions as usual: *"I remember it as though it were yesterday"*

My headache has reached delirium. Where is the thermos with Düdergot? A chamomile would be too much for my stomach, and the just killed boar's head falls on me, smashing me. The lemon will save me. The one cut in transparent slices, constellations the dishes. There will be lemon for me too! Smoke, bones and jellies, cold fish heads, crumpled packs of cigarettes, and Great Nevio's adventurous hunting recounts, this is what the Sunday trip reserves.

The Prophet of the Past comes to life. A resounding noise reverberates through the tavern's enclave. My mother barks four chairs away, telling Nevio to stop, nobody cares about his hunting skills. I remember Angela the giraffe, China the wounded cat, Antonio Villa who dies in his cell at Spielberg prison, and this unlikely congregation of family souls. The man who married my mother is brother to the Erinyes who are bored to death by her, he is the son of the deceased who ran around the kitchen table chasing her daughter-in-law whilst brandishing the rolling pin.

* * *

At the cream labs to pay the rent

They were my first independent sorties in the great world. Finally, an opportunity to make myself useful, as I walked down streets populated by sinister figures and females of dubious repute. I had to venture into a maze full of pitfalls, all for what? All to be able to pay for the first month's rent. "Why don't you go; you might wake up." said my mother. Well yes indeed, I had to start paying my monthly rent.

I was wary all along the way, with some ten thousand lire in my back pocket; but I did not know if I was going to make it. A long stretch of road was honeycombed with arches, arcades and ruined houses of the seventeenth century, they merged into a fantastic architectural prowess called: a decaying city, with its hints of urine and tomatoes scents.

Then there are black caves where you could put both children and pickled olives in. Shady deals were made, within the walls where everything was salty and precarious. The ancient city stretches showed signs of blackened neighbourhoods, where immigrants from the south lived off of small trades, tomato sauce and basil.

Shop signs surrendered to the mould, they flowed down the streets, illuminating bazaars, stacks of cloths and skeins of wool. It was a great casbah, located next to the headquarters of Italy's first parliament.

The area could not be avoided, it was paved with porphyry and leaden stone flakes. Whole stretches of road lay inert, with lowered shutters concealing the magic of lives I had not yet encountered.

Lottery receivers, box offices allowing people to place their bets on horses, dogs and anything you could bet on, kiosks mounted on precarious wheels, packed with postcards, lottery tickets and football teams' flags. A little further on you could see junk dealers, and tailors specialised in both military and clerical apparel.

A gallery with a domed ceiling embroidered with iron snakes opens its belly at my passing. There one could breathe a little, there was some life. Life at the bottom of the cup of coffee resting on the cafés *dehors*, the people seemed different too, they drank Campari and coffee.

On the ground there were boxes, wicker entangled furniture and screens, then the emporium where ropes were made, hemp braids, jute bags cloth sack and straw hats. My time was almost up, and I occasionally felt for the sweating money stashed deep inside my pockets.

I had to go to Via della Basilica. There I would find the EFAM laboratories, and its director, a gentleman of great class and few words. Coincidentally, he was also the owner of our mansard and many others in the building. *"If I send you my son… yes here we go… so even he can start doing something. He will now come and pay the rent, if that is fine with you?"*

Plum, strawberry, aniseed, rhubarb. Harmonious natural dosages filled with a thousand different virtues. That was what the EFAM laboratories for health and beauty focused on. Creams, toothpastes, ointments, syrups, liquorice and mints, this is all it takes to cure depressions, phlegm, warts, bruises, itches and bad breaths. My final destination was close. No more knights with long cloaks and ladies with golden locks would come down the eroded stone stairways, that honour was now only reserved for festering cats.

I did not yet know how paradisiac this new heaven would be. My imagination painted it into grandiose splendour, the only thing fitting for a past ruin. *"Via della Basilica?"*, I asked an inoffensive old man who raised his bony finger towards a stream of gravel. This pebble beach was joined by crumbling bricks. *"EFAM drug therapy laboratories,"* said the writing on the wall. The moisture entered the lungs. The door opened, paradise set forth its thousand angels wielding blades of odorous concoctions, firing arrows of exotic scents. *"I'm… I should pay… Is there the doctor?"*

"No" said a pretty sight. I breathed, luckily the landlord was not home.

"But the doctor did say…" continued the desk angel. I blushed.

Why was I here again? I had sweaty money in my pocket. My knees tumbled with the emotion. I cleared my throat, and in doing so tasted the fragrances lingering in the air. Women looked at me through portholes, like the ones you see on vessels. I told myself they were busy woman bees, workers with a white coat and a cap. They all appeared dressed in white, like the badly compressed mint pills, narrow on the sides with blue straps. Should I have greeted them one at a time? That thought tortured me. What if they asked questions? What could I say? I eagerly awaited the arrival of the queen bee, but access to her quarters was denied.

"Here, this is the rent receipt. I am sorry, but we had to get it ready you know?" Thus, spoke the bee. I pocketed the receipt, thanked her and got

out of the palace. The aspidistra leaves bowed as did my head. I retraced my footsteps down via della Basilica and its adjacent decay; I had finally paid the monthly rent. I had escaped with little to no injury and felt like a lion.

* * *

Mouse face investigates

"Hey, what's your name? Sorry, you know. What's your name? You live upstairs right? On the top floor. Hey ...!? .... Look ... I mean, I think you're the one who lives on the top floor."

"Why?" I said laconically, holding back a: *"How dare you stop me without even knowing who I am?"*

It was Jack Lo Cascio. His stalactite face, hanging from his cave's doorway. He said the opposite of what he thought.

"... Do you live near that lady who has ... two children ...?"

"... What lady?" I ask, suspicious.

"The one upstairs...hey listen, you wouldn't like to... I mean. you know what job I do right? Do you know how to sing? How to dance?" Jack Lo Cascio took me at an unsuitable time. He had played his cards. *"I see you when you walk by. Would you like to be on TV?"*

I don't know ... he had infected me with curiosity.

"Well? If you get ashamed easily, you won't go far. Take me for instance, I managed to get all the way here, not bad eh?"

Mouse face proudly showed his collection of autographs and photos with various half-celebrities hanging from the bulletin board.

"How does one know if they are made for entertainment? Here, this is the address and the phone number. I will call them and tell them you will go there ... all right? An audition ... what's the harm in that? ... Do I know Marlon Brando? That guy's in Hollywood! I still have to go to America but will go there soon. I have a brilliant idea ... anyway, do you live upstairs? That

186

lady with the two children ... ah! they are your friends ... she is called Rambaudo. Ah! A beautiful lady, ... Okay, then I'll see you around. I am here, and it seems to me that you are perfect for television... The woman's name is Rita, right?" He said with his stalactite face. I went up the stairs, as did my swollen chest, was the TV looking for a guy like me?

* * *

Fire eater and women at the pillory

Mouse-face reminded me of it. With his array of words, his questions on Rita Rambaudo, whose white shoulders he most certainly admired. I had not given the TV much thought! But the show currently on display is of a different kind.

There is a crowd, on one of the wide roads preceding the market square, where they sell jackets, fish, fruit and vegetables. On the right is the gallery, with shops selling artefacts made of wicker and rope. Nearby there is the largest concentration of Southerners in the universe, they come from Lo Cascio's land.

This coming and going fuels the storm of southerners and their unspeakable aspect. The woman behaves crazily. I saw her before she warmed up with wine. She yelps. She gets angry with a guy. Here one can admire a collection of cutting pieces of glass and broken beer bottles necks.

They are on a big plate, made of cardboard. The woman shakes them, then pours them on a piece of wood. She rummages inside a cloth sack on the ground and pulls out a three-meter long chain with thick rings.

The savage party dissolves less a stone's throw away from Via della Basilica, and from the EFAM paradise. The woman ruffles. She says she has two sons. One of her incisors is missing, her husband drowned at sea three years ago. She was fine back then. She had lived well with her husband. She recalls the shoes, the clothes, the luxury. Now she looks after her children, with that disgusting job of hers. She growls, and moves her arms around creating whirlpools in the air. The invectives she fires off hither and tither get lost in the crowd. The crowd comes and goes.

Her watery eyes are disturbing; they scan everyone's face. She commands a guy to leave, she arrived here first, and nobody takes her spot. She quickly inspects the curious folk around her to then take her shirt off. She stays there with her crumpled bra.

"This is what I do for a living, gentlemen and kind public. Oh cursed, misfortune!" She raises her hands; a fresh crowd gathers. She places the chain under the cardboard sustaining the glass shards. They fall to the ground. She collects them.

She lies down onto of the broken pieces of glass, all the while recollecting how she always used to go to the Grand Hotel when her husband was there. She does not grimace; she feels no pain.

She rolls around on the glass shards and tells the guy with the yellow shirt to climb on her stomach. *"Careful!"* Last time she had been pierced by a splinter and her stomach broke.

My gaze runs from the blue neon light hanging over the crayfish, octopus and sardines in the fish shed, to the Turkish cafe where people smoke like chimneys and drink litres of coffee, to the shape of lady fakir surviving on the bottle glasses, memories of a better past. The guy with the yellow shirt takes off his shoes, slowly mounts on her stomach. The group melts becomes thicker again, then gets distracted again. The little man wraps Lady Fakir with three turns of the chain. She blows out and rolls her eyes. The fire-handling gentleman slips out from behind the onion sacks. She screams, driving him away, and the stoking fakir negates his steps. He carries half a bottle with him and a twisted cotton rag. A small crowd follows him, as do I.

With large movements of the arms he invites the fire bird to descend upon him, he challenges the fiery cloud in that vitreous autumn sky. Naked pectorals proudly take their stance in the sparkling air. He's almost an old man. And here comes the big blaze, closing in a puff of black smoke at the end of the roaring tongue of fire and alcohol. He spits out a concoction of future fire which hits the torch and makes it look like the blaze comes from the half-naked man's mouth.

The old man comes from far away, from the caravan cities of the Caucasus, or perhaps from the Yemen's stony Styx. He came with Lady Fakir, they crossed time, and they steal the show. They are rags, tired meats and veterans, who give a miserable spectacle to an easily bemused mass of miserable people.

An army of bees was watching over me against the dangers lurking in Via della Basilica and its ancient market. The fragrance of the women of the EFAM laboratory, that had truly bewitched me, not the two street refugees.

* * *

ACT V

Someone is about to fall from the Tower

It had not been ringing for a while, and it was probably a good thing, if only it could stay that way forever. Instead, it rang at the less suitable moment, half-opening China's eyes, we had recently discovered that she urinated out of the box.

"Ah, it's you aunt, how are you?" I loudly answered with my creamy voice.

"Ah aunt ... is not well." One of the two Erinyes had fallen ill. *"Then I'll pass you onto someone else."*

A shadow of reproach grips me as I only ever stay a few seconds on the phone, once a month at the very most, and I still have nothing to say. One needs to be careful when dealing with the Erinyes aunts. I will definitely not inquire more than is strictly necessary. Their cellar withheld some interesting documents, but what is truly worrying is that I cannot even remember the face of the person on the other side of the phone.

"What are you saying? Mom wants to know who I am on the phone with. I did not understand..." I say quite politely.

One speaks from miles away on the other side of the phone, the other shouts from the toilet seat, China, the smart cat comes rubbing her fur on my calves, asking for forgiveness. What on earth have I got to do with the fact that my aunt has fallen ill and that my mother is about to go to the doctor to cure her nervous illness?

I really do not know what to do, why am I on this suspended bridge connecting a phone call with an answer? *"I do not know what to say, so whatever, let it be, I am sorry for the dying aunt, Amen."* My soul has already answered. If I recollect, the sick aunt had also slapped me across the face once. But I was not mad at her for that, oh no!

The news of aunt's departure came while people's sentiments towards the fridge were still dire.

"We are not at her service; she drove me into a frenzy for a whole month last time." Proclaims she who is not at all well.

"Hello? Who is it? … Yes, no, … I am not well as well… And when does she need to go to the hospital? I will go too, I am also going now to the hospital, my bag is already ready. Your brother is at work… and he comes back after seven."

"Remember to tell father that her sister called, his other one is not well… Where is the bag with the doctor's note? I will go with Miss Borgo. Don't cause any problems. Did you understand? And don't open the door to anyone."

I feel as though I have reached a terminus. What on earth do I have to do with the fact that my aunt is sick and will most likely not last until Christmas? I think about the succulent petal women from Efam laboratories, to the fakir woman emerging from the gutters, to the fallacious attempts to covet Angela and the soapy mermaids. A secession is occurring.

* * *

China's disappearance

One has never seen an animal composed of a clown, a snake and a cat. This is what China; the super cat truly is. We could not have known that with age she would have adopted the characteristics of a miniature tiger. But a cat is a cat. The animal becomes nervous, then aggressive. It throws itself at your feet to be forgiven, and only the stripling's mother would fall in her trap and say: *"Oh she is so sweet!"* Hosting the snoring cat on your lap is a pure utopia. A stray cat approaches. Menacing, grim looking. From the roofs. He descends from the sky's electric purple. He menaces our cat and my mother's faith. *"Close the window, she will escape. Just look at her!"* I do, and I notice how her expression has changed. She is no longer a small ball of fluff trying to lose itself in overgrown jumpers, she is now a terrifying creature, perched on the last log of wood onto of the pile, snout against snout, glued to a bastard vagabond, spotted by the cold windowpane. They are looking for one another; they usher that shrieking meow. This is not good. We are raising a small beast. Her master says: *"Had I known she would have become like this… she has become evil… And I took care of her for so long…"*

The cat would like to be outside, she is ready to pounce, to roll on the dormer, to enjoy the balcony's torpor. Cats are like that you know? They cannot be trusted, they are dirty, what the mother does not know is that a cat which is not castrated is just like a permanently charged electrical battery. *"She will come back, dirty and pregnant, if she manages to get away."* Sooner or later she will run away, passing through the crack in the half-closed window. Around the end of November, she takes for the roofs, we will never see her again, and we are quite done with cats.

* * *

Betrayal and reproach.
New hermeneutics are needed

The whole of creation lay under mantles of darkness, lightless pavilions introduced chasms freshly made by the Creator's hand. Clouds of vapor extended over the lands, because the Word had not yet completed its task.

Were these the same clouds that now loomed over the condominium? Depths of darkness traveled at the same wavelength ECT treatments and as lovers' quarrels between me and the giraffe-woman. The grand theatre repeated its show full of fakirs, ambiguous theatrical agents and unapproachable mansard hamlets. I needed a new alphabet, one which encompassed horrifying cellars, where the first bricks of my existence lay, one which could describe the horrid conclaves, imagined more than a thousand times, where new species emerged, an alphabet for the condominium assemblies organised by Basovici, who died of a heart attack during a communist party rally.

When my mother went to the doctor the second time, she was accompanied by the marshal; a widow with a greenish face. She was kind enough to carry my mother's pyjama bag because Rita Rambaudo was dizzy. China's betrayal had influenced my mother's mood more than the breaking of the refrigerator's door handle. New hermeneutics were required to not get lost among the disturbances all these accidents caused and to find a grip in this the condominium's primordial darkness.

One had to avoid giving up at all costs! However, to make matters worse, black socks with lines and red suspenders landed on the washing line, waving in the courtyard's breeze right under Madama Serra's nose. Whose luxurious undergarments, were they? I inquired. The cleaver was about to fall on my hopes for love and the beloved tap-like noses. My Tunisian angel was filling my calendar with sadness. The Prophet of the past's betrothed was about to parade her body for a lingerie house!

The laid-out garments were part of the sample. Plus, she was also thinking about moving! The dazzling vision of underwear and garters, some sparkled as the rays fell on their glitter, had nothing to do with my desire.

Quite on the contrary, it decreed its end. It was dichotomy in its purest state. When the time for passion expired, the fan of threatening stenches took over. Definitely. Angela received a set of underwear from an intimate fashion house. *"How can they get someone like that? She is also stained in the face! What does she hope to become? She wants to be a model. With that tap-nose, oh please! Do not worry, I know the son of a lady who teaches French. You will go to him for your classes, you will not go there anymore. Who does she think she is?"*

With great regret, I abandoned the blue-arm pitted giraffe to her destiny.

* * *

Tagliatelle, roast veal and pasqualina cake

They brought food from their country, hand-knitted pullovers and wool gloves, tablecloths, lampshades, pear-shaped salamis held in place by a net and bottles of Lambrusco. My hermeneutical experiments could not miss the opportunity of closely analysing my relative's convention.

Was a general reconciliation of humans under way? Had it not been for two large rats, which were noticed scuffling around the house, everything could have been considered promising.

The house was almost new. It was part of a newly built complex, near the river, on the town's southern outskirts. It was so soaked with water that it appeared to have come out of a flood. It sweat water, swollen walls, felted wood and tiles but it was almost new. It stood close to a disused factory and the urbanisation included alleys with benches, plots and a fountain. It was the new home of Purusa

Albino, the primordial male and his bride Lory, my scandalous lice-hunting cousin.

"Who knows how she will laugh today. When she laughs like this I really cannot stand Lory." Said mother.

"I am sure she will laugh as she shows you her new house." The newlyweds had done it, apart from the gigantic rats, who anyway would have become victims of urbanisation soon enough.

Lory and Albino had just abandoned the room with the external bathroom giving onto the stairs and proceeded in giving the world a tour along the house's social ladder. Cousin Lory showed the ravenous relatives the entrance to their lair, a green Palladian floor stretched for miles.

"aaahhha! ah! ah," the sturdiness of the lock and door, it had to be fake walnut, made its victim, *"aahhha! ah! ah!"*. The kitchen's suction hood is on show next, it was so powerful that it could take away your underwear, *"aahha! ah! ah!"*

The group of relatives are in silence, some yawn, before such wonders. Not to mention the first plastic shutters, the ones which are easily raised unlike the heavy wooden ones.

"aahhha! ah! ah!" so when you're in bed you have the strength to do something else *"aahha! ah! ah!"* the mammoth red-lined sofa: *"do not sit on it, the velvet will dent!"*

The chandeliers in the living room, the spotlights in the corridor *"oohhh!"* and the tube-shaped lamp in the bathroom, *"aahhh!"* A tiled bathroom, with sparkling faucets, unbelievable!

"The room of love!" stresses the bride as she giggles, for the first time ever I find my cousin void of any vulgarity; in her there is no retention, no intention, no inhibitory brake or guilt or feeling of sin and restraint. Now that I look at her well, in her home broth, or in her nest of fornication adorned by the red sofa, Lory appears to be one of the many divinities of sex. To her, the room was a place where she could enjoy herself with no brakes, following the ways of the old and the new hermeneutics.

"Oh, come on, let's say what we use this for shall we? Ahha! ah! ah! It feels so good to be lying down, isn't it true aunt Ahh ahh!"

This is my cousin Lory, with her slightly pointed tits, with her partially bare legs, with her throat that laughs about sex, and you can see her tonsils. Lory is the happy nymphomaniac dedicated to her primordial groom, she has been assigned to the great forefather of hosts of fornicators.

That gypsy, my cousin, clinks the gold beads on her wrist as she takes you by your hand. She wants you to see the wonders brought by that bed, which looks like a raft in the ocean. My mother pungently asks: *"Who knows what you do there Lory? How much fun you must have!"*

"Aahahhha! ah! ah! Well said aunt, well said. Some quite beautiful things happen there, especially the ones when the bum is in the air! Ah ahh!"

Hermeneutics aside, I sit on a kitchen stool to catch my breath. Everyone travels on their own and in their own way. It's too soon for me to lead. Other people will take the upper hand. It is all about food and its preparation.

Meanwhile, I witness Uncle Bizzarrone's debacle; his mouth wide open, asleep on the new house's biggest armchair. I dare not venture into his arms anymore, as I have grown up and am now endowed with embarrassing limbs which a locust would envy.

Aunt Luigina Uistiti, sits on her chair, the seat is hard, it soothes her haemorrhoids; she is in a ruinous mental abandonment.

Lory's brother is also there. I have only ever seen him once, he had asked for substantial financial relief, forcing aunt Luigina Uistiti into the darkest of discouragements. "Oh, come on, just give him the money" said cousin Lory, quite impudently in an impetus of fraternal solidarity. The hoard quickly passed from Aunt Luigina Uistiti's purse to the elusive cousin, leaving no trace exception being for my aunt's mortified and anxious regret. The florist had also been invited for the tour. He had housed Aunt Prisca back in the day when she was pregnant with Olga. Albino rebukes his parents-in-law, who had just awakened after happily snoring through the initial part of the tour. But everybody wants to see the most luxurious mansard in the world. Albino slaps me on the back and adds: *"Eh! You are putting on weight son!"* I respond with a stuttering and incongruous: *"Why thank you..."* Polar opposite to what I really wanted to say.

"And now everyone to the cellar!" Proclaims Lory. *"No!"* I scream inside, not in the cellar, no, I cannot ... in the cellar, in any cellar in the world, never again, and, while I repeat it to myself, I slither away in the kitchen where the food has been prepared since early morning.

I remain alone, contemplating the food whose preparation, has a mystical significance to it, characteristic of the delta regions we come from. Only those born from those parts know what the Great plains means.

The plains and the fog, the infinitely multiplying clouds, the rows of poplars leading to the farms, the house, the farmyard. Only great poets recognize the value those places have. An aroma of burnt stems, ancient smells arising from gravel, cement, bricks, earth, hints of fungus, rusty iron, underground medicines. Uncle Bizzarrone's land teaches this. The sky smells too. Its odor wanders straight to your stomach. The scarlet scent of spent sunsets on the salt marshes which widen in the sea of fog. All this was dissolved in my relatives' blood and laid out infant of their very eyes. Microcosms admiring their reflections, a message written in the food. Some great thinkers have said that cooking is the art of transforming matter into a poetry of the senses and of taste.

There were traces of that art in my cousin's kitchen. On tables and shelves rested inebriating delicacies.

Spices, roots, horseradish crumbs macerated in vinegar, metallic laurel and nutmeg, freshly grated Parmesan and then eggs, flour, veal slices, scallops with wine and hard-boiled eggs. My eye feasts on that cornucopia. Appetisers rest on a shelf and include tuna pie and capers the shape and size of ping pong balls. There is the roast beef, as delicate as a newborn's cheeks, spare noodles for the evening, memorable sauces, thickened by a tablespoon of flour, vegetables, grilled peppers from Aunt Uistiti's vegetable garden, drowned now in oil and served on steel plates.

Who will touch that cornucopia of food? Who was it prepared for? Was it food for the sake of virtue? Tradition? Or the Absurd? The succulent food crammed on shelves will, in fact, only be tasted to understand if they lack salt. It is as if the diners were not suitable for the very dishes they prepared themselves. As if the perfection of roasts and braised meats, and the filling of ricotta and ravioli vegetables were part of a ritual, one of perfection which must not go tarnished via its phagocytes.

I look at the old men in this place, at the rare young relatives who could not wait to leave, at Bizzarrone, who is rumbling again. Nobody cared to honour the horde of delicacies crammed in my cousin's kitchen. *"Well, if no one is left for dinner, I'll eat everything, ahhhahhaa aah!"* Explodes Lory, the former lice hunter and rumpled nympho.

* * *

Everyone to the hall. Hurray the theater!

The city's Teatro Stabile held an actor's training course. When enrolled, one would undergo diction, vocalisation and interpretation classes, followed by lessons on Macbeth and Santa Giovanna dei Macelli. I saw the good in it, it was a way out to sneak out of the familiar environment after China's disappearance. It was a pretext, a short cut, going to this course would take me away, and maybe place me under Hollywood's spotlight. Perhaps I had found my way after all. The great star in the spotlight, the Prophet of the Past himself! I was destined to move the village's audience to tears, and with it my mother's friends, my clan of scattered relatives and the two Erinyes. You have no idea, what clamour I would raise.

I could not miss an opportunity like this one, but I did not want people to know Jack Lo Cascio, stalactite face, had brought me here.

We were a confused dozen, females and males in the mix. The diction master was a familiar voice on the radio. I confuse one of my work colleagues with the witch of the West's magical broom, Lady Macbeth's bloody crown with a colleague's tiny hat. There was some good to it. I presented myself to the audition with an anxious heart and trembling legs, it was my turn now. My finger touched the sky, and my main worry was not knowing with what pen I would start handing out autographs to crowds of admirers. I had the world in my pocket. I would make everyone see what stuff I was made out of.

When my turn came, so too did a shrill little voice. I was immediately ashamed, I lost all inspiration and the future actor within me died a most high-pitched silent death. However, the diction master did not despair; quite on the contrary, he looked at me with sympathy, confiding that I looked awfully like his young deceased nephew, who had succumbed to an avalanche.

From that moment on, that well-known radio voice took me under his wing and paid particular attention to how I filled my belly with air, thus making the diaphragm vibrate.

Me: name and surname, one eye clearer than the other one, a perfidious instigator, arousing conflict between the condominium boys and the Black Children, consecrated to the tasting of divine food, victim to cousin Lory, the limpid nymphomaniac, and lice hunter, I had finally chosen my true vocation: fiction as a means to try to exist.

There was a smell of dust, cork and linoleum. Among the most attentive pupils, there fluttered a most discomforting ugly broomstick. She was as dry as a herring, and as tender as a rum baba, open and available enough to embarrass you. I do not know what parts she would have gone for, she was certainly not a Cleopatra, or a Clytemnestra, she more like the witches haunting Dunsinane forest.

My protector, the famous voice from the radio, was very demanding on the way in which we there out the air our diaphragm pushed in. Everything starts from here, a mighty inner roar which makes window panes tremble. He could do everything with his voice, at times it was a bronze church bell, other times it was a sword slashing through the air, or a bird sneaking garrulously, there was no sound estranged to his repertoire.

The theatre room was an exquisite candy box, one where people had their shot at stardom; a place where everything was a performance, with some going on to becoming national tours.

But dust lay like dunes on the folds of the armchairs' crimson velvet, it spread like a desert on the carpet, on the

proscenium and behind the stage. The brunette sitting next to me, a fellow classmate, has nothing to do with all this dust. She has a sparkling smile which suggests *"If you like me, we are free to touch each other to a degree, but beyond that, you have to stop, do you understand boy?"*

Even she would like a small part in some Brechtian *pièce*. We look at each other with diffidence, we want to train by ourselves, each one to their own, training for the stage's indivisible glory.

But where are Lana Turner and Lawrence Olivier? And the aspiring Orson Welles and Liz Taylor? There is much better, in their stead comes a guy from the south, black, greasy and lanky, a sort of shaman with hair dropping to his shoulders. He is a spiritual character, he talks about how an individual's energy comes from the solar plexus, or rather, from a little further down, from the intestines; every action commences from the great brain residing in one's intestines. I notice how a few companions touch their lower abdomens, visibly attracted by this new truth.

Among us there are hermeneutics scholars, scientists from the performing arts academy, grand marijuana smokers, playboys, but not a single person studies intestine. Epistemology, maieutic, in Aeschylus' theatre the science of representation and symbolism are confused, but in the end, we always return to the lesson's key points, to the flashes of light, namely the great William and the sagacious Bertoldt. There must certainly be an electric current between the two, a sort of invisible link which keeps them connected through the centuries.

There is a mirror which spans the length of a wall; in it I spy the convergence of male and female bodies with their reflections and icy stares. It is a kind of deforming well, it eats our figures and never spits them back out, all the while we compress air into our diaphragms as we declaim: "Master Eltwood, how far are we into the night?" Or: "Sire, a forest of armies marches against us! Or: *"Who do we have to kill, among these men."*

"No no no, this will not do, we are too rough, too approximate, how can we adhere to the footsteps of Macbeth's marshals? How can we become Jenny the Pirates or Meki Messer? And let's not even dream about interpreting the choir of Supplicants around Agamemnon's tomb. We are not little kids. More life! More blood in those expressionless faces! What are you afraid of?"

Another actor, a massive stage sultan jumps into the spotlight and spits out a Mozartian Leporello Don Giovanni so powerful it makes your head turn and your guts tie knots of emotion. His echoing voice shakes you like dry grass in a storm, while the incredulous Don Giovanni is grabbed by the Stone Guest's hand. You sink into an ice crevice the statue has just torn under your pedestal, your ankles tumble as Don Giovanni Tenorio's voice explodes. The lamentation originates from Edvina, the horned chorus falls, cursing the corrupter, the unscrupulous devilish man.

This is what our master of recital makes you feel in a Mozartian crescendo made of jolts and lamentations. Alto, basso, forte chair, andante con brio, vigorous sentiment. This is Mozart. No, this is the devil who knocks or the breathless Leporello who exclaims: *"Ah misfortune, my master, do you*

save yourself?"

"No!"

"Do you repent?"

"No!"

"Do you redeem yourself?"

"No! I do not know what I should repent for."

"Wretched, I will punish thee."

"Leave me!"

"I curse you. Disappear. Hell, take back this man! Be gone oh supreme shadow, return to your ice incubus. In your justice's grey prison cell…Wretched thou art."

The applause poured spontaneously, effortlessly. Mortified, I returned home, certain I would never attain such interpretative height. Why though? After all, I did have what one could consider as being a small beard.

* * *

Pierina and the wolf

Life had not been clement to Pierina, the seamstress living on our floor. Few words, few greetings from the stairway, followed by two deaths, one after the other; first her daughter, then her husband. Too much, even for Pierina. Allegedly, she even has a lover now to tell the story to.

The man walks in, without riding the doorbell, accompanied by his stealthy steps, as my mother watches and comments.

"She does not visit her brothers in the countryside anymore. What use is going if she has fought with her sister-in-laws? What is hers, is hers. The house, the land, and all the rest. She got a hold of her inheritance even before arguing."

That night, the night when her daughter died, Pierina rang every doorbell, but Fiorillo and Pezzuto were both asleep, as

was everyone else.

"My daughter is not well. She is dying, Help!" Screamed Pierina.

"I remember the heat to this day, a terrible heat, a heart attack. I never really liked her daughter."

"But death is death!"

"So, it is."

"She did not even have a boyfriend. But to be gone so young, because of a breathing issue…"

Pierina had said: *"now she dies,"* and then she closed the door.

"The girl could not stay indoors."

"To die of suffocation, how does one even?" Pierina wept no tears.

The husband came and went. He stayed in the doorway.

"Come inside, please be seated. Let us call the doctor. But it takes time. Please do not stay in the doorway, come in…"

"No, my wife does not want me to."

"And what is this? She wore yellow at the funeral?"

She was always a bit bizarre"

"She invited me over to her place for coffee, but I never went

again, after that."

"She wanted to see me every hour of every day, I had no peace."

"Also, the priest told her something on the day of the funeral, when she walked in with the coffin. What is the meaning of this? Who goes to a cemetery with a light-colored dress and no sleeves? It is not respectful to dress like that."

I thought about the all-conquering stain on the wall. *"The husband stays in the kitchen the whole day, with his hat on, sitting on a stool. They don't have any chairs? She does not want any, if he wants to sit down, it has to be on a stool."*

"She did nothing to save her daughter."

"What could she have done?"

Pierina rings our doorbell around eleven o clock, a couple of months after her daughter's death. The Prophet of the Past's father slips on his slippers and cautiously looks out of the peephole. He says: *"Ah! It is Pierina! It is late. What?!... Dead? Who is dead? Let's not joke about such things. What happened Pierina? Yes, I will come now."* My mother's reaction? *"Absolutely not, I do not want to see a corpse"* Nobody had even asked her. The deceased have a right to their story. Pierina's husband has tread the path from which he shall never return. My father has crossed that path as well, he combs his hair in the bathroom, and then he does not really know what to do, he turns the light on and off. What on earth did he comb his hair for? To go to a dead man? It is ten past eleven now, and my father goes to dress the dead the man. Some doors open, others immediately shut themselves.

"Ancient Egypt" I tell myself. So, it begins. They weigh the liver and the brain in front of Anubis. They weigh Ettore's sadness, Ettore, Pierina's deceased husband.

They perforate your nose and away they go, they judge you, they place you on the weighing scale and decide your fate. I linger on the doorway, undecided. My father does not cut a poor figure, he never does. He knows how to stay silent, it is his strength. He only says: *"I am coming."* My father is great and not only with engines.

Pierina is now wearing the same sleeveless yellow dress for her deceased husband. Her mourning springs from the color yellow. Pierina's apartment is barren, here it lies with its opaque grit floor and felted couches. The doily crotchet rests on the lacquered furniture, two balls of yellow wool and a stranded plastic gondola with a broken oar. Underneath it all; a photo of Venice and a postcard with painted daisies. The entrance is wallpapered with daisies which chase after each other to the very ceiling. The entrance of the dead.

What shall we call this story full of dead people? They will be guarding the accommodation for a while. Pierina will want to invite you to the living room to sip coffee and show you how much the spathiphyllum has grown. My father is now guardian of the dead. He fears nothing, and at this hour he must have already fitted the dead man with a shirt and jacket. He goes on the landing with a tie in his hand, he does not know if it would suit the dead man. What about the shoes? The dead man chill without his shoes. The doctor arrives after the five-floor hike, and understandably snorts. Pierina got up from the stool. Madama Serra leans over and makes the sign of the cross. Rita Rambaudo remains at the doorway; Iotti, who also snorted her way up there, snorts her way back down. Pierina pulls out her black stockings and turns on the gas, intent on making the pasta water boil. The doctor does his job. She will eat with the dead man.

Akhenaton is there for him. He is one of the sacred river's ferry men, and he has come to the corpse's bedside to anoint his legs with holy oils. Pierina's pasta boils. It is quite warm, and that is why she will wear the sleeveless yellow dress, the dress of the dead. The dead have all the space they require, they are accompanied on their journey by the living room couch, onto which the deceased daughter's dolls sleep, by the candid crochet doilies and the fake fruit which will last for an eternity of eternities.

Father and daughter will come in the dead of night to see their old house, after all, the dead get along just fine. They will watch their relative become pale, blur and loose her color, and her reputation.

Seven years from the funeral date. That is how much time has come to pass ever since that yellow dress was last worn.

"What lover?" They ask. The man who sees Pierina now has been a warden and a storekeeper. Nothing remarkable about the man at all, and people murmur as he is walking up the stairs. Our neighbor Pierina owns two pensions, and the bearded man desires her countryside farmhouse. Pierina smoothens the walls with her erratic movements, she hesitates as she crosses the street. She goes shopping less and less because the five-floor climb is draining. She cannot live alone. The bearded man does not only keep her company. He has other widows to farm. You need quite some ability to keep it up.

* * *

To the sea, one last time

Antonia has managed to retain the charm of the pale-as-yogurt virgin. I do not know if her lover continues to cross the mountains by night with his Lambretta to come and visit her. Gastritis forces her to fast for two whole days every three. This is the last time we will go to Cavallotti, after this, who knows?

I furtively smoke Astor, it is a packet of ten and the world smiles at me. I am sprinkled with promises, looks, names and girl tits. I have grown, my limbs are filamentous bean stalks. I always find myself posing, admiring my reflection in the showcases lined up to the sea as I stuff butts in the sand. My omnivore hunger devours all; magazines, movies, women in high heeled boots, tight pants which must surely torture their groins. The shoes I love are found in London. How can one be content with no shoes? However, I adapt, dancing does not require shoes.

Nothing is good for me anymore, my flesh bursts, as does my chest, it starts to hurt. *"Oh, it is nothing. You are becoming a little man."* Says the doctor, a friend of Fergallo, the two-timed dentist.

New sirens are waiting for me, and I do not need to squeeze my eyes through the keyhole, as I had done with Fidelio's daughter. An impetuous torrent flows in my blood, gone are the timid raids in via della Basilica, the eye has changed. There is a strong wind today, the iodine foam rises onto the marina and suddenly falls, devouring the waves below. We still attend the poor-people's beach, and discreetly hide from rich eyes. Deserting the pay-to-enter Leopoldo Baths is unseemly, therefore I camouflage my vacations; one day we are here, another day we are some other place, we have no real fixed summer house, we like to wander. Just like the rich do. To avoid any kind of inconvenience, I sit on the wall overlooking the cabins. I will have to rename situations and emotions. The past is moving. I would have given the world to my Tunisian giraffe in exchange for a promise and her bluish underarms. Now the sacred food is split between invisible diners, diatribes between aunts, cousins, and mother-in-laws. I managed to avoid bringing the decrepit raft on the beach, hurting my father's sensitivity, just for a change. *"You do not want the boat anymore?"*

He calls it a boat. Two inflatable torpedoes with rubber oarlocks inside which you can insert mini plastic oars. This is a boat to him. I am ashamed but at the same time I am sorry for how he feels. All this moderation felts his life. He is someone who suffers. The wife, the sisters, the mother, the life he has to lead, and finally me. I tell him: *"This year, the dinghy is all right."* He senses how I do not care about this rubber tub which he calls a boat. He only wanted to give me a gift for the Summer, and even though I will not become a mechanic, even though I have betrayed him, it was his way of saying: *"It's fine."*

How can I not soften up to such a father? At the same time however, I feel a sleeping rage wake up inside me, how I had wished he took things with greater charisma and resolve, how I'd wish he'd told everyone what his mind told him. He realized how it would all end, far too late. He wanted to leave her, my mother. But how can someone just leave someone like her? There is no instruction booklet, and after all, what would people say? The Leopold Baths have become this holiday's only true reference. A concentration of *baiadere* with pointed breasts buzzing in their honeycomb. My eyes land with horror on the little family which has come to lie down under the sun, on the stretch of free beach.

* * *

206

The incarnation of the cosmic obscene

The swollen little man is sitting on a stool under the coloured morsels of the parasol. His feet are sunk in the wet sand as his half-thigh-shabby wooden Bermuda shorts wave in the wind, announcing his presence to the world. His width surpasses his height, he is obscener than he is pathetic. His calves look like flasks of wine. The shiny tripe forms a wreath on his belly, his smooth reflecting back, is like that of uncle Bizzarrone's pig. His beauteous companion is like a mammoth-like boiled duck, her lemon-yellow costume withholds her overflowing guts. The obscene she-pope is double his size. I am disgustingly attracted to the couple. They are the incarnation of the cosmic obscene. Attentive ears such as mine recognise their dialect. What are these two people from Emilia Romagna doing here in the Ligurian sea? They are part of the confraternity of the obese, of the poor in spirit, of the out-of-life.

Gigantic and ineffable, these biped whales with varicose veins, leave banana peels on the sand. Also, they walk this Earth. The man's gaze is expressionless. His lips are bright with grease, because he is gobbling up immense slices of pizza. He laughs as his wife swims, raising screaming starlets of diamond with every colossal gesture. Delicious female puppies run towards the fat man, shouting: *"Daddy, Daddy!"* Their lightness is only comparable to the untold grace of fantastic creatures. Two twins caught in the coastal breeze of Celle Ligure, two-star fragments; if only stars could release crumbs of light in the night, to form such creatures. The first has an oleander flower woven in her hair, the other has a cap held together by a rubber band. They passed me by, these iridescent minor goddesses, formed by the waves' emulsion.

The smaller one caresses the fat man's swollen face, with her velvety hands lingering on the man's greasy lips. In turn, these nibble away at the little fingers. Shamelessly, an in salivated pizza morsel is dropped onto his thighs, provoking joyous squeals.

The fat man's fingers scoop up this piece of half-chewed pizza, and place it in his mouth, where the ice cream also resides.

The other piece of starlight has a blue costume, jagged at the groin. They laugh. While the mother emerges from the sea.

"Selene!" Screams the whale. *"Enough playing with the sand!"* Selene laughs. *"Fernanda, come eat some banana!"*

Selene and Fernanda, puppies to the woman with amber-coloured skin. Her long-wet hair is stuck to her shoulders, like a cape covered with sand.

One clutches a banana, the other squishes the ice cream cone which unceremoniously drips onto her thigh. I would like to scold them; *"Clumsy Selene!"* The fat man extends a finger, collects the piece of ice cream cone from his child's leg and sticks it into his mouth. For who is all this beauty manifesting itself? Am I the honoured spectator?

"Fernanda, eat the banana, come on!" But Fernanda shrugs, then got to stick the tongue out.

They are squeezed in their narrow blue and orange costumes. Their gums are perfect, their sideburns have been embroidered with silver commas by the sea salt.

"Celeste, Celeste!" They cry.

There is no Celeste at the beach today. *"Why does Celeste not want to play? Why isn't Celeste the dog here? Eat Selene, Celeste will come tomorrow. Why don't you just take a look at yourselves? You look terrible!"* Shouts the despairing mother.

Horrid shiny dark spots appear on their buttocks. Ignominious Tar.

"Come here. Tar!" Desperately screams the fat mother. Both nymphs bear a mark on their little asses, the horrible stain of tar.

"Look where you sat!" Squeals the black whale of a mother, brandishing the bottle of fizzy water. Punishment will fall upon the unconscious duo; they have profaned their little bums by sitting on some bitumen-lined wooden panel.

"They need to be tortured on the spot." I think to myself, as I put my sunglasses back on. The fat woman sweats an ocean as she runs after the little monkeys. But Selene and Fernanda are impregnable; they start crying out of fear of being caught. They circle around with tears in their eyes as they evade the huffing matron. The fat woman chases them in vain, panting, the husband utters giggles,

his belly jolts but he does not intervene. He is too concerned with the unscrewing of a sugar-coated cap, glued to the bottle of coffee. The homunculus laughs, downs the drink and gets fat.

"Soon it will come, ... Oh yes, here it comes! The Castigator! The one who will punish them by clasping their throats with the leather string. Bad children!" I still think to myself. The two reckless beings run around the father in circles screaming in fear. The pizza scraps flutter, the banana sinks beneath their feet, crushed by the fugitives' heels.

"I will call it! If he comes he will make sure to give you a

good beating!"

"Who? Whoo!" Shout the despairing nymphs.

They are terrorised, the banana puree mixes with their tears which migrate towards the streaks of ice cream tattooed on their cheeks.

"Come here!"

"No, we won't!"

"Immediately!"

"No!"

Here comes the Black knight on his imposing steed which snorts and sinks its sentencing hooves in the sand. The black knight will chase after the disobedient girls; with his steel hand he will ruffle the naiads' hair dragging them to the ground in a ruinous fall. He will take them away, on his saddle, tie them with their wrists behind their back, after having ripped off their tar-stained costumes. Daddy nods in approval. We all remain silent; the half-naked and terrified girls do not sob anymore. The great black and shiny beast is immobile, it is drooling blood from its nostrils.

The hooves will rage on the bodies of the two disobedient pups after the black knight has fed on their souls. What can one do with two capricious devils? Better to make a pulp of them under the beasts' hooves! As he is about to drop the iron on their limbs, I hear a sudden burst of laughter.

The two gypsies in the making cling onto their dad's bulk; he finally managed to unscrew the cap. The mother is pleased as she vigorously rubs their backs with a towel. They stand up and the two girls point at me and burst out laughing, I am ashamed. Angrily, I turn my back on them, pursued by Selene's and Fernanda's laughter and by their fat family's apathy.

* * *

Languid kisses, caresses and strokes of sunshine

"… Foals and jade gazelles, hips, transparent navels and heavenly breasts, already tortured by uncultivated hands, foment the deluge of kisses which are flatters destined to collide at the next turn of the clock…" This wrote the poet, and this very verse is what I tried to send to memory, in a bid to whisper it in some woman's ear. I was on a mission with a small group of girls and two other guys as we furiously made our way to Cantalupo Ligure. The group splits climbs and pants on the stone road, it takes the driveway, dispersing on a meadow protected by high hedges. Fire seeks fire. The nymph hugs me. I am like a piece of dry wood, but I am all but embers now, I do not need to ask myself what I should do with those lips that look like those from the toothpaste advert. They approach me, cracking imperceptibly, touching and then pressing onto my lips. I am very hungry, gold flows in my mouth, sweet honey. Could this be love? The following day I drunkenly zigzag my way up to the marina. I am satisfied, and I light an Astor. Now I am really in the adult world, minor adjustments are required. The sun scratches my neck and shoulders with its sharp claws.

"Idiot wake up!" Shouts my internal voice. My bare back will be covered with excruciating sores. The candelabra of the dead are spent … Monica and Cristina's kisses lie on my neck! I did not dream this, it all happened yesterday in Cantalupo. In a delirium of sunshine. They have sucked my soul away. I burn again, with my mouth onto of theirs. Crazy! Nobody will ever take those fiery copper kisses away from me. I think I have become an adult all of a sudden.

* * *

In the clinic's basement.
That's where it all happened

You do not feel the sun ripping your flesh open when it is shining so strong. The sun really did ravage me… *"Will he recover doctor?"* This is what I think I hear in the clinic's penumbra.

I fell asleep in the sun; my skin was on fire. On Cantalupo's hill. Not everyone however goes straight from Cantalupo's hill to the hospital bed, in dark lane stretching into unknown places which deny you any clues, any explanations, threatening unmentionable nightmares.

The superposition of places falls into a nightmare. Uncertainty is part of this hallucination. An internal voice tells me that the confusion will last. I will sleep in different beds, trying to settle insolvable dilemmas in vain. Am I or am I not the Prophet of the Past? Don't I have one eye which is very different from my other one? Am I not capable of being in multiple places at the same time? Am I not the protagonist of every ephemeral passion, the amorous prototype with a thousand parts to play, the code breaker of unfathomable enigmas.

"Rise." Says a voice.

"What? I cannot see you."

"Rise." It repeats. *"Do not be afraid, it is time."*

"What? I don't comprehend, I restlessly stutter."

Voices come and go, voices from the hospital corridor, join the hum from the Tecumseh engine, the pulsating heart of the fridge.

"Did you understand? Come on, the moment has come. We can wait no further."

"Hang on, what are you talking about? Tell me who you are and what do you want."

The voice from the darkness slowly explains:

"It will not be difficult for you to understand. The moment has come."

"What you mean? Do not stay in the shadow, let me see you." I say, with my broken, alarmed voice. This must surely be due to the antibiotics. I have a sore throat. I'm delirious.

Delaying the ghost's command is useless. I must answer the call; I ask the divine William to lend me his prose and what remains of my inner actor answers:

"Who are you, voice? Shadow in the shadows, interpreter of the dark, hound of liquefied silhouettes, as black as the fog, propagator of breathlessness? Who are you? You who from the darkness solicit and spur forward confused alerts, uncertain awakenings? Do you spawn from my fever? Are you the cackle of some demonic prankster? Or are you the equivocal emanation of a restless spirit? Perhaps the night is your sister, and you enjoy shaking children's hearts urging them to undertake scary tasks, tempting them into mortal actions?

...What is it that you want from me? Can you not see? I may not be dead yet, but I can hardly come back to life, the sun's cruel mutilations made certain of that. Evil counsel has brought you to me, apocryphal masters whose sole intent is to poison my mind with anxiety, they do not hesitate as they feed from the despairs of others. Speak! Divert the new anxious thoughts from the antique ones hiding in my mind. Or be gone!"

One word described me: delirious.

* * *

From the refrigerator coffin to the exchange of mothers

I was looking for water, or any kind of refreshment. What I got was the clamour of indistinct voices. I reflected. I fragmented and recomposed my mind various time over, bouts of frenzied confusion took their toll. When I heard the voice again I was not able to determine if it was a dream or rather one of those images which attach themselves to us, adhering to our mind's curtain of fantasies, it could have been the mouthwash advert.

What were my qualifications as Prophet of the Past? Of what use were my powers? What did my love for those unlucky Carbonari mean? And then, in the middle of the night, it scratched and creaked. I did not give it much importance. It creaked some more and vibrated. What was it? I remained motionless and on guard.

212

What was it? I could not believe the incubus could go so far. I was certainly delirious.

... Finally, he got up. Unspeakable. I was dumbfounded at the sight. I thought to myself: *"nothing could have been more flamboyant."* He stayed in front of the bed, his figure, one of indestructible power. A chief of the Shoshone tribe? Or a Pawnee shaman? Maybe. I could not comprehend what was happening. What masquerade was this?

The half-naked shape had a rag on the sides, half man, half wizard. It was Tecumseh, the shaman who lodged in the refrigerator with the broken handle. He was wrapped by a quasi hermetically closed tray canvas, and it slowly unzipped as he raised himself from his white coffin. His pectorals looked like bronze shields, his shoulders, tongs capable of uprooting whole trees. A perfect power, in harmony with the invisible forces. A leather string hung from his right arm, the other had a ribbon of cloth tied to it, of the same texture and color as the one circumventing his cranium.

"Your spirit is ready" he said. *"Your time has come; it is time for you to be born."* I looked at him in amazement. He held out his hand and I could not escape his will.

We descended four flights of stairs, lower and lower in the deserted hospital. Then, we went down into the basement. I was glued to the walls; a sweetish smell of saliva, mixed with that from dish-washing filled the air. A stale stench of things that are boiling, and the bacterial stink from warm pots, which use water horses to make their myriad of foul-smelling messengers traverse the skies. This was the stinking breath of the hospital's kitchens, mixed with the antiseptic smell of medicines. Reluctantly, I joined the figure's pressing invitation. I could not do otherwise. Although my feet never dragged behind, I tried to slow down at every twist and turn, I took my time, I rubbed my arms against the walls, but the walls pushed me away, they let me slip easily, inevitably, towards my destiny. I did not have suction cups to postpone the ... revelation.

The only thing which was strong and clear was my beating heart, which I felt in my throat. I thought to myself: *"It must be yesterday's sun"*. I tried to contrast what was waiting for me in the underground.

"Do not be afraid," hissed Tecumseh's low voice, *"here there is no death, the dead's lamentations do not make it*

down here. Here, there is only life."

We jumped into a corridor's dense darkness, horribly similar to the infinite galleries opening up to the underworld in our building's cellar of horrors, my blood is corrupted. Shrubs of cold spaghetti rolled up on branches: none of this could be seen. The smells evoked incredible epistemological overlaps. Green dorms with neon lights, large windows overlooking blind courtyards, and then other rooms, and labyrinths, all tiled with a medicinal green. The hospital's bowels.

There were tubs, various bits of physiotherapy equipment, badly-crafted tin cabinets, beds with large rubber wheels and pedal brakes, and then lamps, pullers, pliers, rolls of bandages and piles of wipes. On oval basins, syringes and forceps. Other badly lit rooms, other disturbing introductions. And then: Rita Rambaudo, lying on a chair!

I thought: *"What is she doing down here?!"*

"Come," said the shaman, custodian of the subsoil, lord of Tartarus.

I screamed: *"What is she doing down here?"* Our neighbour was in the underground. I was just about to start vomiting my agitation, but I meet a woman with her ankles and wrists tied to the bed handles. Her eyes bulge out of her sockets, and the mouthpiece characteristic of the mentally ill stifles her laments. She has the expression of one who does not understand that I am her son. The woman is showered by a dying yellow light, which is promptly extinguished. How can my mother be there? I am here, she is there, or is she someone who looks like her? And the discharge? I read it you know? They give patients electrical discharges to make them heal. Professor Cerletti said so. They put the sick in place and the *acroagonine* dosage would kill a horse. But the woman bearing my mother's face is really about to give birth. What on earth does giving birth have to do with nervous exhaustion? The point of the matter is that I will be scooped out after having swallowed orange peels for months. In the basement, they give electric shocks to brains and give birth to pups. I cannot seem to find a connection. I am at a woman in labor's bedside. And I do not even know if she truly is my mother.

"It is time." says the Indian. *"It is your turn now."* I tremble, evidently, I cannot wait any longer. The woman's water just broke, and contractions are commencing. I cannot find myself in this dense darkness. I believe I am surrounded by Rita Rambaudo, the nurses, and my future mother, but I cannot say that with certainty. In that gathering dark, I was born once, twice, several times over, expelled indefinitely, in Professor Cerletti's delivery room, where electrical treatments are practiced. I should be blessed by light as I come out of this infernal labor, in which everything is a snort, a sweat, a swear, people talk about their affairs, what they did on Saturday afternoons, even the midwives will blabber as the contractions thrust me out. And there is not even a bit of music to accompany my ascent into the world!

I walk down a path I have just traced, I must quickly follow it, I might catch a cold otherwise, I finally see myself on Rita Rambaudo's bed. I am lying there because my mother clearly told the nurses:

"But this cannot be my son! He must have black hair. Even my husband has black hair. Do you know my husband? Everyone in my family has black hair. This is blonde. Can you not see? What am I supposed to do with a blonde child? There must be a mistake! My husband is working now, but he will be able to tell you if I am right. I do not believe it, you bring me someone else's child!"

For approximately five long minutes the beam of light heralds a bluish-pink bundle of foamy fluff, lying onto Rita Rambaudo's bed. I must be someone's child, I must have slipped out from somewhere!

Rita Rambaudo and her beautiful white shoulders, food to Jack Lo Cascio's insatiable appetite. She had nothing to do with me, she was in the hospital's basement because she had to cure her exhaustion. I had no idea that everything is recorded for security purposes. They might have recorded my birth as well, and I will get to know whose son I am. I was continuously coming to the world, again and again, out of all the ways I had to be born, this one was by far the most bizarre.

I've had two mothers, I've always known this. To them I add a natural father who decided to stay at the factory to measure the bolt's diameter with his caliber, while I was born. I screamed. The shaman, who was previously asleep in the fridge, got me out of trouble, I did not want to get out that warm sack.

I was pointing my feet; I stood sideways, there was no way to get me out of there. This did the doctors say, after a most tumultuous and non-cooperative birth. So how did the American Indian do it? Like lightning, with his long hunting knife. A clean cut, right along the woman's tummy, and then he pulls me out, by the head with his forceps -like hands. I rise to the sky as he says: *"Now."* The forceps' marks are still clear on my temples.

Had I not seen everything with my own eyes, I would have thought this to be a scene from a movie, or Professor Cerletti's ECT.

A fluffy crumpled up figure rises. I have a Bulldog's face, like all newborns, blessed with ignorance, enduring anything that might happen to them, how could they remember it anyhow? The basis of my existence is composed of a confused birth, the loss of sleep, the ontological jumble to fuel my great journey and all this metaphysical trash. I am deposited on a neurotic patient's pillow, she is our neighbour, and mother to two children. My mother comes second. I have an eye different from the other one, this is now an established fact. What would you have done at my place? Have you ever witnessed a birth? I have, my own. This is no joke. You are always one step away from life and a shot away from death. Technology allows you to see the contractions as waves on a monitor, if you miss one, there is always another one. *"Take it easy!"* Who is going anywhere? It is like being on Thor Heyerdahl's Kon-Tiki, drifting into the turmoil overlooking coastline of Rangiroa.

Someone gives you a push and you take off. *"Yaamhh!"* The wave sucks you back, one time, two times, I was tossed here and there too, hiding in the womb, waiting to see the light, not a soul was willing to show me the route and purpose of the journey I would embark on. I was rowing against the current of life, they did not care about the birth, they don't want him, and that's an end to that. Flee! I must flee! Anywhere, everywhere, towards the dark stars, towards the immanent nothingness. The last contraction eradicates me from the surface of the water, thrusting me in into the inner lake formed by the enclosure of corals. So be it, earth, finally. The Indian has disappeared again, he must have returned to his ageless slumber in the icy coffin.

But now it's my turn.
Apparently, I am born.

* * *

Printed in Great Britain
by Amazon

65137163R00132